finding me

Books by Kathryn Cushman

A Promise to Remember

Waiting for Daybreak

Leaving Yesterday

Another Dawn

Almost Amish

Chasing Hope

Finding Me

finding me

KATHRYN CUSHMAN

BETHANYHOUSE
a division of Baker Publishing Group
Minneapolis, Minnesota

Published by Bethany House Publishers
11400 Hampshire Avenue South
Bloomington, Minnesota 55438
www.bethanyhouse.com

Bethany House Publishers is a division of
Baker Publishing Group, Grand Rapids, Michigan

Printed in the United States of America

Library of Congress Cataloging-in-Publication Data
Cushman, Kathryn.
Finding me / Kathryn Cushman.
pages ; cm
Summary: "After her father's death, Kelli Huddleston discovers the entire life she's known has been a lie, but as she seeks to know more about her past and finds family she's never known, ugly secrets threaten to stifle the truth and restoration she seeks"—Provided by publisher.
ISBN 978-0-7642-1261-1 (softcover)
I. Title.
PS3603.U825F56 2015
813′.6—dc23 2014041329

Cover design by John Hamilton Design

Author is represented by Books & Such Literary Agency.

15 16 17 18 19 20 21 7 6 5 4 3 2 1

To Maxine Methvin and Daphene Cope—great mentors
and role models. You've poured yourselves into the lives
of so many young people over the years.
Thank you for believing in me
and encouraging me to be the best I could be.

For the time will come when people will not put up with sound doctrine. Instead, to suit their own desires, they will gather around them a great number of teachers to say what their itching ears want to hear. They will turn their ears away from the truth and turn aside to myths. But you, keep your head in all situations, endure hardship, do the work of an evangelist, discharge all the duties of your ministry.

2 Timothy 4:3–5

Prologue

26 years ago

David Waters slid into his usual corner booth, promising himself once again that today would be the last time. He knew it was a lie. He'd be back again tomorrow. And the next day. And the next. Why should he feel guilty about that? It wasn't like he was doing anything wrong. He was simply eating lunch in a diner. No crime in that.

"Hey, handsome, whatcha having today?" She wore her usual white V-neck, with just enough cleavage spilling out to be provocative, but not so much that she looked, as his wife would call it, trashy. David felt something like happiness for the first time all day.

"I don't know. What do you suggest?" He smiled up at her—not because he was trying to flirt but because just being around her made him smile.

"Ha. I've got several suggestions I could make, but why don't we stick to the issue at hand? I'm thinking . . . how about today's special, which is the buttermilk fried-chicken sandwich. Crispy breaded chicken, buffalo ranch sauce, bleu cheese crumbles, lettuce, and tomato, on a toasted French roll."

This sandwich would not be approved by his cholesterol-watching doctor, and most certainly not by his food-gestapo wife. "Sounds delicious."

"Oh, it is, believe me." She wrote on her order pad, shaking her head as she did so. "Men are so lucky. I eat one of those things and for the next two weeks I've got to do double time in the gym." A quick glance at her lean and toned legs made David think she spent double time in the gym every day, anyway. "I will say, though, I'm glad to see you eat this way. It's just so manly, you know? Never could stand to be around a man who eats salads and tofu."

David was more than a little sure he'd ordered neither during the past few weeks. "Well then, I guess I pass the test."

"Handsome, you pass the test in all sorts of ways." She winked at him. "I'll be right back with your iced tea."

He watched her walk away, the short denim skirt revealing unseasonably tanned legs. One deep sigh later, he had forced his attention to the booth where he was sitting. The red vinyl seats were worn and dull, the Formica tabletop beginning to crack and peel around the edges. *Just like my life,* he thought. David put his elbow on the table and leaned his forehead into the space between his thumb and middle finger. Everything felt so hopeless. Overwhelming to the point of crushing. What was he going to do when his mother's insurance ran out at the end of next year? There was no way he could afford to keep her in Brighton Manor on his own, and the slightly more affordable options offered a greatly decreased level of care. Maybe she had lost enough mental capacity that she wouldn't know it, but he would know it.

"Things that bad?" Her voice cut through his self-pity, and he looked up to see the iced tea sitting on the table before him. "I'm a good listener, if you need someone to talk to."

"Thanks." He took a sip. "I'm fine, really. Just a little tired."

"I'll keep the iced tea coming then, until we get you tanked up enough to make it through the day."

"Thanks."

"I'm just here to help." She tilted her head to the side and winked.

Everything about her was so inviting. So approachable. So . . . alluring.

And it wasn't like his wife had even looked at him in the past week. The kids kept her running in circles, as did the committees she was on at church and school—all of it zapped her time and energy. There was nothing left for him. Not that he blamed her, exactly, but truth was, he felt neglected at home, so he came here to get his daily fix.

There was nothing wrong with him being here like this, nothing wrong at all. All he was doing was eating.

"Here's your lunch. Anything else I can do for you?"

A surge of something completely enjoyable raced through him as she leaned forward to set down the plate. Okay, he should probably stop coming here so often. Maybe just tomorrow, and then he would stop.

Present day

You better watch out. Boss man is looking for you, and he's got that red-faced, eye-bulging look we all know too well."

Kelli Huddleston dropped her purse into the drawer of her desk, glancing over her shoulder toward the front door, resisting the urge to run toward it. Just ten yards away, the threshold of escape. Unfortunately, it was a threshold she couldn't afford to cross—not yet. "Great. Do you know what he's mad about?"

Tammy's face was grim. "Mrs. Layton's son called this morning. Jimmy's been in a rage ever since."

Kelli twisted her bracelet around on her wrist. "Did my name come up—in the phone call?"

"Jimmy took it back in his office so I couldn't say for sure, but judging from the way he came charging out of his office looking for you a few minutes later, I'm guessing the answer is yes."

"I'm sunk." Kelli dropped into her chair.

"Tell me you didn't open your mouth again."

Kelli shrugged. "I might have."

"I've been warning you about that."

"But it's wrong. He didn't do any of that work he was charging her for. Mrs. Layton is in her eighties and the sweetest little lady you could ever know. It would never enter her mind to double-check her contractor's billed hours. Her kids all live hundreds of miles away. What was I supposed to do?"

Tammy shrugged. "Mind your own business, I guess. I'd like to sit around feeling guilty about some of the things I see around here, and sometimes I do, but times are hard right now. This is no time to be out job hunting."

She was right, and Kelli knew it. It had taken eight months after graduation before she'd found this receptionist job, one that on paper she was overqualified for. Still, there were some lines that could not be crossed, no matter how desperate she was. "I'm all for minding my own business, but in cases like this, how can you stand it?"

"I'll tell you how. I've got two kids who look to me to keep them fed and warm. They don't ask me whether I double-checked my boss's numbers, they don't wonder if I'm policing other people's work, but they do know what it's like to be hungry when I'm between jobs. They know what it's like to have the electricity cut off because we couldn't pay the bill, and to have the landlord knocking at our door wanting the overdue rent. They know more about those things than any kid should, and I aim to do my best to help them forget about it."

"Sorry. I didn't mean to judge you."

"Good, because I don't have the time or patience for it." Tammy returned to her desk. "Now, it's time to get busy. We've got lots to do."

"Yeah." Kelli considered whether she should go in search of Jimmy or let him come find her. She finally decided on the latter. Perhaps the extra time would help him cool off. "Need help with anything?" Only now did Kelli notice Tammy's light brown hair. Normally gelled to a manageable amount of wave, today it frizzed into a giant halo around her head, giving something of an Albert Einstein impression. Kelli looked a little closer and noticed the coffee stain on Tammy's shirt. "Are you okay?"

Tammy shuddered. "No, I'm not. My alarm clock didn't go off this morning. Rachel and Billy were late to school, I was late to work, I'm trying to leave early today because Rachel's got a softball game this afternoon, and I'm already so behind from last week that I'm buried—" She threw her hand over her mouth while her face blushed deep purple. "I'm sorry." She shook her head, her face truly repentant. "I didn't mean—oh, Kelli, I can't believe I just said that. I really didn't—"

"I know you didn't. Now tell me what I can do to help." The sooner they got busy, the sooner this awkwardness would be over.

"Would you mind helping me with these bills? I've got everything printed, just have to get them all out with today's mail."

"Of course." Kelli picked up the stack from Tammy's desk and placed it on her own. The phone rang before she sat down. "Good morning, Dalton Construction, how may I help you?" Kelli transferred the caller to Reed's office, then went about her task.

Fold. Stuff. Seal. Fold. Stuff. Seal. It was a mindless duty, one easily accomplished while answering calls and directing clients and salesmen in the appropriate direction. She liked being busy—the more she had to keep her occupied, the less time she had to think.

Jimmy Dalton came sauntering down the hallway. "My, my, look who's here." He grabbed some M&Ms from the jar on Kelli's desk and tossed them into his mouth. His sleeves were starched and pressed, his pants perfectly creased. He looked more like a big-city lawyer than the owner of a smallish construction company. "Kelli, may I see you in my office please?"

"Sure." She followed him down the hall. One of the side effects of grief was that it numbed her to almost every other emotion. She supposed in this case it was a blessing, because other than a vague sense of dread, she felt nothing.

"Have a seat, please." He gestured toward one of the padded chairs opposite his desk. He didn't sit himself, he simply leaned back against his desk, arms folded. "How's your morning been so far?"

Kelli tried to keep her face neutral. "Fine."

"Well, that's good for you. Unfortunately for me, mine's been very upsetting." The office phones were ringing down the hall. "Would you care to guess why my morning was so bad?"

Kelli looked up at him and saw him glaring back. She tried to affect a confused expression. "I have no idea."

"Don't you?" He paused. "What have you been up to?"

"What do you mean?" Kelli's mouth had gone dry. Jimmy remained silent and simply stared at her. The *beep-beep-beep* of the forklift backing up came from just outside the office window, a phone rang somewhere down the hall, and Kelli began to hear her own heart racing in her ears.

"I got a call from Kevin Layton today. He's an old high-school friend of mine, did I tell you that? Anyway, it seems his mother heard some bad things about me and about the remodel work we're doing on her bathroom. You know anything about that?"

"I . . . uh . . . well . . . two weeks ago, you billed her for six hours of design and drafting time."

"Yeah, so? We're remodeling her bathroom—design and drafting is what I do." He put his hands in his trouser pockets, his suntanned face showing not a hint of comprehension.

"You were in Hawaii two weeks ago."

He sat on the corner of his desk and smiled up toward the ceiling. "Mm-hmm, yes, I was. Wish I still was." He shook his head and looked down at Kelli. "Sorry, lost in memories there."

"How could you have worked six hours on Mrs. Layton's project if you were on vacation in Hawaii?"

He made his way over to his leather executive chair and sat. "It's quite simple, Kelli. I'm surprised I have to explain this to you. I was . . . thinking about her project on my trip. The sound of waves crashing nearby always heightens my creativity." He propped his feet on his desk. "And of course, the girls in bikinis and three daiquiris didn't hurt either. Yep, I got a lot accomplished while lying on that beach."

Yeah. Lying is right, just not on the beach. "Jimmy, that's—"

"Listen, Kelli"—he leaned forward—"this company has come upon some hard times financially, and I've realized quite unexpectedly that I'm going to have to lay off an employee. Of course, I hate to have to do it. I always strive to be as loyal to my employees as they are to me." He paused and looked at her for the space of several heartbeats, which were coming faster and faster with each passing second. "But sometimes these things can't be helped." He steepled his hands atop his desk. "Since you were the last one hired, you are the obvious choice of who must be let go. So, I'm—" he coughed into his hands—"sorry—" another cough— "to inform you that we can no longer offer you employment here."

Kelli knew her mouth was hanging open, but she couldn't help it. Jimmy continued to look at her, waiting for her to leave, she supposed. Finally she found her voice. "Is this . . . effective immediately?"

He nodded, and as he did so, he actually grinned. "I'm sorry to say it is. You are still on probation until June, so there is no requirement for longer notice. I'd appreciate it if you'd clean out your desk immediately."

Kelli somehow managed to stumble from his office and back to her desk, where she took her purse out of the drawer, slamming it shut with every bit of her strength. How dare he do this? She gathered the few personal items she kept here—a glass paperweight with an ocean scene inside and the carved wooden pencil box her father had made for her in celebration of her new job. Had he known what a lout Jimmy Dalton was, maybe he wouldn't have bothered. She kicked her desk chair hard enough that it fell over backward. She took a deep breath. "'Bye, Tammy. I'll miss you."

Tammy had already come to her feet during the spectacle. She stood shaking her head. "Tell me he didn't."

"He did."

"Oh, girl." Tammy walked over and threw her arms around Kelli. "I was afraid something like this was going to happen, but I'm so sorry it did. You take care, okay?"

"Okay."

"Kelli?"

"Yeah."

"Be glad you're in a place in your life where you can choose to do the right thing."

That wasn't quite as true as Tammy believed. Everyone seemed to assume that the death of Kelli's parents had left her with some kind of large inheritance. After all, their upscale house had already been in escrow when they died. From the outside, it probably appeared that a large cash payoff was days away. No one knew about the mountains of debt, the long list of creditors that had taken every last dime from the estate. Everything was gone, a complete loss brought on by many years of overspending. Kelli had her own debts, too—college loans, car payments, and rent. Still, she mumbled, "I guess so."

"Be even more grateful for your courage and integrity. Hold tight to them. Once you start to let them go, they're almost impossible to get back. Stay just the way you are, and you'll be fine."

Kelli nodded. "Thanks, Tammy." And with that, she shuffled

out to her car, wondering how all this could possibly ever be fine. She knew the answer. It couldn't.

Oh, Daddy, I wish you were here so I could talk to you.

But Daddy wasn't there, and Kelli was going to have to find her own way. Time to buck up and get on with it. Whatever *it* was.

2

Kelli went to her friends' house, determined not to tell them she'd been fired. The longer she kept it a secret, the less time they would worry.

She turned over the three-hundred-page book Denice had given her, then laid it on the table in front of her. "So . . . what did you say this was for again?" Across the front, *Kelli* was written in perfect calligraphy with gold metallic ink.

"It's a grief journal." Denice walked over to open the book, gesturing toward the lined pages waiting to be filled. "You've got to work through all that's happened, and you need to do it now or else it will come back to haunt you for the rest of your life. I want you to write at least a little in here every day—about your emotions, what you're going through, fond memories, anything at all that's bothering you. It will help speed the healing process."

Denice had been Kelli's best friend since childhood, and for as long as Kelli could remember, she'd been the touchy-feely balance to Kelli's non-emotional self. "And who says this is the way to heal?"

"Everybody who knows anything."

"In other words, says my wife." Jones put his arm around Denice's shoulders and grinned down at her. "Kelli, you know that when it comes to psycho-babble, Denice knows it all."

"It's not babble." Denice elbowed Jones with a bit more force than necessary. "To you people who grew up in a *Leave It to Beaver* kind of family, maybe you can afford to laugh at the rest of us as we try our best to work our way through our stuff, but—"

Jones leaned forward and kissed his wife square on the lips to stop the flow of words. Then, keeping his face less than an inch from hers, he said, "Sorry. I'm sorry." He continued to simply look into her eyes, one hand on the side of her face. Jones might look like an Italian mobster with his mop of dark hair and bearded face, but he had the biggest heart of anyone Kelli knew, and at times like these, he understood what was at stake. Kelli was glad Denice had found him.

"You should be sorry, you big lug." Denice shoved at him again, but there was a grin lurking at the corners of her lips when she turned back to Kelli. "Seriously, this is important. First your breakup with Rick, then your parents' death. That's a lot of bad stuff to deal with."

Kelli had never been able to convince Denice that the breakup with Rick had not been that big of a deal. Yes, she had caught him cheating, but it wasn't like she was in love with the guy. Still, Denice worried about it, because that's who Denice was. Kelli opened the journal and thumbed through the empty pages. "Well, I've got something new to add to my list of woes. I got fired today." She could have kicked herself the moment the words slipped out.

"You're kidding!" Denice walked over to sit beside her. "What happened?"

"Kevin Layton called the office this morning. Obviously he told Jimmy I'd been to see his mother about her remodel bill."

"You did that, really? Like, went to her house and told her she was being cheated?" Jones leaned his head forward, eyes wide with shock.

"Well, yeah. How could I not? She was my parents' neighbor, *my* neighbor for all my growing-up years. She's elderly, and she's one of the nicest people I've ever met. I just couldn't remain silent about what was happening."

"I, for one, am glad you are out of that place. I know that's been hard on you, having to work for that slimeball." Denice took her hand. "I say you're better off."

"I won't miss the job itself, that much is for sure."

Jones smiled. "I sometimes forget how fortunate I am in my wife's choice of BFF and my own brilliant choice in business partner. Good for you for doing the right thing." He stopped then, mouth open, and smacked himself on the forehead. "Business partner! You're going to need part of your money back now, aren't you?"

Just last week, Kelli had taken the entirety of her life insurance money—the one thing her parents' debt wasn't able to take from her—and used every bit of it as a down payment in a business partnership with Denice and Jones.

The three of them had shared a dream for years about starting their own restaurant, ever since Jones had gone to culinary school. He specialized in Southern-style comfort food combined with a healthier, farm-to-table, California sensitivity. Kelli had her degree in business, and Denice had been a waitress all her life—in her mid-teens to help pay the bills for her highly dysfunctional family, at eighteen when she'd moved out on her own, and then to support Jones while he attended culinary school. When the owner of Sam's, a mediocre restaurant in an old Victorian home in downtown Santa Barbara, had announced he was retiring at the end of the summer, the three of them had gone crazy trying to pool together enough money to buy the place. They had talked to loan officers all over town and were not going to be able to swing it until Kelli received the life insurance check after her parents' wreck. It had taken every cent to make it work.

"Will you have enough to hold you over until we get Farmstead up and running?" Denice pulled a twenty-dollar bill out of her wallet and set it on the table between them. "You're being buried under an avalanche of bad stuff right now, there's no doubt about it. But you know you can count on us for anything you need, right?"

Kelli slid the money back toward her. "I'm not desperate yet." She knew the two of them were even more cash-strapped than she was.

Jones reached for Kelli's hand, put the money in her palm, and then balled up her fingers. "Truly, Kelli, please know that anything we have is yours." Somehow, coming from Jones, it was all the more special. She leaned her head against his shoulder and patted him on the arm. "Thank you. But really, I'll be okay."

"Yes, you will, because the three musketeers look out for each other, and right now, I'm planning to do my part." He walked into the kitchen and opened the refrigerator door, calling out, "It's time I whipped us up something delicious."

"There's something really great about a man who cooks and looks good doing it." Denice grinned at her husband, who wiggled his eyebrows in response.

"And don't you forget it, either."

Kelli looked back and forth between them. "I don't know what I'd do without the two of you."

"Well, that's one thing you won't ever have to find out." Denice followed her husband to the kitchen and pulled some plates out of the cupboard. "Do you need any help cleaning out the rest of your parents' place?"

"Nah. There's nothing left but Daddy's office. I guess I have all day tomorrow to get it knocked out while you two are slaving away at your jobs. This extra time is definitely the one benefit of being fired." Kelli thought about the room she'd put off until last. Cleaning it out seemed so final, going through his personal things too invasive. Everything about emptying out that room struck her as being wrong.

She had no idea how wrong it would turn out to be.

Odd that my first entry into this journal isn't about Daddy and Mimi at all. It's about my other family, the one I never knew.

For as long as I can remember, I've had this dream. It's my only "memory" of my mother, brother, and sister, though it's really not a memory at all. It's a figment of my imagination, because this is not at all the way it happened, and I have no idea what they even looked like in real life.

We are in a car. I am in the back seat holding Scruffy, my favorite stuffed dog. My brother is on my right side with his hand stuck out the back window, my sister on my left, leaning forward so that I can see her blond curls. My mother is driving, and they are all singing a completely nonsensical song, something about Scruffy and me. I can never quite make out the words. Everyone is giggling and laughing, right up until the moment the windshield explodes and glass goes flying everywhere. I hear them screaming, and then it goes silent and dark. On the good days, I wake up as soon as the glass shatters. On the bad ones, I lie there alone and frightened in the silent dark for what seems like forever, calling for my mother but hearing no response except my own cries.

This morning was the latter type. I hope this is not a sign of what's ahead.

Even from the road, Dad and Mimi's house felt empty. The *Sold* banner across the realty sign in the front yard reminded Kelli that by this time next year it would be as if she and her parents had never existed here at all, erased from their home of the past twenty-four years. Kelli turned into the driveway, which still held her father's truck, tool chest across the bed, as if waiting for its driver. Only the *For Sale* sign in the back window told the truth of the situation.

Well, sitting in her car, staring at the house was accomplishing nothing. Kelli climbed out of her lime green Ford Fiesta and couldn't help but touch the hood of her father's old white pickup. After several weeks of sitting unused, a layer of grime had settled over it. Kelli made a mental note to wash it soon. She pulled open the driver's side door and climbed in, the torn vinyl of the seat scratching her legs. She wrapped her arms around the steering wheel and leaned her forehead against it. "Oh, Daddy, I wish you were here."

No answer. Only silence.

She climbed out and made a spur-of-the-moment decision to tackle the car cleaning first. She found all the supplies in the garage and got started, soon deciding a wax job was in order, too. Vacuum, tire treatment, dash dressing. She didn't stop until there was absolutely nothing left she could do to the old heap.

Finally, she made her way inside the house. As she entered, she noted that the place had taken on something of a musty smell, with only a hint of Mimi's perfume and Daddy's turpentine still left in the air. She stopped at the door to the living room, looked at the bay window—the place that was always home for the Christmas tree. Twinkling colored lights and tinsel filled her memory, then were jerked away by the realization that this year at Christmas, she would be alone. Yet one more layer of sting added to the constant pain of the past weeks. She shook her head and started down the hall, toward the next task.

Her father had been positively territorial about his office. Kelli had never been allowed in there. Even Mimi kept a wide berth from this room, so cleaning it out for the new owners felt a bit like a violation of her father's sacred space. Especially now that she was armed with the combination to the safe—which she'd come across in some other paperwork just last night. At least it would save her the expense of having to call in a locksmith.

Suddenly, she was five-year-old Kelli again, playing with her Barbies in the living room. She was getting them ready for a ball with the prince, so they were dressed in their finest shiny gowns and wearing all their best jewelry.

She heard the clank of metal coming from inside Daddy's office and knew what that meant. It was just a little safe in the bottom of the closet, and he was always very secretive about what was inside. She looked down at her finely dressed dolls and all the jewelry they were wearing and wondered if maybe Daddy had some jewels in his safe. Probably. Rubies and diamonds, she guessed, and maybe a few sapphires, too.

The rules were very firm. If Daddy was in the office with the door closed, he was not to be disturbed. Today, however, the door remained slightly ajar, which meant it was okay to go see him, right?

Kelli really, really, really wanted to see the jewels. So, as quietly as she could, she tiptoed down the hall. The door was cracked open a couple of inches, but since the safe was against the back of the hallway wall, there was no way to see it without entering the room and looking back toward the closet. She pushed at the door oh so slowly, hoping it wouldn't make a squeaking sound and give her away. It didn't.

She crept inside and finally came to the point where she could see her father. Just then, a board creaked beneath her feet, causing her father to jerk around. "Kelli, what do think you're doing, coming in here? You know the rules!" He shouted the words at her, and his face turned bright red. "Never, ever, ever, are you allowed to come in here when the door is shut. You know that."

"But, Daddy, the door wasn't shut—"

"Don't you dare lie to me, young lady." He stood up and started toward her, and Kelli could see the vein bulging at the side of his forehead. Usually that only happened when he was really mad at Mimi. "You get out of here right now. Do you understand?" He pulled the door open and pointed her out toward the hallway.

Kelli had her head down and tears streaming down her cheeks as she walked past him. Daddy had never talked to her that way before, and she had been telling the truth. As she got beside him, she mumbled, "The door wasn't closed."

The swat that landed on her rear end hurt all the more because she hadn't seen it coming. "Ouch."

"You ever sneak in here like that again, and you'll get worse." He slammed the door behind her, leaving Kelli crying in a crumpled heap in the hallway. The next day, he'd installed a lock on the inside of the office door. It was the only time in all her life Kelli could remember that kind of anger from her father directed at her.

Now, twenty years later, she stood at the door to his office, once again wondering what kind of treasure her father had hidden in his safe. She moved toward it, her heart pounding like it had all those years ago. She reached forward and turned the dial to the right, confirming the number on the piece of paper. Then back left. Then right. Then left.

As the light from the room filtered inside the safe, Kelli saw a stack of extra-large manila envelopes. She pulled them out and flipped them over to see them neatly labeled across the front with a black Sharpie. She recognized her father's block handwriting, which came as no surprise. The first envelope read *Starting Investments*. She pulled out a stack of official-looking documents. The top sheet was a statement from Smith Barney, as was the next page and the next. All investment stuff. An account opened in 1989, with regular deposits every few months. It wasn't a particularly large sum, and since it was over twenty years old, she couldn't figure out why he'd kept this, much less locked it in his safe. All of his current investment information had been in his filing cabinets.

1989?

That's when it hit her. These papers couldn't be from 1989, because the house fire that took the lives of Kelli's mother, brother, and sister had happened in 1991. That same fire had destroyed every single one of their family photos and mementos. Any paperwork also would have been destroyed.

It took only a few seconds before Kelli realized that these documents could have easily been copies made from the broker's office. Of course they could make duplicates.

She skimmed over page after page. Opening investments, deposits made, securities bought and sold until numbers all melted into one another and became nothing but an amorphous blob of indecipherable information. There was no reason she could discern as to why these particular documents would have been placed inside the safe. "So much for the mystery and excitement in here."

She pulled up the next envelope. It was simply labeled *Documents*. She opened it to find Social Security cards for Dad and Mimi. Hers had likely been kept there too when she'd been a child. Her vaccination reports were in there, and various licensing paperwork. All these things would have been placed there to prevent fire damage, she supposed.

"You found your way into the elusive safe. No wonder you didn't want any help, you were planning to keep all the riches for yourself." Denice's voice behind her caught her by surprise.

"I didn't hear you come in."

"Obviously. It's a good thing I'm not a robber."

Kelli shrugged. "Wouldn't matter much if you were. This thing is filled with old investment paperwork and Social Security cards. Nothing too exciting, that's for sure." She tilted her head. "What are you doing here?"

"Just came by to check on you. You're not answering your phone."

"Oh shoot. I must have left it on silent again." Kelli picked up her phone, saw that she'd missed six calls, and sighed. "I don't know why I always do that."

Denice rolled her eyes. "I'm willing to forgive you yet again, and I came by to tell you that Jones is about to throw some stuffed burgers on the grill, and he's made your favorite. You in?"

Kelli glanced at the next two envelopes. One marked *Miscellaneous,* the other *Odds and Ends*. Not exactly compelling. She looked at her watch and was surprised to see how late it was. "I must have spent more time on Daddy's truck than I realized. Come to think of it, I haven't eaten since breakfast. Jones's burgers sound good."

"Great. I'll see you at our place in twenty minutes."

"Okay, let me just lock this stuff back in the safe—for whatever reason, it must need to be in the safe. I'll finish dealing with it tomorrow." Kelli flipped off the lights as they left her father's office, but an uneasy feeling followed her down the hall. It poured itself into her and made its presence felt for the rest of the evening, although she couldn't give a reason for it. Something wasn't right, she just didn't know what or why. Yet.

It was almost noon when Kelli pulled into her parents' driveway the next day. She went straight to the office, determined to finish the cleaning today.

She opened the safe and pulled out the final envelopes. The first, the one marked *Miscellaneous,* was misshapen, the bottom much thicker than the top. She opened the flap and peeked down inside to see what looked like mostly photographs. She dumped the contents into her lap and picked up the photo on top.

A younger version of her father sat on the bank of a creek, fishing next to a small red-haired boy. Kelli had no idea who the boy might be—was it possible that it was Preston? No, it couldn't be. Not a single picture had survived the fire. Knowing her father always labeled pictures, she flipped it over. *Max, age 3, May 1987.*

Who was Max? And how had Daddy come by a photograph from 1987? The only explanation that made sense was that this Max person had given her father this picture after the fire. As a thank-you for taking him fishing? But why would her father keep it in his safe?

All of her life, Kelli had known that her mother, brother

Preston, and sister Kaitlin had been killed in a house fire in rural Louisiana when she was barely one. She knew no other details because her father could never bring himself to speak of it. Even Mimi, her stepmother, seemed to know little about it, and she always insisted they never speak of it because it upset Kelli's father so.

Kelli turned her attention back to the pile of pictures. The next was Daddy holding a chubby baby with short, curly hair. She had her arms locked around his neck, offering a huge smile to the camera. Kelli flipped over the picture. *Beth, age 1, May 1987.*

Kelli began to flip rapidly through the pictures now. There were more of Max and Beth individually and together. Dad was in some of the pictures, but not all of them. Toward the end, Kelli came to a picture of a woman she didn't recognize. She was pretty and elegant looking in a non-pretentious, Laura Bush sort of way. She held her hand up over her eyes, shading the sun as she smiled at the camera. Kelli flipped the picture over. *Alison, 1988.* The very last picture showed all four of them—Daddy, Alison, Beth, and Max—standing together in front of a couple of huge sequoia trees. Kelli turned it over, afraid of what she would see. *Family vacation, Kings Canyon National Park, 1988.* The photo dropped from Kelli's hand and fluttered to the carpet.

There was still another envelope yet to be opened. Kelli simply stared at it, minute after minute ticking by.

Odds and Ends.

Finally, she dumped the contents on the floor beside her and found a mishmash of newspaper clippings, notebook paper, and some official-looking paperwork. She picked up the top article from the group, prepared to read about the horrific house fire that had trapped a woman and her two small children, that had left not one single thing in the home uncharred. Her eye fell immediately to the two large photos on the page. The first was a tiny girl, little more than a baby, dressed in a frilly dress, wearing lacy socks and a floppy hat. The other was a middle-aged man, wearing a coat and tie and a broad smile.

The headline read, "Local Man and 1-Year-Old Daughter Missing After Boating Mishap." Beneath the photos was a sentence in bold type: "An overnight search was launched off the South Carolina coast for David Waters and his young daughter Darcy, when the skiff the two were last seen in washed ashore in foul weather. The Coast Guard captain says he is 'cautiously optimistic.'"

Kelli studied the pictures. The little girl looked like . . . But she could be anyone, there was no way to know for sure. The man, however, she did know. Her hands started shaking so hard the paper fell from her grasp and fluttered to the ground. The implications of what she was seeing began to take shape, and she ran to the bathroom and puked in the toilet. As she stood at the sink, rinsing her mouth, she looked up at the mirror and spoke her question aloud. "David Waters? Darcy Waters? Who are they, and what is going on here?"

She walked from the room, knowing that the complete and truthful answers to those questions were something she had to find out. And she knew more than enough at this point to know the answers were going to be devastating.

Ken Moore, known to everyone in the sleepy town of Shoal Creek, Tennessee, as simply Kenmore, looked over the ledgers yet again, seeing month after month of negative numbers. It was times like this he was thankful that he hadn't bowed to Shane's insistence that he computerize all his accounting. At least he wasn't stuck looking at his impending demise decreed in bright red numbers. He slid the ledger book into the desk drawer, which he proceeded to lock.

He leaned back in the wooden swivel desk chair. It creaked and tottered backward at an alarming angle—signaling that it, too, had just about reached the end of its usefulness here. How many times had Kenmore seen his father sitting in this same chair, working on essentially the same ledgers, his face deep in concentration? This office still carried the faintest hint of his smell—wood shavings and Old Spice—even though he'd been gone for over fifteen years. It was the clearest memory Kenmore had of his childhood—a memory he'd hoped to pass down to Shane. And he supposed he had to some extent. Shane's memories would just be clouded by the closing of the place. At least he wouldn't be losing his job in the process. That was something to be thankful about.

Kenmore shook his head and pushed to his feet. Now was not the time to get sentimental. He pocketed the key to the desk and walked down the two steps into the store itself. Time to sweep up and go home.

His back and hips ached something fierce as he pushed the broom across the cement floor. He was halfway down the first aisle when he heard the back door squeak open. He looked toward the storeroom and made a point of standing up straighter and pushing the broom with a bit more gusto than before, trying not to grit his teeth in the process. Sure enough, his son Shane emerged, took one look at him, and shook his head. "Pop, you should have been home an hour ago. What are you still doing here?"

"It makes for a better morning if you arrive at a clean store." He focused his attention on the pile of dust, paper, and debris as he shoved it up the aisle. "You know I've always done it this way."

"Let Frieda sweep in the morning. You pay her way more than you should, I don't think asking her to sweep is a problem. Know what I mean?"

Kenmore shrugged. "Since she's leaving in a couple of days, now's not the time to start new habits. Know what I mean?" He parked the debris pile near the front door and walked to the end of the aisle with mostly grocery items and began the process again.

"No, I don't. In fact, I think it's the best possible time to start something new. When you find Frieda's replacement, he or she won't think a thing about it."

"Like I told you, I'm not replacing Frieda." By having one less salary to pay, and if everything went relatively well, it should be financially feasible to keep the store a little longer. October 27 would be the fiftieth anniversary of the grand opening. Kenmore owed it to his parents' memories to take it that far.

"Pop, get serious. Dr. Craviotto told you months ago that you need to have your hip replaced. You can't work twelve-hour days and have surgery, too. I don't know why you're still working so many hours anyway. At your age, it's time to hire more help and start relaxing a little."

There would be plenty of time to relax come November—more time than Kenmore wanted—but he wasn't going to say any of that to Shane right now. "It takes more work and effort to break in a new employee than it does to just do everything myself."

"What about Ashley, then? Have her come in extra."

"She works weekends only, you know that. She spends her weekdays watching her grandkids while her daughter works."

"I knew you were going to say that."

"Then why do you keep bringing it up?"

"Because this time, I brought the solution to the problem." Shane lifted his hand to reveal a *Help Wanted* sign. Without saying another word, he went behind the counter and got some tape, then hung the sign in the window right beside the door.

Kenmore walked over and pulled it down. "I've told you, I don't want to hire more help. It took me nearly two years to get Frieda broken in to where she was any use to me. That was seven or eight years ago, when I was younger and more patient. I don't have the time or energy to do that again."

"It did not take two years. Frieda's a good worker, and she caught on fast."

"Yeah, well, it's not so much the doing-the-work part, it's the staying-out-of-my-way part that people seem to have a hard time figuring out. Like my own son, for instance, who is standing here inside my own store telling me what I should and shouldn't be doing."

"We both know the thing you should be doing is taking better care of yourself. So, since you've chosen not to do that, I'm choosing to help you along." Shane took the sign from Kenmore's hand and put it back in the window.

"I don't want anyone else in my store. Period." Kenmore reached right over and pulled it down again. "I've got Keith afternoons and weekends for all the heavy lifting, and Ashley lets me have weekends mostly off. That's more help than I need. Truth be told, I'd prefer to do it all myself."

"Pop, you're overdoing it. Summer's almost here, and you know it's your busiest season. Now is the time to start planning ahead. You need more help."

"Not my fault Frieda decided to get married and move off to Kansas."

"But you won't even try to replace her. Why?"

"Told you. I like doing things my own way." He planned to keep silent about the financial situation until after the summer season, then slowly leak out word that the place would be closing because he'd decided to retire. Best case scenario, he would walk away from this place with no one ever realizing that shuttering it was something he'd done from necessity rather than choice.

Shane growled, then grabbed the broom handle and began working the area around the counter. "You have got to be the most stubborn man alive."

"Give me my broom back."

"I've got it."

"Who did you say is stubborn? I'm not an invalid. I can sweep my own store. Looks like there won't be any choice about it from here on out."

"Oh, I think there will be." Shane picked up the *Help Wanted* sign and returned it to the window without relinquishing control of the broom.

"You can hang that sign there if you want to, but I'm telling you now, I'm not going to talk to anybody about it. I'm not taking any applications, I'm not checking any references, and I'm not offering a job. Me and Keith can handle it just fine."

Shane studied Kenmore for a few seconds, then nodded. "Well, all right, then." Much to Kenmore's relief, he pulled the sign out of the window. That had been easier than he'd expected.

Shane carried the sign behind the counter and pulled out a Sharpie. After writing something at the bottom, he tore off a few pieces of fresh tape and put the sign back in the window.

"What'd you write on there?"

"My cell number. You said you weren't going to take any applications, and if that's how you want to play it, that's fine. But me, I'm willing to consider anyone. Whoever might be looking for a job is welcome to talk to me."

"Well, they can go to work for you then, 'cause they're not coming here."

"We'll just see about that."

Kelli pulled her knees up to her chest and rocked back and forth on the old beige carpet. There were several more articles to read, but she wasn't ready yet. Her mind raced, trying to make sense of what she knew already.

First of all, her father had a whole set of pictures with another family—a family he was apparently a part of, yet none of their names matched the names Kelli knew as her deceased mother and siblings. And apparently her father had gone missing in South Carolina, but he had always said they came from Louisiana. Third, if there was a harmless explanation for what she was seeing, why would her father have kept this all so secret? Locked in a safe in a room where no one else was allowed?

She reached for the next article. This one was written a week after the first. The search had been called off in spite of the fact that no bodies had been found. The photograph this time showed a mother, her lips turned down at an impossible angle, puffy eyes drooping, as if the weight of grief had pulled down and elongated her entire face. She had her right arm around the shoulder of a young girl, her left arm around a slightly older boy. The caption beneath the photograph said, "Alison Waters, shown with her two children, says that she will not give up hope that her husband and daughter may yet turn up alive." Kelli leaned forward and took a closer look, then she reached into the pile of pictures she'd already looked through. She picked up a couple in particular and set them beside the newspaper clipping.

He had grown, but there could be no doubt about who she was seeing. This was the boy named Max from the other photos. The girl was Beth.

Kelli skimmed the article. One particular paragraph gripped her. "When asked about a memorial service, Mrs. Waters declared that she would schedule no such service while she had even a small hope that her husband and daughter were still alive somewhere. She noted the contradiction that the Coast Guard called off the search, but the coroner's office refused to issue a death certificate until bodies were found. 'What kind of wife and mother gives up hope before some government agency?'"

Kelli stood and started to pace. She put her right hand around the gold cuff bracelet on her left wrist and began to spin it around and around. Over and under. Over and under. Its scratchy surface pulled at the skin on her wrist.

Denice. She had to talk to Denice. She pulled out her cell phone and saw that she had missed three calls from her friend because the phone was on silent again. She pressed the button to return the call and tried to hold herself together.

"'Bout time you called back. I was about to send out a search party."

"Denice, I . . ." The words choked her. She took a deep breath. "I've found something awful."

"Where are you?"

"Dad and Mimi's house."

"I'll leave work as soon as the afternoon crowd dies down. In the meantime, tell me what's going on."

"I can't talk about it over the phone. Can you just come here, please? As soon as possible."

"I don't like the way you sound right now."

"I don't like the way I feel right now." She looked at the piles of papers and photos on the floor. "You're not going to believe this, you're just not going to believe it." She pushed the disconnect button and sank down to the floor, where she curled up in a tight ball and closed her eyes. That did nothing to stop the shaking that had begun in her hands and now worked its way through her entire body.

By the time she heard Denice's car in the driveway, the shakes had stopped, but she couldn't find the energy to sit up. The door screeched open, and footsteps pounded down the hall. "Kelli? Kelli!" Denice rushed into the office and dropped to the ground beside her. "What's happened? Are you hurt?" Denice leaned over her in concern. "What's going on?"

Kelli sat up, drew her knees to her chest again, and buried her face in her hands. "It's my dad."

"What about him?"

She pointed to the piles of various photos and pictures. "I don't think he was who I thought he was—who he claimed to be." She looked toward Denice, knowing she could help her make sense of all this.

Denice looked down at the photo of the family vacation, studied it, then nodded her head. She took a deep breath. "Why don't you tell me exactly what you've found out?"

Kelli reached for the picture. "I'm not really sure what it all means yet, but it seems pretty evident to me that his entire past is something different than what I've always been told it was."

Denice put her arm around Kelli's shoulders and drew her close. "Oh, honey, I'm sorry." She waited a few heartbeats before she followed it up with, "Does that completely surprise you? Honestly?"

"Of course it does! What would make you even ask that?" Kelli pulled away from her, stunned.

"It's just that, deep down, I've always believed there was something he was hiding. I never knew what it was, but I always felt it."

"What would make you say that?"

"He avoided the subject of anything from the past like Ebola, no matter how insignificant it seemed. Remember that time Jones asked him if he'd played any sports in high school? You'd have thought he'd been asked to reveal a national secret from his reaction."

Kelli found her strength in a surge of anger and stood up. She began pacing the room. "Of course he never talked about his past. What man alive would want to talk about something that tragic?" Even as she asked the question, Kelli's anger began to dissolve into the fog of doubt. She knew about the accident she'd been told about all her life—the tragic fire that happened in Louisiana. Yet now she was confronted with newspaper articles about a different kind of accident altogether, in a different state, with different victims.

Denice held up her hands in truce. "Hey, I'm on your side here. I'm just saying that I am not surprised that you've found something unusual. He was a good dad, and you had a happy life—of course you didn't think anything about it. Those of us who were raised in a bit less conventional families, who have a bit less . . . faith . . . in others, well, it's people like me who notice there are things not quite copacetic about people like your father. Now, why don't you tell me what it is you've found and let's talk about it."

Kelli started from the beginning and showed Denice what she'd discovered. "Unbelievable." Denice just kept mumbling the word. Finally, she said, "Let's take all this back to my place. We can keep looking through it, and Jones should be home by now, so we can get his input."

Half an hour later, they were once again seated around the little kitchen table in Denice's house. Kelli locked her hands behind her neck and slumped forward. "This can't be real, it just can't." But she knew, even as she said the words, that all of it was true, that her father had had another family. She sat up and rested her elbows on the table. "Except, when I think about it, there were all these little clues, like the way my father always avoided downtown Santa Barbara, especially during tourist season. He blamed it on hating crowds—which was true enough—but was the fact that he was in hiding a bigger part of the reason? He was afraid he'd see someone from his old life and they would recognize him? My own father, my best friend for all of my life, constantly looked over his shoulder, and I never suspected a thing."

"These pictures, then—they are of your mother and your sister and brother?" Jones looked up from where he'd been methodically going through a stack, one photo at a time.

"That's my assumption. It's the first time I've ever seen any of them."

"You're kidding. Your father didn't have any pictures of them around the house?"

"Not a one—not that I knew of, anyway. I'd always been told that all the old pictures burned in the fire, and there was absolutely nothing left."

"But I mean, online. Didn't you ever try to look them up?"

"Sure. Lots of times. But I was always looking for Maria and Preston and Kaitlin Huddleston in Louisiana. Apparently I should have been looking for Alison and Max and Beth Waters in either South Carolina or Tennessee. I'm still not clear where they actually lived. I've spent my entire life wondering what my family looked like, and he had these pictures all the time."

Kelli moved to the chair beside Jones and traced the photo with her hand. "Why wouldn't he have shown these to me? He still could have told me they died, but why would he be that cruel, to have these pictures and not share them with me, knowing that I wanted to know?"

"I can answer that question for you, without even thinking about it," Denice said from across the table. "Mimi."

Even as she started to deny it, Kelli knew it was the truth. Knew it beyond a doubt. "You're right. Had to be."

Jones looked up. "Why Mimi? Wouldn't she have wanted you to have a picture of your family?"

Kelli shook her head. "Mimi took the word *jealous* to a whole new level. Any time Dad even spoke to another woman, she'd pitch a fit, and if the woman was pretty, well . . ."

"Which is ironic, considering she's the one who caroused around all night. I always wondered why your father just took it when she was out at some club, why he never got mad. Seeing all this, it's obvious." He flipped to the next picture.

"Really? What's obvious? Because quite frankly none of this makes sense to me." Between the new information, and partial information, Kelli now possessed, none of it added up to answers for anything.

"It was guilt. Your father must have felt so guilty about what he'd done—to his kids at least, if not to his own wife, that it must have eaten him up. He deserved what he got, and he knew it. Then, he looked at you, the only remaining child he hadn't betrayed and abandoned, and the last thing he wanted to do was get a divorce. Besides, he was probably afraid Mimi would get mad and tell his secret—surely she knew it."

"Why wouldn't he just have divorced Kelli's mother back at the start of all this?" Denice asked. "That's what doesn't make sense."

"There would be custody issues, financial settlements. This way, he got Kelli free and clear."

"But why would he take only me?"

"Your siblings were older, right? Too old to believe some cockeyed story, and even if they did, they were definitely too old to change their names without eventually spilling the beans to someone." Jones stroked his beard, nodding thoughtfully.

Kelli had to agree that the pieces seemed to fall into place just a little. "You may be right. Maybe knowing all this is what drove Mimi to drink as much as she did."

"Makes you wonder, doesn't it." Jones was looking at a picture of Alison. "If your dad put up with Mimi all these years without a bit of fuss, it makes me think your mother must be a real piece of work. I mean, your dad is a pretty docile guy, so there has to be a reason he was desperate enough to do something like this."

Denice reached over and shoved his shoulder. "Watch what you say, you big lug. We're talking about Kelli's mother. You can't just insult her like that."

"I'm just saying, it makes me wonder. But then again, why would he have left your brother and sister to face that all alone?"

Kelli rubbed her forehead with her thumb and middle finger, the way she'd watched her father do all his life when he was overwhelmed. She pulled her hand away. "It doesn't make sense. None of it does."

"These are answers that you are going to need to find. You need to figure out and accept what happened before so you can start moving forward to the life ahead of you."

Jones looked up. "You mean she should call her mother and tell her who she is?"

"Are you crazy? Of course not. She might be a raving lunatic, for all we know. It is imperative that the secret stay in this room only."

"Agreed."

"Agreed."

They did an around-the-circle handshake in their own little custom of promise-making.

"It's a good thing you have that journal I gave you, because you need to focus all your energy on getting through this. Don't you even think about anything else. We've got you covered as far as anything at the restaurant goes, right, Jones?"

"Absolutely. You do what you need to do, Kelli."

"Thanks, you two. Figuring out what happened in my past is the black bog I'm about to have to wade through. Opening our restaurant in the fall, well, that is going to be the solid ground ahead where I keep my eyes fixed. As long as I have that, it gives me a reason to keep going. To tell you the truth, I'm concerned that for a while, it might be the only thing that does."

7

My dad took me camping every summer when I was growing up. It was always just the two of us—Mimi wasn't much of an outdoor girl—and we'd spend a week at El Capitan Beach.

By the time I rolled my groggy little self out of my sleeping bag each morning, he would have the camp stove burning full tilt. I'd unzip the tent and follow my nose toward the smell of bacon and scrambled eggs, my mouth watering in anticipation. He'd have a spatula in one hand, and he'd gesture toward the sky with the other. "'Bout time you got up. We're burning daylight," and with that, the adventure would begin. Days spent hiking the cliffs, digging in the sand, and playing in the waves. He never grew tired of building sandcastles and pretending for hour after hour that seashells were magical chariots with pebble princes and princesses riding them all around the moat.

By the time the sun started to set across the ocean, Daddy would throw me on his shoulders and carry me up the hill to the campground. The whole way up, he made neighing sounds and bucking motions, like he was a renegade horse. People looked at us like we were idiots, but we didn't care. We were happy. Completely happy.

Actually, maybe it was only me.

The printer whirred and zipped as it printed out page after page. By the time Kelli left her laptop to check on the progress, there were well over thirty pages in the tray. She pulled them out and began to sort it all by subject. So far, everything fit into one of four categories: Mother. Sister. Brother. And her father's friend named Ken Moore, who was a little easier to find information about.

Knock. Knock.

Kelli turned the stacks upside down before she went to answer the door of her apartment. Probably her landlady. Since Kelli lived in the mother-in-law unit above Mrs. Rohling's garage, she dropped by for one reason or other several times a week. Although she wasn't the nosy sort, she did tend to tidy up as she talked, a habit she acknowledged as being annoying but unbreakable.

It was a relief to find Denice at the door instead. "How's the research coming?" She hurried inside and kept her voice low. "I've been doing some of my own, and then it occurred to me that we could accomplish more by working together. You know, pooling our collective wisdom." She reached into her purse and pulled out her iPad.

"Sounds like a good idea, although I seem to have more or less hit the dead end of having found most everything there is on the Internet."

"I've got the same problem, that's why I came over."

"Aren't you supposed to be at work?"

"I called in sick."

"Why?"

"So I can help you figure this out. I'm not leaving you out here all alone to suffer like this. We are best friends, and this is what friends do for each other."

"I doubt seriously your boss would agree."

Denice grinned. "He won't be my boss for much longer. Three more months and then I am free of that man forever. I'll be in charge of my own destiny."

"*You'll* be in charge, huh? What about your partners?" Kelli smiled.

"Eh, they're pushovers. I'll rule the place as a kind, humble, yet firm queen."

That made Kelli actually laugh out loud. "I don't know that I've ever heard Jones's name and pushover in the same sentence before." Jones had a heart of gold, there was no denying that, but he also had a mile-wide stubborn streak.

"Well, that's because Jones isn't crazy about everyone else the way he is about me. Basically, he'll do whatever I tell him." It was a joke, yet at least half true at the same time.

"Well, I, for one, have not fallen into your evil little spell. I'm not a pushover. I'm a stickler, even if you are a queen."

"But, just like my husband, you love me to your own detriment. Yep, I'm planning to kick back and relax and enjoy the fruits of your labor soon enough. But first"—she opened her iPad case—"I've got to help my best friend figure out what exactly is going on here. What's your story, so far as you've found?"

"Best I can figure, we lived in a small town in Tennessee. We were supposed to take a family trip to a coastal cabin in South Carolina. Dad and I went a couple of days earlier than the rest of the family—something about looking over a cabin he was thinking about buying. The day before everyone else was due to arrive, Dad rented a little boat, the two of us went for a ride, and the boat washed ashore twelve hours later in a storm. He must have planned it all pretty carefully. The timing, the boat. His car was left at the dock. All our things were still in the hotel room. He must have hidden another car somewhere up the coast, I don't know, then somehow set the boat adrift, knowing a storm was coming."

"It seems pretty farfetched."

"Yes, it does, but everything about this seems farfetched."

"Okay, so what have you found about your family in recent years? I haven't seen much other than a notice in the local newspaper that your sister got married about four years ago."

"You did? Where'd you find that?"

"The *Shoal Creek Tribune*. Here, I copied it." She shuffled through her papers until she found the right one, then slid it across the table. "The two of you favor each other a fair amount."

Kelli looked at the wedding picture of the sister she'd believed dead for the past twenty-four years. Her smile was huge as she stood beside her groom, a lake in the background. What had her wedding day been like?

Kelli handed the picture back to Denice. "I don't see a resemblance at all."

"That's because she's got a fancy wedding updo and makeup. Take all that away, and I'm saying there are several similarities." Denice didn't bother to look as she put the article back into her file. "Your brother has been a little harder to track down."

"For me, too. You know what? I think I'm going to need to take a trip back there and see a few things for myself."

"Go back there? Absolutely not. Nothing good would come of that."

"Maybe. Maybe not. You're the one who keeps telling me I have to work forward and get some closure. Maybe my father had some reason to do what he did. Maybe my mother is an addict, or an abuser, or mentally unstable. Even Jones said she must be a piece of work for this to have been necessary."

Denice looked doubtful, but she nodded her head slowly. "Perhaps if you went back there and saw the truth, you could move forward with your life with a sense of peace, and quite frankly, that's what is at stake here. I still think it is very risky. You would need to set some boundaries and hold firm to them, and I do mean hold firm."

"Of course."

"You know I'd come with you if I could."

"I know you would, but this is something I've got to do myself." Kelli turned back to her stacks of paperwork. "I wonder if there are other members of the family, too—aunts, cousins, grandparents . . . Grandparents! Why didn't I think of this before?"

"Think of what?"

"Opal. I wonder if she knows anything."

"Mimi's mother?"

"Yes."

"Your father and Mimi married after the two of you moved here, right? Surely even if Mimi knew the whole truth, or even if she was involved, they wouldn't have told Opal."

"I'm not so sure. Mimi tells Opal pretty much everything. Who could say what she might know?" She nodded her head, liking the thought more and more. She picked up her cell and scrolled to Opal's number in her contacts. "Opal? I was thinking I might come visit tomorrow afternoon. Can I take you out for dinner?"

Kelli drove past mile after mile of central California vineyards on her way to Opal's house. The house itself was on an acre of land completely surrounded by hillside wineries. The owners on each side had, on several occasions, offered her twice what her house was worth if she would sell, but she had refused. "She likes the appearance of being a major landowner," her father had said. "Somehow she just knows that people who drive by here believe she owns every bit of those grapes up on the hill. Your grandmother has always been more concerned about appearances than common sense."

The fact that she did not allow any kind of grandmotherly nickname, but preferred for Kelli to call her by her first name—because "Mam-maw is a name for old people"—leant some credibility to what Daddy had said. Fact was, Opal wasn't much like a grandmother at all. She was more like Mimi's slightly older best friend—something that had driven Daddy crazy.

Opal flung open the door as soon as Kelli pulled up in front of the house. Today's outfit included a white turban, a white vest made of some sort of shaggy material, white shirt, and white jeans.

Opal never did anything halfway. She rushed forward and met Kelli at the side of her car. "Oh, my darling, how are you doing? I'm just so glad to see you. We've got to stick together at a time like this, yes we do." She wrapped her thin arms around Kelli and hugged tight.

"How are you, Opal?"

"I honestly don't know how much longer I will be able to go on. No woman should have to bury her own daughter. It's just too much for me to bear."

What about Daddy's parents? Had he left them behind to believe he was dead? Had they spent their lives grieving their son? Or did they know what he'd done and never come to visit because it would be too risky? What do you know, Opal?

"How about you, dear? Are you holding up okay?" She dabbed at her eyes with a tissue she had produced from a pocket in her vest.

"I'm doing all—"

"You've always been strong. You can surely thank your lucky stars that you were raised by such a wonderful woman, because I guarantee that's where you learned it. What a blessing it has been for you to have such a terrific role model to guide you through your growing-up years. I know all your friends wish they'd had such a good mother, and I was so fortunate to have her for a daughter. We were both lucky, that's what we were."

Kelli wondered how lucky Opal would feel if she knew what apparently was the truth about her daughter. Or did she know already? Kelli had no intention of being the one to tell her, but if Opal did know something . . . "Yes, we were both lucky."

Mimi, whose real name was Suze, had been the light of Opal's existence. She had loved and adored her with every fiber of her being. Somehow, though, this love had often manifested itself in tiny little digs against Kelli's dad, and sometimes all-out criticism.

Because of this, Kelli had never been that close to her grandmother.

"Oh, darling, there are some days I just don't think I'll be able to make it through."

"I miss them both so much."

"Of course you do." Opal took her by the elbow and led her toward the front door. "Come inside and let's have a drink and chat for a while before we head down to the restaurant. Now, you come right on in the kitchen and I'll pour us both a glass of something. What would you like, dear?"

"Diet Coke would be great."

"Little rum for good measure?" She quirked a penciled-on eyebrow.

"No thanks. I'm driving, you know."

"I don't think one shot of rum would hurt anything, but whatever you say, I won't argue." Opal pulled out two highball glasses and put ice in each. In one, she poured Diet Coke, in the other, a generous helping of scotch. While Opal busied herself pouring the drinks, Kelli took a seat at the table and once again thought through the best way to present her questions in order to get the most honest answers.

"Opal, how did you meet my dad?"

She brought the glass over and set it in front of Kelli, took a sip of her own drink, then wiped her palm across her forehead. "I'm sure you've heard this all before, but let's see. It wasn't long after he moved here. Suze herself had just returned to the area after living for a few years in Tennessee." She shook her head. "I was proud of her for making it through like she did."

"Making it through?"

"Broken heart." She rubbed her forehead as if she had a headache. "Not long after Suze graduated from high school, she went down to visit some friends at Cal Poly, and she met Jonas. He was playing at a club there and supposedly moving up the country-music food chain pretty rapidly. He was something else, I'll tell you that. He drove a big fancy truck, always had his shirts pressed just so, his jeans, too. And good-looking—woo-wee." She fanned herself and took another drink. "They were a beautiful couple, just stunning. Next thing I knew, they were packing up and moving to Nashville."

"Funny, I've never heard of him."

"I guess I'm not surprised." Opal looked out the window and sighed. "Suze was such a pretty girl. All the men were just gaga over her, and she always had a long trail of admirers. If it hadn't been for Jonas, she'd . . ."

"So what happened?"

"Apparently, once they got to Nashville, some girl set her sights on him and would not give up—her father was a big shot in the music industry, that's the only way she could have taken him away from Suze, we all knew that—and she connived and contrived and finally convinced Jonas to leave Suze and move in with her." Opal wiped a tear at this point. "Somehow, he managed to take every bit of Suze's money before he broke things off, though. Left her alone and broke, he did. The only satisfaction I got out of the matter is that he never did amount to anything. We heard a few years ago he was working in a bar on the seedy side of Nashville. That's better than he deserves, if you ask me."

"So that's when Mimi moved back to California? After they broke up?" At least Kelli was getting more detail than she'd ever gotten about her parents' former life. She suspected that if she could keep Opal talking about Mimi long enough, there might be some true answers.

"Heavens, no. My Suze would never want to be a burden to anyone, or for us to worry, so she didn't even tell us it had happened. She went and got herself a job as a waitress, worked long hours and saved every penny until she was back on her feet. You know what a hard worker she was."

To Kelli's knowledge, no one had ever referred to her stepmother as a hard worker—fun to be around and energetic, yes, but hard worker, no. And money saver? Definitely not.

"Good for her."

"Yes. By the time we knew things had gone wrong, she was already on the road to recovery. She moved to Santa Barbara and bought that house, got her job at the gym. A couple months later, you and your father came to town looking for a room to rent."

She took another sip and then another before continuing. "She was a smart businesswoman, so renting out a room made sense. It's a good idea to get some extra income when you're first starting out. Your father was so much older than she was, and she'd never wanted kids, so of course it never entered anyone's mind that he would convince her to marry him." She glanced toward Kelli then, and the mist seemed to clear from her eyes.

Opal seemed perfectly sincere in her answers, but somewhere deep inside she had to know that with the high prices of Santa Barbara real estate, there was no way a single woman who worked as a gym assistant manager could possibly have afforded to buy that house. Not without help. A lot of it.

"So, she didn't know my dad until he moved here?"

Opal paused for a moment, seeming to consider her answer. Was she trying to remember the official storyline they'd all agreed upon? "That's right." She tugged at the fringe on her vest. "One day, she called me and told me they'd just gone to the courthouse and got married. I was . . . stunned." She shook her head. "It wasn't exactly the way I had thought her life would go." She glanced up at Kelli. "Well, let me just give you some advice. When it comes to love, you've got to use your heart *and* your brain."

By now, they were in familiar territory, and Kelli had no

patience to listen to it today. "Opal, I just wanted you to know I'm leaving town in a few days. I don't plan to be gone for more than a couple of weeks. I should be back by the end of the month at the latest."

"Leaving? Where are you going?"

"Tennessee. There's a little town south of Nashville called Shoal Creek."

"Shoal Creek?" Opal's voice came out deep, scratchy. She looked at Kelli hard, her eyes squinted. The grandfather clock behind her chimed the quarter hour, breaking the long silence. Opal slammed back the rest of her drink. "Don't believe I've ever heard of it."

"Really? Because I thought maybe Mimi—"

"Time to head out. We don't want to be late for our reservation." She stood up and grabbed her purse. "Let's get this show on the road."

I am a nonexistent person. Apparently the person I've believed myself to be for the entirety of my life does not truly exist. Which leads me to ask these questions: 1) Why have I been thrust into this nonexistent life by my father who claimed to love me? 2) Who is my real family and what do they know? 3) What am I supposed to do?

If Opal knows anything, she's keeping quiet about it. I thought about pushing a little harder, but what if she really doesn't know anything? I don't want to crush the good memories she has left—and she has definitely self-edited most of her memories to make them all good (the ones about Mimi, anyway). In a couple of days, I'm driving to Tennessee. I'm planning to spend a week there and hopefully find out some more answers. Enough that I can go on with my life. Right now, I'm not sure how that's possible.

I changed the cover of this journal. It used to say Kelli, *but now it says* Finding Kelli. *That's what I hope to do.*

Find Kelli.

Kelli went to her parents' house for the final time on Saturday. Even now, with everything moved out and the place completely empty, she expected to see her father walking down the steps, grin on his face, asking her if she wanted to go hiking up at Lizard's Mouth, or paddleboarding at Goleta Beach, or kayaking at Leadbetter. It didn't seem possible that he would never again do any of those things.

After her final walk-through with the Realtor, she handed over the keys. "I'd like to just sit on the steps for a few minutes before I go."

Marian nodded. "Take all the time you need." She squeezed Kelli's arm, then hurried to her car as if afraid somehow the grief was contagious.

Kelli buried her face in her hands. This place had been her whole world for all of her growing-up years. Happy times and not so happy times, just like any other family. Only in this case there seemed to be one thing that most families didn't have—it was all built on a lie. There had to be some sort of logical explanation for all that had happened, and Kelli intended to find out what it was.

"Sorry to see you go, neighbor." Kelli looked up to see Julie Layton coming up the driveway toward her. Julie lived in Colorado but flew out to visit her mother on a regular basis. "I saw you over here and wanted to come tell you good-bye, and to tell you how sorry I am. About everything." At fifty-something, Julie easily looked ten years younger, even with the no-makeup, slightly unkempt look she'd always favored.

Kelli remained seated on the steps but nodded her appreciation. "Thank you. It's been rough around here lately."

"For all of us." Julie dropped down beside her, extending her tan legs in front of her so that her Birkenstocks rested on the edge of the lawn.

Kelli liked Julie, so she bit back her sarcastic response—her week wouldn't have been nearly so rough if she hadn't gotten fired for trying to help Julie's mother. But Julie hadn't been the one to make the call, and either way, it was done now, no reason to burn bridges.

There had been Dalton Construction trucks parked at Mrs. Layton's all week without even a pause. Kelli wasn't sure how that translated into a tough time "for all of them," as it seemed more than apparent things were fine for the Laytons.

"How is your mom?" Kelli asked. Mrs. Layton had seemed to believe Kelli when she confided about the overbilling. Had she approved of, or even known about, Kevin's phone call that ended Kelli's job?

"She's devastated."

"Devastated?" Kelli glanced down the street toward her house. "Please tell her not to worry on my account. We've got the restaurant opening in the fall, and I'm sure I'll be able to find another job to tide me over in the meantime."

"You lost your job over this?" Julie's voice held true surprise.

"Yes. Jimmy fired me as soon as I walked in the door on Monday morning."

"Because Kevin called him about Mom?"

"Yes." Kelli looked toward Julie, truly confused. "I assumed you knew that."

"No. And please do me a favor and don't tell Mom. I think that would put her over the edge. She's so upset already."

"What is she so upset about, then? Because Kevin didn't believe it when I told him about the dishonesty?"

Julie inhaled, cranked her face up toward the sky as if to drink in the sunlight, then slowly exhaled and lowered her head. "Mom's moving to San Francisco."

"Why?"

"Kevin called an emergency teleconference of all us siblings on Sunday evening. Due to all that has transpired, he declared it too much of a burden to watch over Mom from afar. Since he is the one who handles all her financial affairs, and is the closest geographically, he is the one who has to drive down when there are health issues and whatnot. He found an assisted living facility close to his home and has made arrangements for her to live there starting next week. So tomorrow, instead of having a nice Mother's Day brunch as usual, we're packing up Mom's things and getting her ready to move out."

Tomorrow was Mother's Day? Back when Kelli still lived at home, she and Dad had always made a point of fixing a nice breakfast in bed for Mimi, usually accompanied by a gift certificate for a day at a spa. This year, Kelli wondered how her real mother would be celebrating. "Your mom has always been such a do-it-yourself-type person. I'm surprised he could convince her to agree to a move like that."

"You wouldn't be so surprised if you knew Kevin better. He's a master manipulator. He played it off to Mom that he wanted her to be closer to the grandkids, yada yada, and when she didn't go for that, he threw in a whopping dose of guilt about what a burden it is on the family to have her so far away. That's what got her to give in." Julie shook her head. "Her independence was the one thing she always valued most, and now she's lost it just that quick."

"That is so sad."

"I was the only one of the four kids against it, so I was overruled. Poor Mom, I heard her crying after she went to bed last night."

"If she's leaving, why are they continuing the remodel?"

"It'll make the place look better when it goes on the market next month."

"Can I go over and tell her good-bye?"

"I don't think it's a good idea." She put a hand on Kelli's arm. "I don't blame you a bit, you did the right thing. But last night, Mom said she wished she'd never answered the door when you came over. Seeing you right now would not be a good thing for her."

Kelli looked toward the Layton house and thought about the wonderful woman who had lived there for at least fifty years and now was having to leave because Kelli had tried to help her by telling the truth. Why hadn't she just kept her mouth shut? It would have been better for everybody. "Will you . . . tell her something for me? When you think she is ready to hear it?"

"What?"

"Tell her I'm sorry."

Julie sighed and stood up. She kept her eyes focused toward her mother's house. "Yes, when the time is right, I'll tell her." She turned and walked away without looking back.

Kenmore made it just in time. He'd been putting money in the floor safe when he'd realized it wasn't going to be so easy to get back to his feet. He reached for the nearby chair, barely able to grasp it with his right hand, and slid it toward him. Finally, he was able to push himself up. He'd just made it to standing when Shane pranced into his office.

"What's the matter with you? You're huffing and puffing like you just ran a marathon."

Kenmore glared at his son. "What exactly are you doing here?" He reached forward and pretended to wipe a spot on the desk. In truth, he simply needed a place to lean.

"Glad to see you too, Pop." Shane crossed his arms across his chest and grinned. "I could ask you the same question. It's Saturday evening, supposedly your day off."

"Two of Ashley's grandkids have the stomach flu—apparently so does her daughter. She called me and asked if I could take over so she could help out, not that it's any of your business."

"Maybe it's time you think about selling this place."

"And do what?"

"Spend your days fishing. Learn to relax a little. You're sixty-two. A lot of people retire at sixty-two."

Did Shane know something or was he just talking? "Sit around by myself and get old, you mean. You can peddle that snake oil somewhere else."

"Then why aren't you getting serious about hiring someone to replace Frieda? Today is the perfect example of why you need another person."

"Frieda didn't work Saturdays anyway." He made a point of looking Shane up and down. "You're looking downright pretty." He nodded slowly and grinned. "Fancy-looking dress shirt and khakis. I'm betting there was a tie at some point today. The real estate business is making quite the fine gentleman out of you."

"Quit trying to change the subject. Why wouldn't you hire Ronny? He was perfect for the job."

Ronny was a nineteen-year-old that Shane had sent in a couple of days ago. He was nice enough, but it was the point of the thing. Nobody was going to tell Kenmore who to hire in his own store. "I didn't like him."

"What didn't you like? He's young and strong enough to lift heavy things that you can't lift anymore. He has some experience with a cash register. Comes from a nice family. What's not to like?"

"I don't like the idea of him. I told you, I don't need to hire anybody. I'll do just fine here." Kenmore walked out of the office and into the store proper. "How'd your walk-through of the Miller place go?"

"'Needs a fair amount of work' is a gross understatement." Shane pulled a piece of bubble gum out of a jar on the counter. "I'm not asking you to hire a complete staff, I'm just saying replace the one you had."

"I'd rather do the extra work myself than have someone underfoot and driving me crazy."

Shane shook his head. "How did such a nice guy like me get such a stubborn old coot for a father? I must have my mother's genes."

"Your mother took stubborn to a whole new meaning, I guarantee you that. She could . . ." The rest of the argument died in his throat. "Stubborn about different things, though." He looked toward his son, the result of her stubborn resolution to carry her baby to term, even when the doctors said it was too dangerous. Even when they were proven to be correct. Kenmore shook his head, and something between a choking sound and a laugh came out of his throat. "I wonder if she's not up in heaven now, making a stand about something she feels strongly about."

"Yeah, like telling the angels to come down here and tell you that you need to hire some help. I'm sure she's on my side, we all know it."

"I'll tell you what, you start praying that God will send me somebody that won't get on my nerves. When that person walks in, I'll hire 'im on the spot. Until then, you're wasting my window space with that ridiculous sign."

"Okay, okay, I give up." Shane tossed up his hands in surrender and jumped down off the counter. "I got that new smoker set up. You ready to come home and have some ribs?"

"Let me just sweep the store real quick."

"I'll do that while you finish up whatever else you've got to do. A man could starve to death waiting on you to get closed up."

Fifteen minutes later, the two of them walked out to the parking lot in amiable silence, but Kenmore knew it was not the silence of resignation. Shane was determined to see some help hired at the store, and when it came to being stubborn, Kenmore had more than met his match in his son. Still, in this case, he would prevail. There wasn't really any other choice.

Kelli put her suitcase in the back of her car and closed the hatch. It felt so weird to be taking off like this, but she wouldn't have any peace until she made some attempt to sort out the past. "Well, I guess I'm off." She held out her hands, palms up, and shrugged, hoping this gesture would keep Denice from guessing exactly how freaked out she was.

"Oh, sweetie." Denice reached out and hugged her. "I really, really wish I were coming with you."

"I'll be fine. Don't worry about a thing."

Denice pulled away and wiped at her eyes. "Yeah, like that's going to happen. Worrying is what I do, we all know that."

"Yes, I guess we do." Kelli reached out and took her friend's hand. "I promise I'll obey all traffic laws, drive safely, and avoid talking to strangers—at least until I reach Tennessee and actually find the strangers I'm making this trip to go talk to."

"What about your route? Do you have it all mapped out?"

"Today's route, anyway. I'm going to hit I-40 and end up somewhere around Flagstaff, Arizona. It's about nine or ten hours from here, so I think it will be a good stopping point."

"Stop before then if you get too tired."

"Ma'am, yes ma'am." Kelli did a military-style salute.

"Did you make reservations for a hotel?"

"No, I decided not to, in case I need to stop earlier."

"Not later, though. Promise me you won't go any farther than Flagstaff."

"I don't think you have to worry about that. You know I've never been one to enjoy driving. I'm pretty sure I'll be prepared to turn around and come home by that point."

Denice folded her arms. "I hope so. As I've said before—"

"—This is not a good idea." Kelli finished the sentence with her. "Relax. I promise I'll be careful."

"Okay." Denice squeezed Kelli's hand. "We are here for you, you know that, right?"

"I do. Thank you." Kelli gave her friend one last hug, then climbed into the Fiesta and drove toward her past.

Kelli was exhausted and stiff by the time she saw the distant mountain peaks she knew surrounded Flagstaff. She kept her eyes focused on her goal as the sun sank beneath the horizon and the world turned dark.

She found a room in an older downtown hotel, then went in search of something to eat. It was almost eight on Sunday evening, but a fair number of people still roamed the sidewalks. She was happy to join them and work out some of the kinks from a long day in the car. The streets in the area were lined with small cafés and pubs, with music spilling out from several nightclubs.

Finally, she found a diner, '50s themed, which was mostly empty. She sat down and ordered a cheeseburger, fries, and chocolate shake, knowing she would regret this high-calorie splurge, but for tonight, she was willing to pay the price.

She pulled up a note-taking app on her phone and began to type in a list of plans for when she arrived in Tennessee. She made a column header:

What are my goals for this trip?

To actually lay eyes on my mother, brother, and/or sister.

To find out as much as possible about what happened without telling anyone who I am.

I REALLY, REALLY, REALLY need to find out the reason my father did this.

To come back home and pick up my life without looking back.

Even as she typed out the goals she knew that meeting any or all of them was going to be difficult. At least by making this trip, she would always be able to say she had done everything in her power to find out what'd happened. She could move on without regret at not having done something.

That was the hope.

"Here you are." The waitress was a teenager, long hair, bright eyes. "Need anything else?"

"No thanks."

"Alrighty then. I'll check back in a few minutes." She nodded at the milkshake in the old-fashioned soda glass. "You better watch those things. They're addictive."

"They look it."

The waitress walked over to the next table and began wiping it down, humming beneath her breath. It was so easy to be happy when you were young, innocent, and didn't know your entire life had been a lie.

Kelli picked up a French fry and started another list:

What am I going to say when people ask me why I'm in town?

Just traveling through (seems lame and unlikely)

Visiting some friends (except in a small town like that, people are likely to ask who I'm visiting)

Looking for inspiration for my jewelry collection?

Kelli looked down at the bracelet on her wrist. She did make bracelets and necklaces in her spare time. Sometimes she even sold them at craft fairs, but it was not even a real hobby, just something she did when she felt like doing it. Still, she could come up with some sort of story about hoping to start her own little business and wanting to be inspired by another part of the country. It was weak, but it might work if she couldn't come up with anything else.

Then again, why not just tell the truth?

Looking for my long-lost family

She erased the last line almost as soon as she'd typed it, but somehow putting down the words made her feel better.

By now, the screen cover on her phone was smeared with greasy fingerprints, so Kelli set it aside and concentrated on the burger and fries in front of her. After she ate, maybe she would go for a walk, try to burn off a few of these calories, and figure out more of a plan.

Daddy always had this goal of driving Route 66 from Los Angeles to Chicago. Every summer he would declare that this would be the year, pull out a handful of maps, and start planning. He would wax eloquent about all the old Americana we'd see along the way, then he'd go into one of his tirades about how people were too used to immediate gratification and that freeways, along with the Internet, were mostly responsible for the downfall of modern society. Every summer, Mimi would tell him something to the effect of "Have a nice trip." She was never much of a car traveler, and certainly not when it involved two lanes and traffic lights. Those things didn't much appeal to me, either, so I always took her side and wished him well on his solo journey.

He never went.

Now, here I am in Flagstaff, Arizona, where part of Route 66 runs directly through the center of town, less than a block from the hotel where I am staying. There are signs about it everywhere, all over the interstate, all around Flagstaff. What I wouldn't give now, if I had taken him up on that trip.

He spent plenty of time doing the things I wanted to do, that much was for sure. It was selfish of me not to return the favor. Maybe if we had done this thing, this long road trip that Daddy chose, maybe we would have talked in a way that we never talked. Maybe then, in the midst of doing what he wanted to do, away from all the pressures of his regular life, maybe then he would have opened up to me and told me I had another family.

I went for a walk tonight after dinner. I walked beside the very road where we might have had that talk. This car drove by, and there was a teenage girl in the passenger seat, and her father was driving. I started screaming, "Tell your daughter the truth. Tell her before it's too late." They kept driving. If they heard me, they gave no indication of it (probably thought I was crazy or drunk). It occurred to me that it really wouldn't help anything if I ended up in jail for disturbing the peace, so from then on, I walked in silence. The same kind of silence my dad chose for the past twenty-four years.

Silence is not a comfortable thing. But it is the easy thing.

Tomorrow I head for Amarillo. Hopefully there is something besides silence somewhere up ahead.

By the time Beth woke up, she was sitting straight up, covered in sweat and gasping for air. She could not seem to get enough.

"Beth! Beth!" Rand pulled her close to him. "It's just a dream, baby, just another bad dream."

In the comfort of his embrace, the beating of her heart slowed and quieted. Her lungs finally seemed to get their fill of oxygen. "I'm okay. Sorry, didn't mean to wake you up."

"Those pregnancy hormones are really working a number on your dream life, aren't they? That's the third time this week."

"Yes, hormones." But even as Beth agreed with her husband in words, in her mind she knew that he was wrong. This wasn't hormones. This was buried grief, clawing its way to the top. "I'm okay now." She climbed out of bed and made her way to the bathroom, where she splashed cold water on her face and tried to change the direction of her thoughts.

When she went back into the bedroom, Rand was sitting up in bed with his reading lamp on. "What is it you keep dreaming?"

She climbed under the covers and snuggled up against him. "It's always about me and the baby. Sometimes I get to work and realize at the end of the day that I've left the baby in the back seat on a hot day. Sometimes I'm sitting watching a movie and eating popcorn, and then I realize the toy I just gave the baby was a knife, not a rattle. I run into the nursery, but it's too late. There's blood everywhere." The dreams were so vivid, just telling Rand about them made her start shaking again.

"Rand, I'm just not sure I'll be a good mother. You know how I am—flighty, forgetful. What if I'm a complete failure? What if I do something to hurt our baby?"

"Oh, honey, there is no way you would ever hurt anyone, much less your own child. You don't have a hurtful bone in your body."

"I know you're right that I wouldn't hurt my baby, not intentionally anyway, but what if the dreams are right? What if I just forget?"

"Okay, I can't argue with the fact that you are a bit of a space cadet, we all know that and love you in spite of it. But you have the sweetest, tenderest heart I know. There is no way that kind of love forgets her own child."

"My parents were so completely perfect. There's no way I can live up to that. There's no way."

"Perhaps your parents were the perfect parents *for you*—or as close as they could be to it—but you are the perfect mother for *our baby*, that's why God is giving her to you. Or him. Whichever."

"You really think so?"

"Of course I do. And in spite of your doubts about yourself, I know you believe that God is in control and knows what He's doing. It doesn't seem all that likely that He would make a mistake in this one case, does it?"

"I guess if you put it that way . . ." Beth began to calm a little. "But what about all the abusive parents? God gave their kids to them, too."

"Babe, your theological questions are going a little beyond

what I have an answer for right now. But I do know that you have prayed, and I have prayed, and our families have prayed, that God would finally grant us the gift of a child, and that He would show us how to raise that child to the best of our abilities. It took several years, but God has answered those prayers. Now, let's not go doubting whether or not He has figured out all the details right down to this kid's future prom date, although I believe that He has. Let's just be thankful that in spite of what the doctors predicted, we are going to be parents."

Comforted, Beth settled back against her pillow and pulled the blanket up under her chin. She began to get drowsy. "Rand?"

"Yes?"

"God knew what He was doing when He gave me you, too."

He kissed her forehead. "That goes both ways. Now get some sleep."

I arrived in Amarillo this evening. To be honest, everything about this place is painful.

Today's travels were almost entirely on Route 66. I stopped at a place just outside of a town called Cadillac Ranch. There are a couple dozen old Cadillacs, their noses buried in the ground, all leaning exactly the same way, but painted in all sorts of crazy variations, graffiti being chief among it all. I heard one man say that the cars were all set at the same angle as the pyramids of Giza. Go figure. My father would have gotten such a kick out of that.

Then I pulled into town and they have all these painted horses all over the place. Big quarter horse statues with scenes painted on their sides and backs. Again, just the kind of offbeat thing Dad would have loved.

He used to take me to Art From Scrap in Santa Barbara. They had a big store they called the ReUse store and it had everything imaginable—yarn, buttons, tiles. We would go and load up a bag full of these treasures, bring them home, and make ourselves a sculpture, or a greeting card, or robot. We would spend the entire day together laughing and dreaming and having a grand old time.

Most people, Mimi most especially, didn't see the beauty in what we had created from junk, but I sure did. I think Daddy did, too. The woodcarving he did for a living was serious art, and our projects most certainly were not. But he always went on and on about how much he liked them.

Is any memory I have of my father true, or was it all seen through the lens of a naïve kid who just didn't know any better?

It was late Thursday night when Kelli drove past the city limits sign for Shoal Creek, Tennessee. She drove around the town square, lined by quaint brick storefronts that were perhaps a bit run down, but still charming. The center of the square held a large gazebo, which was lit and pumping out music from speakers that Kelli didn't see.

What must it be like to grow up in a place like this? It was a far cry from her home in California, but something about it seemed welcoming. Familiar almost.

She was too tired to do any more exploring tonight, so she found a hotel on the main strip and checked in, relieved to see the rooms were clean and quite nice. This would be a good place to call home for the next week. Yes, this would work just fine.

The next morning she was up early. She ate the continental breakfast in the hotel lobby, sipped her hot tea, and reviewed her plans for the day. She would drive out to the store Ken Moore owned and just check out the situation. Did he work back in an office, or was he out somewhere that would lend itself to conversation? After that, she would drive by the address for the home she would have lived in for the first year of her life. She wasn't sure if her mother still lived there or not, but it seemed like a good place to start. These two excursions ought to give her some idea of what to do next.

She pulled up the map on her phone and studied the route she would use to get to the store. It was about fifteen miles from town, situated out on a country road. Kelli glanced toward the sun streaming through the window of the hotel lobby. It was a beautiful day outside, the perfect time to start something new. She stood up, her stomach already starting to flutter. The search for answers started right now.

It was almost forty-five minutes later when Kelli pulled into the parking lot of Moore's More Store. The landscape on the drive was gorgeous—rolling green hills, huge lawns that were thick and neatly mowed, and an abundance of trees—their leaves just sprouting out green and new.

The store building itself was mostly nondescript. It appeared to be forty or fifty years old, concrete block, brown shingles, high windows plastered with advertisements for everything from soda to paper towels to spark plugs.

Kelli sat in her car, thinking through her options. Would she just do a walk-through or was she planning to strike up a conversation if the opportunity presented itself? This store was too far off the beaten path for a "just passing through" kind of visit—those kinds of stores were back on the highway. The only reason to have followed this winding and twisting road this far into the country was because you had business or family in this immediate area.

Then she noticed the *Help Wanted* sign in the window. Perfect. She could go in, feign interest in the job, and ask questions without seeming overly suspicious. She could go so far as to take a job application with her. Of course she would never bring it back, but it gave her the perfect cover story as to what she was doing here and gave an excuse to ask a few questions of her own.

As she crossed the parking lot, two women walked out of the store. One was dressed in a nice sundress and sandals. She was saying to her companion, "I'm telling you, he didn't even look at my résumé. I don't think he's really even looking for someone else to work here. That's why it's his son's phone number on the sign."

That interesting tidbit of information might make Kelli's new plan a bit less helpful than she'd hoped, but also less dangerous. She looked down at her Bermuda shorts and blouse and wondered if it would be believable that she was looking for a job, dressed in this casual way. Well, it was time to find out just how far she could take it. Maybe she wouldn't even say anything on this visit, she'd just wait and see what felt right.

The door opened with a whoosh, releasing the smell of mothballs and dust. Once her eyes adjusted to the interior lighting, she saw a long shop with five or six rows, each overflowing with merchandise of all imaginable kinds. Behind the counter, just to the left and in front of the door, was the man she believed to be Ken Moore. This was her first stroke of luck. At least he wasn't back in an office somewhere.

In spite of the fact that he had to be in his sixties, there wasn't a single apparent gray hair in his sandy-blond mop that hung just a little too long across his forehead. He looked like an old surfer, or hippie, or some combination of the two. He wore little reading glasses, which he peered over.

He looked at her and nodded a greeting, and at that moment, she lost her nerve. She turned right down the first aisle and scanned the snack foods and small grocery items on the shelf, then she turned to look at the drink cooler behind her back. Her mouth had gone completely dry, so she reached for a water bottle, took it in her hand, then meandered around the store. There was everything from plumbing and painting supplies to sewing goods and knickknacks. It was a conglomeration unlike anything she'd ever seen—at least for its size.

She started back up the aisle, realizing she was not acting like a job applicant, so that plan was blown. Plan B would involve improvising.

"Looking for anything in particular?" He was watching her approach with a puzzled expression on his face. They appeared to be the only two people in the store.

"Well, uh . . . no, not really. I was just looking around. You've got a little bit of everything here. It's a really interesting store."

"Why, thank you. You're not from around here, are you?"

"No. Not yet anyway." With a last jab of determination she plunged forward. "I was kind of thinking of moving to this part of the country for a while. I, uh . . . make jewelry, you see, and I live in California, which is beautiful, but I've been thinking of moving out this way and seeing if I can find new forms of inspiration."

"California, you say?" His eyes narrowed just a fraction. "What part?"

"Central coast. Just outside of Santa Barbara."

"I see." He studied her face for several seconds too long. "Well, I think you'd like it around here if you decided to stay. Lots of natural beauty, if that's the kind of thing that inspires you."

"Yes, yes it is lovely. Thing is, I'd need to find a job. Are there many available in town?"

"Thought you designed jewelry."

"I do, but, you know, it doesn't really pay the rent yet. I'm hoping it will, someday. But I've got bills in the meanwhile."

His eyes had never left her face. He cocked his head to the side and said, "I'm sure you could find a place to work without too much trouble."

"Good to know." She nodded back toward the store. "This is an amazing place. I've never seen anything quite like it."

"So you said." He gestured around with his hand. "This store is the place the country folk come to when they don't want to make the thirty-minute drive into Lawrenceburg to go to the Walmart."

"Makes sense." She nodded, frantically trying to come up with more conversation ideas. "Have you always worked here, at this store?" She knew the second she asked it, the question was too prying, was going to tip him off that she was up to something. And he did pause a long time before he finally answered.

"You ask a lot of questions."

She shrugged, trying to sound nonchalant. "I guess I do. It's just that I've never been in the South before. This is all so new and different. Yet something about it feels so—" she paused, thinking about what she might say, when the word just seemed to pop out—"familiar."

"That so?" He continued to study her. "Well, to answer your question, yes and no. It's my family's store, has been since my father was a young man, so I grew up working here. I moved on for a while, then came back."

"Got it." She looked around, making an effort to back off yet still keep some thread of conversation going.

"Just for a while, huh?"

He was looking at her as if he knew she was hiding something. "Oh, you know, sometimes in life you realize the grass really was greener on your own side of the fence."

"I guess you're right. I'm not sure whether or not I hope that proves true."

"Planning to climb out of your own pasture for a while, are you?"

"I guess maybe I am. Actually, to tell you the truth, I got kicked out of mine. I got fired last week." At that, he looked at her with such blatant disapproval that she felt she had to explain herself.

For some reason, she couldn't stand the thought of this man she'd only just met thinking ill of her. "See, I got a job out of college as a receptionist for a contractor, but then I found out he was cheating people, including a dear old woman who lived down the street from my parents. I told her about it, and the boss found out I told. I got fired. She got sent to an assisted living facility. I figured I'd done enough damage to that part of the country for a while, decided it was time for a road trip so I could mess up people's lives somewhere else." She faked a little laugh.

He tilted his head back, as if considering whether or not this was a story to be believed. Finally, he said, "Honesty. It's a good trait. You don't see it all that often these days."

"Apparently not, unfortunately for me."

"You're better off away from that place. You mark my word, before long you'd be included in the cheating—either by helping him cheat people or by him cheating you. Yep, you're much better off away from there." He nodded and stared off into the distance. Then he turned to look at her straight on. "I'll bet your parents are proud."

Kelli shrugged. "I'm sure they would have been." She hated how her voice cracked at the end.

"Would have been? So, they are . . . ?"

Kelli just nodded. She didn't trust her voice just then.

"I'm so sorry. How long?"

"A little over a month. Car wreck. Killed them both." Kelli put the water bottle on the counter, as she had run out of conversation ideas. "I guess this is it for me."

The keys on the cash register made a beeping sound as he entered the price. "That'll be one dollar."

Kelli fished a dollar out of her wallet. "Thanks." She started toward the door.

"Hey, you know what, if you're interested in a job, I've been kind of thinking of hiring some help here, just for the summer. Would you be interested in something like that?"

"Well, I . . ." Kelli was getting ready to answer no when she realized this might be the opening to more conversations with Ken Moore. She could pretend to be interested all week long and see what else she could find out. "Yes, I think I might be."

"Here, write down your name and number and I'll give you a call in a day or two so we can talk more about it. Are you going to be in town for a while?"

"A few more days anyway. I was thinking of spending a few days just poking through downtown." Kelli wrote down her name and cell number on the piece of paper he held out.

"It's a nice little town. You should check out the City Center Church on Sunday. Nice place, nice people. I'm sure they'd make you feel right at home."

"City Center Church, huh? Maybe I'll just do that." In fact, one of the few things Kelli had found about her mother involved City Center Church, so she had already planned to go there and see if she could get at least a glimpse of her. She turned back to him. "Do you want me to take an application or anything?"

"Nah. I work off my gut, not some mindless, formulaic paperwork. Besides, you already told me you got fired from your last job. I don't reckon there's any reason for me to check that reference."

"I guess not."

"I'll be in touch. My name's Kenmore, by the way."

"Kenmore?"

"Ken Moore, actually, but nobody calls me anything but Kenmore."

"Got it. Well, nice to meet you, Kenmore." Kelli walked away, not certain whether she was glad he had her number or whether she should have lied and given him a fake one. She supposed the next few days would tell.

Kelli waited until evening, then drove toward the address she had long since memorized. She had no idea if Alison Waters still lived at the house, she only knew this was where the candlelight vigils were held when David and Darcy Waters were missing—or Don and Kelli Huddleston, depending on which parts of history you chose to accept as true. It appeared that in this case, truth might be a little bit . . . relative.

She found Beuerlein Avenue and drove up it slowly, checking house numbers as she went. The homes here weren't new, but they were all larger and more upscale than those she'd seen in the rest of Shoal Creek. When she came to a large two-story Tudor-style home, she looked at the number on the mailbox just to be sure. This was the place. She pulled her car to the opposite curb and looked at this piece of her history.

Five windows were visible on the second floor, the nursery had likely been behind one of them. Kelli looked from one side of the house to the other, wondering where her crib had once stood. As an infant, perhaps she'd gazed over her parents' shoulders out these very windows at this very yard. Maybe she took her first steps here. Had she cried a lot? Who held and comforted her when teething kept her awake at night? She imagined her father peering out the window, her infant self in his arms feeling completely safe and secure and loved.

What had happened in this place that set the gears in motion for her to be where she was today? "Daddy, I know you had a reason for what you did. Help me find it."

There were two cars in the driveway. Jutting up above the shrubs surrounding the backyard, she could see a swing set, and just beneath the front porch there was the outline of some sort of toy—it appeared to be a plastic lawnmower. Did these belong to her nieces and nephews, or did some other family live here now?

She could see shadows moving behind the curtains just to the right of the door, a fair amount of activity. Kelli imagined small children wrestling with their father just inside. Had she wrestled with Daddy in that very room?

A woman came toward her down the street, walking a border collie on a long leash. Kelli needed to leave before the woman came close enough to see her sitting here and got suspicious. She started the car and headed back toward the hotel, feeling a strange mixture of satisfaction and longing for what she'd found so far.

She knew that Alison Waters taught history at the local junior high school and that they would be out of session for the summer next week. She had to act fast if she was going to get the chance to see her. She just needed to come up with some plausible explanation to get close to her. She needed to make out this woman's character. Surely there must be something about her that had caused Daddy to do what he did. Surely there was.

Shane looked through the glass door at his father limping down the first aisle of the store. For the life of him, he couldn't understand what drove his father to want to keep this place going. It was such an overwhelming amount of work with no significant payback. Shane walked in, prepared to make a stand.

"Come on in, and before you start your lecturing, you'll be happy to know I offered somebody a job here today."

"Pop! Way to go! I can't believe you finally did it."

"Gah." Pop waved him off. "You can wipe that smile right off your face. I find it offensive."

"You find my smile offensive?"

"It's your victory smile. I've seen it a thousand times after you hit a home run or caught someone trying to steal second base. I want you to know, young man, that I made my own decision."

"Of course, of course." Shane focused his energy on trying to keep his expression neutral, but he knew his father saw right through him. "Erica was a nice girl, though, wasn't she? I knew you'd like her if you gave her a chance."

"Erica? Who's that?"

"She's the girl I sent you today that I'd prescreened. The one you just told me you hired."

Pop waved his hand in a dismissive gesture. "Oh, her. Didn't like her. Sent her away."

"What? But you just said . . . you said you offered her the job."

"Wrong. I said I offered somebody a job, I didn't say anything about Erica."

"All right, Mr. Argue-with-a-signpost, who did you offer the job, then?"

"Her name is . . ." Pop fished around in his pocket and pulled out a scrap piece of paper. "Kelli Huddleston. She's not from around here."

"Where's her job application? Did you check her references?"

"My gut is reference enough, and my gut tells me she's the right person for the job."

"Your gut, huh?" Shane shook his head and jumped up on the counter, already reaching for a piece of bubble gum from the large glass jar beside the cash register. "It's amazing to me that you have made it this far in this cruel world with your naïveté. Dad, you've got to look at hard facts, not just feelings. You've lived long enough to know this."

"Thank you for the advice. I'm sure I'll take it into consideration."

"Yeah, I'm sure you will."

"Can I at least meet this Kelli-who's-not-from-around-here?"

"Sure, you can meet her when she starts work."

"Pop, this is all so sudden, especially for you. What's going on?"

"You're the one who is so desperate for your old man to get some help. I've found someone, end of story." He looked at Shane with a dare in his eyes, then rubbed the back of his neck. "Although, she hasn't accepted the offer yet, not technically. We're going to talk again in the next day or two."

"You said she's not from around here. Where's she from?"

"California. She needed a little getaway, and her road trip led her straight to me."

"Really? Right to your store from California, huh?" Shane shook his head. His father had done some unconventional things over the years, but this one was taking the cake. "Let me see that paper."

"Nothing doing." Pop put the paper back into his pocket. "Like I said, you can meet her after she starts work."

Right then and there, Shane silently vowed to track down this Kelli girl and find out what she was all about.

I met my father's old best friend today." Kelli sat propped against the headboard in her hotel bed. "Seems like a nice man. Kind of rough around the edges, but he's just the kind of person my father would like."

"You didn't tell him who you were, right?" Denice sounded worried in spite of the fact that she certainly knew better.

"No, of course not. I did exactly what I told you I was going to do. I went in, assessed, and left." Kelli decided it was probably best to leave out any more specific details.

"Good girl. By the way, I've been doing some research, and I guess you are not completely alone in your situation."

"What do you mean?"

"So far I've found two similar cases. The first happened in the late seventies. A father in Massachusetts picked up his two girls for visitation. He never returned. He didn't try to fake their deaths or anything, but he took them away, changed everyone's name, and started a new life. It was almost twenty years later when they finally found them—the girls were both in their twenties by then. All this time, he had been telling them that their mother died in a car wreck. He took the Social Security number from a boy who had just died and managed to fly under the radar."

"So when they found them, the mother was still alive?"

"Yep."

"What happened?"

"He claimed that he had taken the girls because his ex-wife was an unfit mother. The girls loved their father and defended him wholeheartedly. In the end, it went to court and he got probation, but from what I've been able to find, the girls never did reunite with their mother. I'm still looking into that, though, so I'm not completely sure yet."

"If my mother was abusive, why would my father have left my sister and brother there alone? What kind of father would do that?"

"Good question. And that brings me to the second scenario I found. A married father of five disappeared while on a business trip to San Diego. They found some of his stuff scattered in a rough part of town, so it looked as though he might have been robbed and killed, but they never found the body. Several years later they finally had him declared dead, and a life insurance policy was paid out to his children. More than sixteen years later he reappeared. Turns out, he had been living all over the place, and apparently he'd left because he was gay and wanted to start a new life. Best I can tell, for the past few years there has been a big fight going on about whether the kids have to pay back the insurance company."

"Pay them back?"

"They paid out on a life insurance policy for a man who was still alive."

"Wow. I'd never thought of that." Kelli shook her head. "I wonder if there was life insurance money involved here. I guess it doesn't matter in this case, though, since my father is dead."

"Yeah, but he wasn't dead twenty-four years ago, if there was indeed a policy paid out back then. That's just one more reason to keep things quiet."

"In your second story, did the family reconcile?"

"I don't think he's winning any Father of the Year awards. Sounds like most of his kids are pretty angry."

"I guess they would be."

"I know. I'm thinking this one is more in line with your father. Maybe he just wanted to start a new life."

"Maybe you're right." Kelli thought about what Denice had just said. "This just makes me all the more certain that you're right about not telling my family who I am. Being the wife or kid who was left behind without a word could not be a healthy thing to find out, insurance money or not."

"Exactly." Denice paused for a minute. "So what is your next step?"

"I've been doing some research, too. Other than being a history teacher, and teaching music lessons on the side, the only thing I can really find out about my mother is that she is on the Women's Ministry Team at her church. I figure showing up at church is the least obvious way to maybe get a look at her. I'm hoping I'll get some sort of inspiration for the next step after that. I'm still trying to figure out about my brother and sister."

"All right, then. Go forth and quietly conquer."

"That's my hope. Although in all honesty I have to doubt anything good will come out of my going to church. . . ."

Denice laughed. "That could be taken more than one way."

"And pretty much any way you choose to take it, it's still true."

My dad was hot and cold about the whole church thing. Every now and then he would get on a kick that we needed to start going regularly, or sometimes just that I needed to be going regularly. Most of the time, though, he avoided the place altogether.

I asked him once if we needed to go to church to go to heaven. He said being in church didn't make a person a real Christian any more than being in a garage made you a car. He said the people there just wanted our money and they were judgmental but no better than us. I threw these lines back at him a few years later, after an incident in high school put him back on one of his jags about me needing to attend more consistently. Somehow, when he had said those lines, they were true and acceptable. When his teenage daughter who had been caught ditching class said them, he came back with, "That's what someone with a guilty conscience says."

Looking back on it, it seems he was right.

15

Alison Waters pulled the last of the banana bread out of the oven. Tomorrow was her group's turn to provide snacks for the greeting area at church, so she'd been baking all morning. Now she was ready to go spend some time in her garden before her first piano student arrived.

A loud bang rumbled from the ceiling, followed by a scraping sound. Probably the neighbor's cat stuck on the roof again. Alison opened the back door, preparing to coax the thing down if she could. Likely a can of tuna would be required before it was all over.

"Good morning." Kenmore nodded down from a stepladder he had set up at the corner of the house.

"Kenmore, whatever are you doing?"

"Cleaning out your gutters. They say it's going to be a rainy summer, so it's best to be prepared."

"You don't have to do that, you know." Since David's death twenty-four years ago, Kenmore had made it a habit to randomly show up at Alison's and do a chore or two that he considered "man work."

"I do it 'cause I want to. Just finished cleaning out my gutters at the house, figured I might as well come get yours while I was in the right frame of mind."

"You are too good to me."

"Bah." He scooped a pile of leaves and debris into his trowel and dumped it into the large trash bag he'd hung on the side of his ladder.

"How about you come in for some ice water and banana bread when you make your way around to the door?"

"You've got yourself a deal." Kenmore loved baked goods, and since Alison enjoyed baking, she always found a way to offer a token of thanks for his help.

Since her house was small, it was less than half an hour before Kenmore was seated at the kitchen table with her. "How are things going with the kids?"

"Fine." She took a sip of her water. "I'm worried about Beth, though."

"How so?" He cut another slice of banana bread and put a thick chunk of butter on it.

"Ever since they moved back to town, she's just sort of been floundering. Most of her friends from high school don't live here anymore, and the ones that do all have their own lives and friends and children. You know how she is—the helpful side of her personality can be a little overwhelming at times. I think, no I *know*, it makes it harder for her to make friends. By the time someone would realize that Beth really is a sweetheart, they are long gone."

He laughed. "She's maybe a little over the top sometimes, but who wouldn't want a friend like that? They've only been back in town a few weeks, give it time."

"I know. I just worry, that's all."

"Shane tells me she's been calling him three or four times a week about finding a property to buy as a home for single mothers. You know anything about that?"

Alison sighed. "Yes. There was a nice facility where she used to volunteer up near Knoxville. I think it was good for her because it gave her a channel for some of that surplus helpfulness. Now she's got the idea in her head that since there is nothing like that around here, and since she has an abundance of time on her hands, she should start her own place."

"What does Rand think about that?"

"You know Rand, he gives Beth a pretty wide berth with her schemes, but he does keep telling her that there is no way they could afford to do it. And we all keep reminding her that come the fall, she's not going to have an abundance of free time anymore."

Kenmore grinned and shook his head. "Your third grandchild. What do you think about that?"

"Finally I'll have one close enough that I can actually see him or her on a regular basis. It's torture having Max and his family so far away."

"Yes, it's going to be nice having this one nearby." He took another bite of bread and moaned. "This is your best yet."

"You say that every time."

"You get a little better every time. Improving with practice." His eyes danced as he looked at her. His humorous side was something other people rarely understood. Most people saw him as cranky and serious. Alison was one of the few who knew better. "I'd like your opinion about something."

"Really? It's my lucky day." She grinned at him, waiting for the comeback, but he didn't seem to notice.

"A girl came by the store yesterday, just sort of passing through town but thinking of staying, too. She's looking for a job, and I'm thinking of hiring her for the summer."

"Sounds good."

"I'd like to know what you think of her."

"Since when do you ask my opinion about anything even remotely having to do with that store?"

"It's just that this girl—there's something about her that makes me think I want to help her. Then, listening to you talk right now about Beth, well, she's fairly close to Beth's age. I heard enough of this girl's story yesterday to think she could use a friend right now, and I'm considering not only offering her the job but also renting her the duplex for the summer."

"That would put her right down the street from Beth."

"Exactly." He rubbed his chin. "I'm not one to be impulsive, you know that, but I think I might make an exception here, although I'm still not sure of the reason. Yesterday when we were talking, I recommended your church as a good one to visit, and I think she might just show up. If you see her there, will you make a point of trying to meet her? I'd love to hear your impressions."

"Of course I will." Alison took a small bite of the bread. "What made you send her to my church instead of inviting her to yours?"

"A small country church isn't the right place for a young person who doesn't know anyone. Besides, like I said, I think she might be a perfect friend for Beth."

"Then you can count on me to be watching for new faces tomorrow. What does she look like?"

"Long brown hair, pretty girl in a sort of earthy way, early to mid-twenties, I'd guess."

"Any unfamiliar faces who remotely fit that description will be thoroughly investigated during the course of tomorrow's service."

"That's what I wanted to hear." Kenmore stood up and carried his plate and glass to the sink. "Now I've got to finish your gutters so I can get out to the store."

"I thought Saturday was your day off. Shane says you need to slow down."

"Saturday's your day off from school, too, but how many music lessons are you teaching today?"

"A few."

"Exactly." He nodded as he walked out the back door.

Kelli drove through the parking lot of the beige brick church with dark brown trim. Her heart was pounding, her hopes for this day so scattered she didn't even know what her actual hope was. There were several empty spaces near the front door, with large white signs declaring *Visitor Parking* in bright blue letters. To park there seemed a bit too conspicuous and almost certain to garner unwanted attention. She drove around and pulled into a spot at the back corner.

For a moment, she sat and watched, wondering if she was underdressed, or overdressed, or just too much of a heathen to be able to fit in here. An older couple walked by, he in a gray suit and tie, she in a green jacket and skirt with heels. Then a young family came behind them. The mother wore a flowing sundress and sandals, the daughter a frilly dress, the son khakis, and the husband jeans and a golf shirt. This was the first moment of relief. Her geometric-patterned green maxi dress ought to work just fine.

As she walked slowly toward the three sets of double doors at the front of the church, she was still pondering the best place to sit. If she slid into the very back, she would likely be less noticeable, but what if the person she was here to see sat up front? Too bad asking someone, "So where does Alison Waters usually sit?" would be a little too much of a giveaway.

As she entered through the back door, a balding middle-aged man in a seersucker sport coat handed her some type of paper. She mumbled her thanks, took a deep breath, and walked into the sanctuary. It was larger than she'd guessed it would be. She stood at the back of the central aisle, wondering if maybe the sides offered a safer choice. She was just getting ready to make for the left when a circle of women farther up the middle caught her attention. One of the women, standing in a profile view from Kelli's angle, was almost surely Alison Waters.

Kelli stopped breathing. She simply held her breath and stared for the space of three heartbeats at the woman who was her mother. She was a little shorter than Kelli had expected, but her smile was every bit as bright as in her pictures—the entire group of women basked in its light. Alison turned and glanced toward Kelli, her gaze seeming to stay on her for just a second longer than normal. Kelli hurried to take a seat in an almost empty pew just to her right. She was still roughly ten rows back from the women, close enough to watch them, but far enough away she could observe unnoticed until she decided what to do. Except Alison seemed to be looking toward her again. Surely it was just the imaginings of a guilty conscience. Organ music filled the brick and wood church with an almost holy sound that Kelli found somehow less uncomfortable than she would have expected.

The group of women hugged and laughed together for another minute before breaking up to go their separate ways. Kelli pulled out the piece of paper she'd been given on arrival and pretended to be studying it while glancing up to see where Alison Waters would sit.

And then suddenly she was walking toward Kelli. Coming closer. Kelli forced her head down and had to abandon peeking for fear of giving herself away.

"Good mornin'. You're new here, aren't you?" The voice was sweet, and thick with southern charm.

Kelli looked up into the eyes of her mother. "Uh, yes. Just visiting, actually."

"Well, welcome. My name's Alison, and oh—" she glanced over Kelli's shoulder and gestured toward a couple walking up the central aisle—"here comes my daughter, Beth, and her husband, Rand. Beth and Rand, we have a visitor today. Come meet . . ." Alison looked toward her. "I'm sorry. I didn't get your name."

Her daughter Beth? The couple came to stand beside Alison, and then all three of them stood there, staring at Kelli. Were they looking at her because they were noting a family resemblance? Then Kelli realized she hadn't answered the question yet. "Kelli. Kelli Huddleston."

"Come meet Kelli."

Beth's smile was large and toothy. Her reddish-brown hair was just past shoulder length, straight like Kelli's but much thicker. Any resemblance that Denice had thought she saw in that old wedding photo was definitely called into doubt in a big way. "Welcome," Beth said. "Good to have you here. Where are you visiting from?" Her accent wasn't quite as strong as her mother's, but still obvious and charming.

"California. Just passing through, really."

"Cal-i-forn-ia?" From Beth's reaction, one would have thought Kelli had just told her she was from Buckingham Palace. "Oh, we've been talking and talking about going out there on vacation someday. Is it as beautiful as they say?"

Kelli nodded. "Yes, I guess I'd have to say that it is. Tennessee is beautiful, too. So green and lush."

Just then, a man walked to the podium. "Good morning, everyone."

"Good morning." About a third of the crowd answered in reply. And Kelli supposed that was the cue for everyone to take their seats and quit talking.

"Nice to meet you, Kelli," Beth whispered as the three of them sat down directly in front of her.

The man at the podium said, "Don't forget about the churchwide picnic as soon as the service is over. I want everyone to stay and enjoy a little fellowship. The Ladies Hospitality Committee has prepared barbecue sandwiches and all the fixings. If you're still hungry after that, the college group is having a bake sale to raise money for their upcoming trip to Kenya."

Beth turned then, reached back to touch Kelli's hands, which were clasped by her knees, and whispered, "Oh, please stay. I want to hear all about California."

"Uh . . . well . . . I'm not sure . . ." Kelli was too stunned to think of the correct reply. This had happened in a much faster and more direct manner than she'd thought possible. She had come here simply hoping for a glimpse of Alison. Now Alison *and Beth* were sitting just a few feet in front of her and inviting her to stay for lunch.

As the service commenced, Kelli couldn't do anything but look at the two women in front of her. Beth's presence here was an unexpected stroke of luck. Now if only her brother would show up, Kelli's goal would be almost accomplished.

This was her biological family, sitting so close in front of her she could reach out and touch them. She began to study them, even now, searching for clues, any signs about who they were and how Kelli might have once fit into the equation. Beth's hair was the identical shade as her mother's, not enough red in it be to called auburn but with too many red undertones to be truly brown. Kelli's own hair was true brown, but in direct sunlight, people often commented about reddish highlights. Was there a family resemblance otherwise?

Beth and Alison both had oval faces, but Kelli had more of her father's square jaw. Beth and Alison were both petite, while Kelli was taller, like her father. When it got right down to it, Kelli could find nothing about these women that would make for anything more than a casual similarity.

They sang a song Kelli had never heard, and then everyone sat down. Quite unexpectedly, Kelli's mother stood and walked up the center aisle to the front of the church. She walked right up to the podium, nodded her head toward someone at the back of the church, and suddenly recorded background music filled the sanctuary. And then Alison Waters began to sing.

At first, Kelli couldn't make out the words, she was so overcome by the beauty of this woman's voice. It was incredible. Something far beyond that, really. At some point, she did begin to hear some of the words—something about God sending His greatest blessings in the form of trouble. If that were true, Kelli had been more than a little blessed in the past month.

Each note seemed to vibrate through her very soul. The beauty of the song, of her mother's voice, of simply being in the same space as the mother she'd never known, it was all becoming too much for her. She remembered her own attempt at singing during tryouts for the junior high play. She still cringed when she remembered how embarrassed her father had been when he heard what she'd done. Kelli had never sung in public since, and something about hearing the beauty in her mother's voice and knowing the discord in her own seemed to draw them that much farther apart.

When Alison finished singing, the whole room erupted in a chorus of "Amen." Alison walked back to her seat, and Beth reached over and hugged her. She left her arm on the back of the seat as the service moved forward. It all seemed so natural and comfortable, Kelli couldn't take her eyes off the casual way Beth's arm encircled her mother. What must their relationship be like? Something different than Kelli and Mimi had shared, that seemed apparent.

The pastor stood up and preached for a while. Kelli heard none of it. Her brain was in complete overload with all that was happening. One thing she did do, much to her horror, was start crying.

It was slow at first, just a single tear running down her right cheek. She reached up to wipe it away, thankful no one was sitting beside her to notice. But another followed, and then another, until her shoulders were shaking. Somehow she managed to remain mostly silent, although she knew her ragged breathing was loud enough to tip off those close by, and the people behind her could undoubtedly see her shoulders shaking. Thankfully, by the time the sermon ended, she had gotten herself more or less under control.

As soon as everyone was dismissed, she stood up, thinking it might be best to make a quick escape. The emotional basket case she had become was certainly not strong enough to spend the next hour or two putting on a charade in front of the people who were once her family. She picked up her purse and turned toward the aisle, ready to hurry out.

Unfortunately, there was a middle-aged couple who had been sitting behind her. The woman reached out and grasped her by the arm. "Is there anything I can do for you?"

Kelli shook her head. "No, I'm fine. Thanks."

"If you say so, then I'll accept that, but let me give you something real quick." She fished in her purse, then pulled out a piece of paper and pen. She wrote something down and handed it to Kelli. *Peggy Johnson 555-1789.* "You call me if you need someone to talk to, okay?"

Kelli nodded. She folded the paper and slipped it into the pocket of her dress, thinking to head out before anyone else who had seen her disgrace came by and offered to help.

"So, Kelli, come sit with us at lunch." Beth smiled and nodded toward the door.

"I don't think I can stay." Kelli was more than certain they had heard the sound of her crying, and even if they hadn't, her eyes had to be puffy and bloodshot. One thing she did not want to be was an object of sympathy, or worse yet, a project for the church people.

Beth's husband put his arm around his wife's shoulders and said, "Please stay. Without some fresh blood and new stories, we're going to have to spend the entire hour and a half listening to my wife and my mother-in-law discuss whether rocking horses or carousel horses are a more appropriate decoration for the nursery. I've heard the same arguments so many times by now, I'm not sure I can handle any more."

Kelli looked at Beth, daring a quick glance at her stomach. "Are you . . ."

Beth's entire face lit up. "Yes! Yes, I am." She nudged her husband with her elbow. "And it took several years and lots of medical intervention before I arrived at this blessed state, so I don't think a little bit of conversation about nursery decorations is going to hurt anyone."

Her husband shrugged, smiling good-naturedly. "Come sit with us. We can talk about the West Coast for a while, maybe come up with a nursery theme of palm trees, surfboards, and sailboats."

"I think that would be cute, especially for a boy." Kelli smiled at Beth's husband, whose name she could not remember. Ralph? Rick? Something that started with an R, she was pretty sure.

"Or a girl. None of that prissy froufrou stuff at my house. I'm going to raise a daddy's girl."

A daddy's girl.

A second eruption of tears was working its way to the surface. Kelli took a deep breath and held it, fearing to release it lest the waterworks come out with the expelled air. Everything inside her wanted to turn and run out of this place. But there was a second voice, the one deep inside her, and it remained consistent and unwavering. *You came all this way because you wanted to meet these people. Here they are practically begging you to spend time with them. Buck up and quit being a baby. This is the chance of a lifetime. You probably will never even see them again after today.*

One more deep breath in and out and Kelli was a little more confident she could control herself enough to answer. "Sure. I'll stay."

As they walked out the door together, Beth said, "How long are you planning to be in town?"

Kelli shrugged, trying to be noncommittal. "I'm not sure, really. The end of the week for certain. After that it depends."

"On what?"

"Beth, you're being nosy," her husband said.

"Am not." Beth shoved at him and whispered loud enough for everyone to hear, "If Rand had his way, we would never have a meaningful conversation about anything, because as far as he is concerned, everything is private."

Rand. This time she would remember. Kelli looked at him and smiled, thinking he might be a good person to have as an ally. Still, she didn't want to offend Beth, so she gave the truthful answer she'd rehearsed just in case she ran into Alison. "I really just came for a visit to check out the place. It's so pretty here. I did speak with a man about a job a couple of days ago. I don't think anything will come of it, though."

"Really? Where?"

"Beth, mind your own business." Rand looked at Kelli. "Please forgive my wife's overly inquisitive nature."

Kelli laughed. "Not to worry, it's fine."

"See, Rand, it is fine, because all I'm doing is making casual conversation. She told me she applied for a job, so it's obviously not a secret. Where'd you say that was?" She cast a quick look in Rand's direction before turning innocent eyes on Kelli.

Kelli supposed there was no reason to hide the truth. If Beth and her family were still closely connected with Kenmore, they might hear about her anyway. If they weren't, then it wouldn't matter. "I talked to a man called Kenmore over at Moore's More Store."

Beth squealed with enough volume that everyone in the near area looked in their direction. She didn't seem to notice. Instead, she raised her hand and signaled to her mother, who had stopped to talk to an elderly couple. "Mom, you better get over here. Kelli's about to go to work for Kenmore."

More eyes turned, and Alison Waters hurried toward them smiling. "I actually knew that already. I spoke to Kenmore yesterday, and he told me to keep a lookout for you today, because he thought you might be visiting the church."

"He did?" Kelli barely choked out the words. Why would he have done that?

"Yes. He told me he had met a very nice young lady and that the two of you were talking a potential job."

They continued walking toward the back lawn of the church, where a couple dozen round picnic tables were covered by a shade tent. Beth and Alison both put their purses at a place on one of the tables, so Kelli did the same. "Well, I don't know for sure," she told Alison. "He said he would call me so we could talk about it, but it's all up in the air. He might find someone else, or I might go somewhere else. It's all just theory at this point."

"Of course he won't find someone else. Mom, you need to call him right now and tell him that she wants the job and that he's got to hire her."

Alison Waters laughed. "I'm happy to call, but I don't think I can tell Kenmore he's *got* to do anything."

Beth snorted. "Right. He's always done everything you've

asked him to do for as long as I can remember. If you tell him to hire Kelli, then Kelli is hired, and we both know it. So you'll call him, right?"

At that moment, Kelli realized she might have trod a little too close to danger.

16

You have a really beautiful voice. I've never heard anything like it." Kelli found herself staring at Alison, so she focused her attention on the plate full of food in front of her. She didn't think she could eat a single bite.

"Thank you." Alison took a sip of sweet tea. "What about you? Do you enjoy music?"

"I enjoy listening, that's about it."

"Mom plays every musical instrument known to man. Don't you, Mom?" Beth leaned across the table toward her mother.

Alison shook her head and smiled at Kelli. "My daughter is blessed with the gift of exaggeration, as you have already witnessed several times this afternoon."

"She's witnessed nothing of the sort." Beth made a snarly face as she took a bite of corn on the cob. The teasing affection between mother and daughter was foreign to Kelli. Surely it couldn't truly be this simple and uncomplicated and . . . loving. There was no way her father would have taken her from this to a life with Mimi. Obviously there was something darker here. They were just putting on a good front for the church people.

Kelli cleared her throat. "How many instruments do you play?"

"I'm fairly proficient in piano, guitar, and violin—I teach piano lessons two afternoons a week and on Saturday. I can pick at a mandolin and a flute. But I'm pretty sure there are a lot more instruments out there than those."

"My mother has the gift of modesty to the point of outright lying. Fairly proficient? Really? She used to be a professional musician, in a band that traveled all around the South playing events."

"Really?" How had Kelli missed this in her research?

Alison actually blushed. "It was nothing, really. There were four of us. We got some local jobs, things like that."

"If by 'local' you mean any state in the Southeast, then yes, you played locally. Kenmore always says that if you hadn't quit, you would have been famous by now. He said there was some guy talking to y'all about a record deal when you stopped playing."

Alison waved her hand dismissively and took a bite of her sandwich.

The polite thing to do at this point was to let the subject drop, as Alison obviously wanted. Yet there was one question Kelli knew she simply had to get an answer for. "What made you quit?"

Alison shrugged. "A lot of things, really." She stirred the baked beans on her paper plate.

"There was an accident." Beth glanced toward her mother. "My father and sister were killed in a boating mishap in South Carolina, while my mother, brother, and I were at a show in Tennessee. It was the last concert she ever did."

"Their accident made you stop doing the thing you loved, something you have such a gift for?" The words flew out of Kelli's mouth too soon for her to stop them.

Alison shrugged. "Beth and her brother were still young, and the grief was overwhelming and confusing. I didn't want to do anything that would take me away from them when they needed me most."

Beth reached over and hugged her mother. "And she was always there for us."

"I'm so sorry." Kelli didn't know what else she could say.

"What she's not telling you is that same daughter and son begged her to take up music again a couple of years later, and she wouldn't."

"To tell you the truth, I just didn't have the heart to do it anymore."

"Do you sing, Beth?"

"Nope. Not at all. My brother inherited the musical gene, somehow it skipped me altogether. What about you?"

Kelli shook her head. "My singing is so awful I don't even sing along to the radio if there are people around. It's one of my great regrets, because I really love music."

Beth smiled and clapped her hands together. "You know what? You should take a singing lesson from Mom while you're here. I guarantee she can free your inner musician."

Alison shook her head. "Beth, you need to lay off. You're backing Kelli into a corner, and you just met the poor thing."

Rand added, "My wife likes to take on 'projects.'" He made air quotes around the word. "Looks like you might be the next victim in her crosshairs. Better run for cover while you still can."

Beth cocked her head to the side, opened her mouth to speak, then stopped. A few seconds later she turned to Kelli. "I hate to admit it, they are right. I do apologize. Usually I don't get this worked up with someone I've just met. Weird though, I feel like I know you better than I do, for some reason. Please forgive me."

"Nothing to forgive. Now, tell me about your baby. Do you know if it's a boy or girl yet?"

Beth put both hands on her stomach. "We are being very

intentional about not finding out the baby's sex. We want to be surprised."

Kelli nodded. "Good for you. When are you due?"

"Not until October. That gives me plenty of time to check out carousels and rocking horses"—she glanced toward Rand—"and decide what I'm going to do with Sprout's room."

"Sprout?"

"Like I said, we don't want to know the sex, but it drives me crazy when people call my baby 'it.' So we went in for the first ultrasound, and Rand commented that the baby kind of looked like a bean with a heartbeat. After that, we bestowed the temporary name of Bean Sprout, which I've shortened to Sprout, and the terms *he* and *she* are always alternated. No one is going to call my baby an 'it.'"

"But it's okay to call her Sprout?"

"Yes, I'm sure he won't mind a bit." She folded her arms across her chest. "See how easy that was? You said 'her,' I said 'he.' It's the perfect solution, don't you think?"

"Sounds perfect to me." Truth was, Beth's quirkiness reminded Kelli of the part of Denice she loved best. And she completely understood Beth's earlier comment when she'd said she felt like she'd known Kelli longer.

All of a sudden, Kelli was overcome by a deep ache. For the past twenty-four years, she had not even known these women existed, and now she sat here speaking with them and realized what an empty spot there had been inside her all these years. Why would her father have done this?

I met my mother and sister (that was an unexpected surprise) at church today. So far, they seem like really nice people. Super nice. I can't think of one reason why my father would have chosen

Mimi over the Alison that I met (except that she was fifteen years younger and more of a hottie, maybe). I'm sure there's more to the story, though, there usually is. Beth seems pretty free and loose with information. If I could arrange to be around her another time or two before I leave town, it would definitely be helpful for gathering information. She's not going to know anything about why my father left, I suppose, but she can fill in a few blanks. I'll see how I can finagle myself into contact with her again this week.

It might mean staying long enough to go back to church next Sunday.

Kelli spent most of the rest of Sunday in a funk. She walked around the town square, then visited the only shop that was open on Sunday—a pharmacy that carried a little bit of everything, from toys, to porcelain figurines, to T-shirts. A young family was standing in the toy aisle, dressed liked they'd probably just come from church—father, mother, young boy, and an infant. Had her own family come to this very store when she was a baby? Had she been in this aisle before, feeling loved and secure, part of a happy family unit like this family appeared to be?

This line of thought cannot be healthy. She went back to the hotel, planning to pack and get out. She'd done what she'd come to do—see her family, everyone but her brother at least. It had been foolish to think she could waltz in here and dredge up some deep, dark secret that would help her understand what had happened, then waltz out again without any problem. It was time to move on.

She pulled her cell phone out of her purse, where she'd had it turned off all day. There were three messages—two from Denice just checking in and a third from Kenmore.

"I called to offer you the job at the store—hopefully you're still interested. I'm about to spend the afternoon fishing, so I'll be out of pocket for the rest of the day. Why don't you come by tomorrow, so we can talk face-to-face? I'll be there all day, from about seven to seven. Stop by whenever it works out for you 'cause I'm not going anywhere."

Seven to seven? No wonder the poor man was willing to offer a job to any stranger who darkened his door. At that moment, Kelli regretted that she wouldn't be staying around to spend more time with him.

She fell back on the bed and stared at the ceiling for a long time, her stomach hurting with the conflicting knowledge and emotions and memories from her entire life. Where was the truth?

Was she going to return home now and act as if nothing had changed? Keep moving forward while always wondering what had happened behind her?

No. Not if she could help it. Not if she could find some answers.

She put her clothes back in the closet. She was going to see Kenmore tomorrow. Who knew what would happen from there, but she wasn't ready to give up just yet.

For my fifteenth birthday, we threw a party at our house. This was a big deal, probably fifty kids, biggest event I'd ever thrown. Dad and Mimi barbecued hamburgers and hotdogs for everyone and then retreated back into the house while the yard full of teenagers cranked up the music and acted like teenagers.

Janine Bradley, one of the popular girls who I'd invited more for reasons of social pressure than because I really wanted her there, came stumbling over. Her eyes were at half-mast and she reeked of alcohol. "Killer party, Kel," she said, like we were the best of friends. She took a big swig from her 7-Up bottle, which obviously contained something other than soda.

"Janine, I promised my folks there wouldn't be any alcohol here. You need to get rid of it."

"Ha!" The party had suddenly grown quiet. I could feel the eyes staring at us from all around. "Your mother's the one that gave it to me. I think we should get her out here to do shots with us."

"That's enough, Janine." Denice had come to stand beside me, her shoulder just touching mine.

Janine looked around, suddenly seeming to realize that we were drawing all the attention. "Hey, it's not like we all don't like her or anything. Especially you, right, Randy?" She turned toward Randy Staggs, the boy who I'd spent the entire year crushing on, and laughed that kind of laugh fueled by a moment in the spotlight and too much alcohol. "All of you boys have a crush on her, am I right?"

The yard had gone deathly quiet by now, Gwen Stefani's voice coming through the speakers providing the only other sound.

Randy came strutting over, nudged right up against Janine. "You've got to admit, she is hot." He reached over and took the bottle from Janine's hand and poured the rest of the contents down his throat. He seemed to choke for a second, but then wiped his hand across his mouth. That's when he looked toward the back door, a big smile on his face. "Definitely hot."

Mimi had come out on the back porch, a drink in her hand that had no pretense of being anything other than the 7 and 7 that I knew it was. Her tank top was low-cut, showing off the rewards of her most recent foray into plastic surgery. She stuck her hand in the air, moving in time with the music. "Great song. You all should be dancing." And she began to sway back and forth in time with the beat, showing absolutely no restraint, occasionally screeching along with the lyrics, "Ain't no hollaback girl."

The boys all moved a little closer, which prompted several of the girls to start doing their own dance in order to draw some of the attention away from Mimi. Everyone was laughing and hooting and having a grand old time.

Denice whispered in my ear, "Forget her. She's not worth it and neither are any of them."

That was the last time I ever invited anyone to my house, birthday or not, with the exception of Denice—and then Jones, once he came along a few years later. For the past ten years, it's been only them. I was too embarrassed to do otherwise.

Kelli rolled over and opened her left eye only. Sunlight streamed around the edges of the blackout curtains. She glanced toward the clock. 11:45. That brought her bolt upright in bed. She'd slept until almost noon.

She pulled her knees up to her chest and stretched her arms out straight. What was going on with her? She never slept in.

Of course, perhaps someone who didn't actually exist didn't actually have routines, either. She shook her head, trying to clear those kinds of thoughts. She needed to focus on the positive—the wonderful life she'd had for the past twenty-four years, the fact that her friends had all envied the way she and her father were so close.

Unable to face the day ahead just yet, she stayed in bed and channel-surfed until she couldn't stand it any longer. Finally, she dragged herself into the shower and somehow managed to more or less pull herself together. She hadn't eaten since the picnic yesterday, but she wasn't hungry. Besides, she needed to get out to Kenmore's store.

As she drove the winding country roads, Kelli wondered what

her life would have been like if she'd grown up here. Would she have made regular trips to this store as a child? And what about having Alison for a mother? From what she'd seen, it seemed so ideal, she knew it was too good to be true.

The homes were mostly brick, set on several country acres each, and though not large or fancy, they were well kept. On one driveway, a group of teenagers were gathered around a truck. They were all wearing T-shirts and shorts and flip-flops. She saw that they were removing coolers and inner tubes from the truck bed, which explained the wet ponytails sported by all the girls. There must be a lake or a river somewhere nearby. Kelli found herself wishing she would be around long enough to find out the answer.

The parking lot at Moore's More Store held several cars. Would Kenmore be too busy to talk? She'd driven all the way out here—best to go in and wait it out.

Kelli opened the door and saw that there was a couple standing at the cash register and a woman lined up behind them. Nothing to do but wander down the aisles until Kenmore was free. She made it about two steps before she heard his voice.

"Hey, Kelli, come on over here. I was just telling Morris and Cheryl about you."

The man looked to be in his sixties, gray hair, pleasant smile. "So you're the young lady that's going to come work with this old coot, huh? Well, good luck to you. I've known him all my life, and I can tell you right now, he'd drive me crazy if I had to spend more than a minute or two with him."

"If that's so, how is it you manage to fish with him for several hours at a time at least once a week?" The woman smiled a dare in her husband's direction.

"That's fishing. You don't actually talk when you fish. He's bearable until he opens his mouth." There was much laughing all around the group as the man picked up his bag from the counter.

"Let me be the first to tell you welcome and I'm glad you're here. This place has been sorely lacking in the class department since Frieda ran off and got married. I for one will be happy to see an improvement in that area."

"Get out of here, you old pain in the rear." Kenmore waved him toward the door and reached for the soda the woman next in line had put on the counter. As the door jangled its opening, Kenmore looked toward it. "See you at five-thirty tomorrow."

"Yeah, yeah, see you then." And Morris and Cheryl disappeared out the door.

Kelli pretended to study the rack of gum and candy while the soda buying was completed. Absently, she picked up a pack of Juicy Fruit and turned it over and over in her hands until she heard the cash drawer close after the transaction.

When she turned around, Kenmore was watching her. "So what do you say? How soon can you start?"

The determination to get even one more tidbit of information warred with Kelli's prerehearsed plan to get out of here politely. She did manage to spit out her rehearsed line. "As much as I'd like to, I'm sure I wouldn't be able to find a place to live so soon, especially since it would just be for the summer. I do thank you so much for the offer, though."

"I've got a place you can rent. My son and I own a couple of rental units in town, and one just went vacant. Should be ready for you to move in in a couple of days. It's one half of a duplex on a corner lot, nice place, if perhaps a bit old-fashioned. Nice older lady lives in the other half. Beth and Rand Thomas live just a couple of doors down. I think I heard them mention that they met you yesterday, and it would be nice for you to move near someone familiar, right?"

For a moment, Kelli simply stood there, too stunned to answer. "But I . . ."

Kenmore waved a hand in dismissal. “Don’t bother thanking me. It works out for both of us. Let’s see, I know there’s some paperwork we’ve got to fill out, so I’ll get that together this evening. Why don’t you stop back by here in the morning, and we’ll do everything all legal-like? You can start work next week, which gives you some time to settle in.” Kenmore reached for the bag of chips and soda a teenage girl had just set on the counter and started ringing it up. Conversation over.

“All right, then. I’ll see you tomorrow.” Kelli was too surprised to say more. After she stumbled out the door and to her car, she thought about what had just transpired. What had she just agreed to?

The coals were glowing nice and hot when Shane heard his father’s truck pull into the driveway. He flipped the burgers onto the grill and sat back in the lawn chair, waiting for Pop to make his way outside.

“Got some good news for you.” Pop grimaced as he walked.

“Oh yeah, what kind?”

“I got us a renter for the duplex.”

“What? I’ve already started packing my stuff. Or have you forgotten you were the one who was anxious to have me move out of your house?”

“Yeah, well, it won’t hurt to have you with me for a few more months. The lease is just for the summer. And it’s not like you’ve got all that much, so it shouldn’t be a big deal to unpack.”

“We’ve never done short-term leases. I think you were the one who made that rule.”

“The only way Kelli could take the job was if she could find somewhere to rent. Since you have been the one insisting that I need to hire more help, I’m sure you’re willing to make the sacrifice of putting off your move for just a little bit.”

"Kelli? Are you kidding me?" Shane's father was stubborn to a fault and never did anything on impulse, yet this Kelli girl had waltzed into town and had him spinning circles for her. There had to be some sort of con involved with what she was doing. "What's her last name again?"

Pop shook his head. "I forget. It's written down with her phone number. Anyway, she needs somewhere to live, and I told her we had the perfect place."

"What do you even know about this Kelli girl? When you're hiring someone for your own store, then it is your right to 'use your gut,' as you like to say. When you are putting someone in *our* duplex—I'm co-owner, remember? I want something a little more concrete."

"She's a nice girl. It will be fine. Trust me, you'll like her."

"I don't know that you are qualified to decide who I will and won't like."

"Tomorrow you will get the chance to decide for yourself."

"When?"

"When you meet her over there and show her around the place."

"You know what, I think that's a good idea. Real good. And I'm going to get to the bottom of who exactly she is and what she thinks she is doing here. I'm telling you, there is more to this story than meets the eye." Shane thought perhaps it was a good thing he had moved back home. His father obviously needed some help protecting his own best interests.

The duplex was easily fifty years old, one-story yellow brick and L-shaped so that half faced Fall River Road and the other half faced Crockett Lane. From the outside, it appeared that each half was fairly large—much larger than the dorm rooms and over-the-garage units Kelli had lived in for the past eight years.

She had been up for most of the night, trying to figure out how to get herself out of this mess without completely alienating Kenmore—just in case she decided to pursue this again at some point further down the road. Plus, she didn't want to hurt Alison and Beth after they'd been so kind to her and, whether or not they knew it, were her family. She'd finally arrived at a brilliant plan. Kenmore had said his son was half owner of the duplex and would be the one to show her around and get her all signed up. She could make certain to give him enough of a reason not to rent the unit to her.

As she pulled into the driveway, she still hadn't come up with a concrete plan for what exactly she would do. She could tell him she'd been kicked out of a previous place because she didn't pay the rent, but she didn't want to blatantly lie, and besides, if his father was going to be the one paying her, it would be easy enough for him to get his money one way or the other. No, it needed to be something a bit more subtle, but still troubling enough that he would want to back out of the deal. For starters, she had worn her comfortable old sweats and an "Elvis Forever" T-shirt. She figured this would at least get the doubts started.

There was a red BMW convertible sitting in the driveway. Kelli pulled up behind it and walked toward the front door, her mind racing through different scenarios. She reached out to ring the doorbell, but the front door flew open before she had the chance to push the button.

To say that Kenmore's son did not look anything like she'd expected would be a gross understatement. She had imagined him as short, overweight, and kind of dumpy. Instead, the man she saw was tall, broad shouldered, and downright good-looking in an all-American sort of way. His face was one that she'd often heard Mimi refer to as a "baby face"—boyish and charming and almost always the kind that led to trouble. His dark brown hair hung low on his forehead, and his short-sleeved shirt revealed arms that were lean yet well muscled.

"Hi. I'm Kelli."

He nodded once. "So I guessed. I'm Shane Moore." He reached out to shake her hand, seeming to size her up as he did. "Tell me again what it is that brought you to town, Miss—"

"Huddleston. As for what brought me to town, nothing in particular. I guess you might say I just sort of happened through."

"Happened through Shoal Creek, some thirty miles off the closest interstate? And then just happened to drive way down Thompson Lane, and then happened to stop at a tiny little store at the end of Thompson Lane that just happened to have a job opening? That's a lot of 'just happening,' wouldn't you say?"

Kelli could feel a cold sweat on the back of her neck. Shane Moore was much too intuitive for Kelli's own good. She shrugged. "I guess so."

"Something about this whole thing feels fishy to me. What exactly are you hoping to gain here?" His arrogance, his downright condescension, grated deep on Kelli's nerves. Who did he think he was?

"I'm offering to pay rent for a place to live and to work for a paycheck. I'm not sure how anyone could make something devious out of that, even with a very strong imagination, but somehow you seem to have been able to do it quite nicely."

Shane opened his mouth and drew in a deep breath, but before he said anything, he burst out laughing. "You know what? I think you might be right. I don't know why I've been so worked up about all this. I apologize if I was rude. Come on inside, and I'll show you around." Something about the way he continued to watch her made her doubt the sincerity of his apology. He didn't trust her, that much was obvious, and maybe she could use that to her benefit if she thought carefully.

"Who lives on the other side of the duplex?"

"An older woman named Miss Birdyshaw. She's super nice, mostly keeps to herself, but consider yourself warned—if she ever catches you on the sidewalk, or heaven forbid you should ask her in for a visit . . . well, she likes to talk. She's a retired teacher, never married. I think she's just lonely." He led Kelli into the back two rooms. "This is the only wall that the two units share. She's the early-to-bed, early-to-rise type, so if you don't like the sound of classical music early in the morning, you might want to sleep in the second bedroom."

Think, think, think. This was the opportunity she'd been waiting for, but how to use it to her best advantage? "Really? I was kind of thinking I would put my drums back here." It was the only thing that came to mind. "Do you think that would bother her?"

"Drums?"

"Yeah, I like to play at night before bedtime. It helps me wind down."

Shane rubbed the back of his neck. "Um, I'm thinking that might not be such a good idea. Especially back here."

"Oh, then it's probably best if I look elsewhere for a place to live. Too bad things didn't work out for me to stay and work for your dad, but I do thank you for your time." It was a flawed excuse, but she was determined to make it work.

The doorbell rang. Shane went to answer it, and Kelli followed, relieved to have found such an easy out.

The woman at the door was heavyset and slightly stooped. She was carrying a plate of cookies, which she held out with a smile. "Is this my new neighbor?"

"Apparently not, Miss Birdyshaw. Kelli was just telling me that she plays the drums at night, and we were thinking that would not be the best situation for the two of you." Shane seemed every bit as relieved as Kelli was, which for some reason irritated her.

"Drums, you say?" Miss Birdyshaw's forehead wrinkled as she considered this. She held the plate of cookies a little farther out. "Won't bother me a bit. I like drums. Please, these are for you."

Kelli tried to pretend she didn't notice the extended plate. No reason to prolong this more than necessary. "Oh, but I wouldn't want to keep you awake. I'm sure I can find another place that would work better for everyone concerned."

"I can sleep through most anything, so your drums won't bother me a bit. And it will be nice to have another single lady living under this roof. We'll make for good friends, I think."

Shane shook his head "Are you sure? Miss Birdyshaw, you've

been our tenant for several years now, obviously you are our top priority. I would not want to—"

"Completely sure. When I was younger, I always wished I could play the drums, but mostly boys did it back in those days. My mother had me in piano lessons from the time I was about three, but I never was much good at it. Maybe you can teach me about the drums while you're here. That'll be the incentive this old dog needs to learn a couple of new tricks."

Shane cut a glance toward Kelli, barely suppressing a smile. "That does sound like a good thing, then."

"Of course it does. Now"—Miss Birdyshaw extended the cookies farther still—"take these things off my hands. I've got a couple more deliveries to make."

Kelli finally took the plate. "Thank you."

"You're more than welcome. And welcome to the neighborhood." She turned and moved slowly off the front porch.

Kelli smiled as she watched the woman walk away. "I like her." Which was more than a little true. What would it be like to have a grandmother like that, one who brought cookies and chattered about music lessons? It certainly wasn't Opal's style, that much was for sure. *What were my real grandmothers like? Did they make cookies, visit people up and down the street, and attend all the school events so they could cheer on their grandkids?*

Before Kelli knew what had happened, she was standing at the kitchen counter, scribbling her name on paperwork she hardly took the time to read.

"I'll need a check for the deposit, and the first and last months' rent."

The money! What had she been thinking? She couldn't afford to pay rent on this place while still paying rent back home. "But I'm only going to be here for three months. By the time I pay all that, I will basically pay my entire summer's rent before I move in."

"Basically." He continued to watch her. "Is that a problem?"

Yes. "No, as a matter of fact, it's not." She pulled her checkbook out of her purse and wrote out a check for the amount he'd requested, her hand trembling slightly as she did so. This check would not clear, but something about Shane's arrogance would not let her back down.

He picked up the papers and tapped them on the counter to even the edges. "Thank you very much. I'll just deposit this and run all the paperwork. If everything comes back good, you should be clear to move in by the end of the week." The tone in his voice implied he doubted this would be the case.

"I guess I'll see you at the end of the week, then." She needed to get her hands on some money. Fast.

19

I've taken a little job." Kelli held her breath, waiting for what she knew was going to be a strong reaction.

"A job?" A long silence followed. It grew longer and longer, the television in the neighboring room offering the only sound at all. Finally Denice said, "What are you thinking, Kelli?"

"I start next week. It's a small convenience store out in the country. I think the change of pace will be good for me, and give me some alone time to help with the healing process. I also thought it would be a good idea to earn a little extra income cushion before the grand opening." She hoped that by starting Denice out on the emotional healing angle, it would soften the blow when she asked the favor.

"Income cushion has nothing to do with this, and we both know it."

"All right. The man who owns the store was Daddy's best friend, and I'm thinking there are some things I need to know, and maybe by just being around him, I will get the answers I need—and I *need* them, Denice. I know you want to protect me from all of this, but I'd rather know the worst than to always wonder. Can't you understand that?" Kelli sat on the side of the hotel bed, her feet resting on a green flower in the carpet design.

"Kelli, you are so incredibly fragile right now. Your parents' death alone would have caused enough grief that any counselor worth her salt would tell you that now is not the time to make any major life decisions. You are plunging headlong into dangerous territory, and you are doing it during a time when you should be hunkered down in recovery mode."

"Did you hear what you just said? You said my *parents' death*, but Mimi wasn't my parent, was she?" Kelli stood up and paced, walking between the television and the small work desk, back and forth, until she finally gave up and dropped into the wing-back chair in the corner. She propped up her feet on the otto-man, but then shoved it out of the way, stood up, and retraced her steps.

"And you've known that all your life. The fact that Mimi is your stepmother is nothing new to you, but her death is. It's still a grief process, no matter the blood relation. Not to mention, your bond with your father was unusually close by any definition. His death alone would be more than enough to put you in dangerous psychological territory."

"Thanks for being concerned about me, Denice, but I've got to know why my father took me away from here—a life that, from first glance, seems so perfect. I'm going to the local library tomorrow to look through the newspaper archives, but some things, I believe I've just got to see for myself."

"At first glance, is right. I'm sure there are plenty of people who would look at my family and, at first glance, think we were just fine, too." Denice's father, a successful attorney, had taken emotional abuse to a whole new level, mixed in with regular bouts of physical abuse to match. Her mother had more or less checked out and allowed it to happen, putting on a brave face publicly when necessary but staying numbed down on booze and pills most of the time.

"I know you're right, and I promise I'll be careful. It's just that I've arrived at the perfect time to try and get some answers. This job just happened to be available, Kenmore just happens to own an empty place I can rent, and I met my mother and sister my first visit at church. She's pregnant, did I tell you that? My sister? If I walk away now, I think I'll spend the rest of my life regretting it."

"How long are you planning to stay?"

"The job is just through the summer, but I don't think I'll need to stay that long. As soon as I get enough information that I'm satisfied, I can invent some sort of emergency that calls me back to California. I'll give my notice and be on my way. But there is one big problem, and I need to ask you a couple of really huge favors."

"What do you need?"

"First, Frank Stevenson needs to come by my apartment sometime today. Can you let him in?"

"Sure, but what's he coming for?"

"Picking up the bear."

"Wait, what? Tell me you have not sold your bear to that man. You've been refusing to even talk to him about it for years."

"There's not enough room for it at my place, we all know that's true. A six-foot carved bear does not belong in a tiny one-bedroom. Besides, I don't have any choice. I wrote a check today for the deposit and rent and it won't clear unless I get some money in my account fast. Not to mention, I'll run out of food money by the end of the week."

"You can't sell that! You've lugged that thing with you all your life. We nearly broke Jones's back and dented his truck bed hauling that thing over to your current place. And for as many years as Frank Stevenson has been trying to get you to sell that to him, we both know he's not offering you anywhere near market value for it."

"Well, I don't have time to look for a better deal. I need the money today."

"If I had the money, I'd lend it to you."

"I know you would. But since you don't, can you grab a deposit slip out of my desk drawer and take his check to the bank for me?"

"This is not a good idea on so many levels." She paused. "What if your other family figures out who you are? Staying longer like this, I still say it's too dangerous."

"I've been thinking about that. Maybe I should just tell them who I am."

"Absolutely not! We talked all about this before you left California, and you know that is a bad idea on so many levels—emotionally, financially—any way you look at it, it's a bad idea."

"I don't think they could hurt me financially. Dad and Mimi were overextended to the point of bankruptcy, so they didn't leave any kind of inheritance to be fought over."

"But you still have a bunch of your dad's carvings, and those things could sell for several thousand dollars. And the furniture he made for your bedroom—well, I'm betting it would bring in a fair chunk of change at auction."

Kelli thought of her headboard back home. The entire piece was a carving in relief, showing an elfin village nestled in a forest. The smell of the alder wood still reminded her of Daddy and the months he had spent perfecting this particular piece for her during her *Lord of the Rings* phase. "All of those things are worth way more to me than the money."

"And that's what I'm saying. You've got to protect them, and the only way you can do that for sure is to keep your identity an absolute secret."

"But wouldn't they want to know? After the initial shock, I'm thrilled to know that my mother and siblings are still alive."

"Yes, but your mother and siblings didn't decide to leave and start a new life without you. Can you imagine how that would feel to them? To know that the man they loved and trusted and probably have fond memories about, dumped them and never looked back?"

"You're right. Of course you are." Being the one who was chosen was crushing; to be the one left behind would be all-out annihilating. "Well, I'm keeping the job, but I promise I will use excessive caution with what I say."

"You better. For your own sake, and for theirs, as well."

Kelli drove to the Shoal Creek Public Library. She had been delighted to learn it held a large collection of old newspapers on microfilm, and that the microfilm readers were set up so that she could copy articles onto a USB flash drive. She planned to spend the afternoon searching for anything and everything she could find about her family.

She entered the keywords *David Waters* and found several articles about various awards he'd received as a broker. She found a picture of her father and Kenmore at the ribbon-cutting ceremony when they'd opened their new office. That photo alone made her believe she was doing the right thing by taking this job. Kenmore would have been around her father more than just about anyone else. He would be the best possible source of information for her.

Missing Father and Daughter Declared Dead. The emotional force of the headline knocked Kelli back in her chair. The only article she had seen even mentioning this possibility was early on when they were newly missing. Her mother had refused to have even a memorial service for them, but now, two years later, she had gone to court to have them declared dead. It felt almost like a betrayal. *Why didn't you look for me and find me?*

According to attorneys for the Waters family, probate judge Joseph Vandiver signed an order Thursday afternoon declaring David Waters and Darcy Waters legally dead.

David Waters (41) and Darcy Waters (1) went missing after a boating accident in South Carolina over two years ago. Since then, the family has held out hope, hiring investigators and doing their own repeated searches of the area. No bodies have ever been found.

Alison Waters requested the legal declaration in order to become eligible to receive her husband's life insurance benefits. She and her two remaining children still live in the Shoal Creek area.

Life insurance? Of course her father had provided life insurance. It would have helped her mother and the kids stay financially stable. Had he planned this far enough in advance that the policy had been sizable and intentional? Somehow, knowing that her family had been provided for in some way eased her guilt. Her father hadn't run off and left them helpless.

This better feeling lasted only until she remembered what Denice had told her last week--about the other family, the one that was still being sued for return of life insurance money when the father showed up alive sixteen years after disappearing. If Kelli revealed the truth, would Alison and Beth be able to return the money, or would it ruin them?

She downloaded the remaining articles onto her USB drive and got up to leave. When she got back to the hotel, away from any prying eyes, she would print all this out in their tiny little business center. No one would see her there.

She carried the microfilm canister back up to the librarian, thanked her, then made for the door. She needed to go back and spend some time really digging through all the information she had. There had to be answers somewhere.

"Alison, I need to ask your advice about something, because I really don't know what to do."

Alison waved Rand into her house. The young man looked exhausted. "Of course. Tell me what's wrong."

He followed her just inside the door, then stopped. "Nothing's wrong, exactly. Maybe it's normal, for all I know about these things. It's just that, well, Beth keeps having these nightmares. Two, three, four times a week she wakes up screaming. It's always dreams about how she has done something to hurt or neglect the baby."

Alison exhaled slowly, relieved that the problem was nothing more than bad dreams. "Pregnancy hormones play all sorts of tricks on a woman. I know it's not easy on you or her, but other than maybe reading something soothing at bedtime, I'm not sure what kind of helpful suggestions I have for you."

"The problem is"—Rand looked at Alison, dark circles under his eyes—"Beth seems overly obsessed with us being as good at being parents as David and you were. She's putting all this pressure on herself, and on me, to live up to this unobtainable goal."

Alison laughed outright. "We were far from the perfect parents."

"You know that you've already been sainted in my eyes, and I'm sure David was much the same, but I guess what I'm asking is, do you think maybe the next time you are together, you could tell her some stories of the times when things didn't go right? Especially when she was a baby? Let her see that everyone makes mistakes every now and then?"

"Some of the stories of our mistakes would probably terrify the poor kid, but you can count on me. I'll spend some time thinking up some of our more spectacular failures, and make sure I bring them up at reasonable intervals. In fact, I'm planning to stop by your place in a couple of hours. I'll start then."

"Thanks. I knew I could count on you." Rand leaned over and hugged her. "I've got to get back to work. You won't tell her I came by?"

"Are you kidding? We both know better than that. This is our little secret."

"Perfect. Thanks again, Alison." He hurried out the door, and Alison walked out to wave from the porch.

Stories of their mistakes as parents. Wow. She could fill a few books with those. She wondered if mistakes as a wife and couple should be included in that list.

Definitely not. It was better to remember the good times and to try to forget the rest.

Still, as she revisited her and David's years as parents, the memories didn't want to segregate by theme, so she ended up remembering a lot of things she would rather have forgotten. Angry words, slamming doors, broken promises.

She kept getting drawn back into one particular memory. David had said he'd be home from work just after five because Alison needed to be at the school to help set up the silent auction. Four-year-old Beth had been whiny and fussy all day, and Max had come home from school with a big project he needed to work on and a swollen elbow from falling off the swings.

When Alison finally wrangled them to the table at a quarter after five, David still wasn't home. She supposed she should go ahead and start feeding them, David would be home any minute. She set the beef stroganoff on the table.

"This is yucky," "Want plain noodles," and "Blech," were the comments flung at her.

"Sorry guys, this is tonight's dinner. It's your daddy's favorite, so if you want to be just like him, you can eat some, too. He'll be here to eat with you in just a minute."

Time ticked past, and still he did not come. She tried calling his office, but there was no answer. Finally, at a quarter after six he walked through the door. By then, she knew there was no way she could get everything ready for the silent auction. She rushed out the door, barely taking time to listen to his excuse about a hard day, and hurried to the school to salvage things as best she could.

It was well after ten when she got home that night, and the house was all dark—not surprising since David went to bed early. She was exhausted, and embarrassed at how ill prepared she had been, but things had turned out reasonably well, all things considered. She walked in to find the dinner plates still on the table, the platter of stroganoff still out, and the milk—long since warm—on the counter.

Tired as she was, she spent the next twenty minutes putting things away and scrubbing dried sauce off the plates, table, and counters. She felt like bursting into tears as she walked up the stairs, so great was her exhaustion. David was snoring as she tiptoed into their room and made her way through to the bathroom. She brushed her teeth and changed into her pajamas as quietly as possible, then crept through the dark bedroom.

The snoring stopped, and David rolled over and yawned. "How'd it go?"

She bit back an angry response, which wasn't going to help anything. "All right, I guess." She climbed into bed. "Can I ask you something?"

"What?"

"Why didn't you clean up after dinner?"

"I was tired." He reached over and pulled her to him, obviously not quite so tired anymore. "Besides, that's your job."

Alison pulled away and moved to the far edge of the bed. "Not tonight. I'm exhausted."

He flopped over onto his back hard enough to shake the bed.

"You're always too tired. What's a guy have to do to get some attention around here?"

Alison almost told him he might have started by being on time and then cleaning up the kitchen, but she didn't. She put her back to him and hoped things would get better. Someday.

You say you're planning to stay there the entire summer?" Opal's voice carried the shrill quality of a woman who'd just seen a large cockroach.

"Yes. Until late August. Then I'll be back to open up the restaurant with my friends."

"Right, the restaurant. May I ask why you are not back here now, preparing for the opening? I don't think you should be squandering your time like this."

"There's really not all that much for me to do there yet. And when I came to visit this little town, I found it to be so beautiful and peaceful. I thought it would be a nice area to stay in for a while and begin the healing process. Then I found a job and a little duplex to rent temporarily, so it all just fell into place." Opal had never been overly concerned with Kelli's comings and goings, so her reaction was quite a bit stronger than Kelli had expected.

"Tell me again, how did you end up in that particular town in Tennessee? You have a friend who lives there, is that what you told me?"

Kelli considered her answer for just a second. "I know someone who used to live here. She's not here anymore, but I grew so interested in the place because of her that I wanted to come check it out."

Opal's breathing was slow and deliberate on the other end of the line. "I hope you are being smart—about the way you're spending your time, I mean." There seemed to be a warning in her tone.

"I am, Opal. I'm just doing what I need to do."

"I see." A couple more deep breaths. "At least give me your address there so I can drop you a line every now and then."

"Sure, I've got it written down here somewhere." Kelli fished it out of her purse, but even as she did so she wondered at the reason. Opal had never in her life sent a "line"—not even birthday cards. "Okay, here it is, you ready?" Maybe it was just a formality, or perhaps Mimi's death had caused Opal to grow nostalgic.

"All right, then. You stay safe and keep in touch. You'll let me know . . . before you make any kind of major decision, right?"

Major decision? Opal had to be talking about the past—what else could it be? Well, now was a good time for Kelli to begin practicing her discretion. "Sure, Opal, I'll let you know if anything big comes up."

"Good-bye for now." Opal hung up the phone with a surprising swiftness. The woman was in panic mode.

Beth pulled up at the Richland Inn, fruit bowl in hand. She walked into the lobby and was happy to find Donna Renfro at the front desk. "Hey, girl, how are you doing?"

"Splendid, just splendid." Donna's tone and expression were as perky as ever. "I'd heard you just moved back to town. How are you?" Beth had known Donna since grade school. After graduation, Donna had married her high school sweetheart while Beth had gone away to college. The only way they'd been in touch over the past decade was Christmas cards—Donna's showing two adorable children.

"Couldn't be better." Beth's left hand went to her stomach out of reflex. "Listen, I brought by a little gift for Kelli Huddleston. I think she's one of your guests here. Can you tell me what room she's in so I can take this to her?"

"According to the rules, I'm not allowed to give out room numbers. It's a safety issue—"

"Are you kidding me? I mean, you've known me all my life. It's not like I'm a murderer or anything. I'm just bringing by a fruit bowl."

"Judging from the black eye you gave Jason Harley junior year, your status as a potential murderer could be debatable." She grinned. "I'm just telling you what the rules are. But"—she nodded toward the lobby—"I do need to straighten the newspapers over on the table over there. If I just happen"—she winked—"to leave the room number written on a piece of paper right here, it wouldn't be my fault if you happened to see it . . . by accident."

"Right." Beth nodded. "Thanks, Donna."

"Thanks for what? I'm not doing anything." She pulled out a Post-it note, wrote *204* in big numbers, then walked into the small lobby and neatly arranged the *Lawrence County Advocate* right next to the *Tennessean*. "There, that looks better, don't you think?"

"Absolutely it does. Thank you so much." Beth went through the lobby, out the door, and up the stairs. When she reached room 204, there was a *Do Not Disturb* sign hanging on the knob. Beth looked at her watch. It was almost ten o'clock, but she supposed Kelli could still be asleep. She went back to the car. She'd run some errands and then stop back by.

When she pulled into the parking lot of Kroger, she noticed a small lime green car with California plates. It wasn't like there were California plates in this area all that often, so she went inside, grabbed a cart, and made a point of looking down every aisle she passed.

When she turned down the produce aisle, Kelli was just putting some grapes in her cart. "Hello there. I just came by to see you."

Kelli looked up, clearly startled. "Oh, Beth, hi." She paused for a moment. "You came by to see me?"

"At the hotel. I brought you a little welcome gift, but I saw the *Do Not Disturb* sign on your door, and I thought you must still be asleep."

"Oh. How'd you know where to find me?"

"It wasn't that hard. The Richland Inn is the newest hotel in the area—it's an obvious choice."

"What were you doing there, again?"

"Bringing you by a bowl of fruit, as a sort of welcome-to-town present. I'm not much of a baker or I would have made you some banana bread or cookies or something. I was just trying to be neighborly."

Kelli smiled. "Well, thanks for that. The need for fruit is what brought me here today. I've been eating nothing but junk food since I've been in town."

Beth looked at her cart. "Well, you can keep those grapes, but if I were you, I'd put those apples and bananas away. I don't think you'll be needing them."

"Thanks." Kelli grinned. "Well, I guess these grapes and some juice are all I need, then."

"My fruit bowl is still in the car, and I've got a little more shopping to do. Can I stop by the hotel after I'm done here?"

"Sure, that would be nice."

Beth hurried through her shopping, and when she finally stood outside room 204 again, the *Do Not Disturb* sign was still on the knob. Surely Kelli was back by now. She hadn't mentioned another stop.

Kelli opened almost immediately upon Beth's knock. She looked at the bowl in Beth's hands. "Thank you so much for that. It's really sweet. Do you want to come in?"

"Just for a second. I've got groceries in the car." Beth reached for the sign. "This is still out, do you want me to bring it in for you?"

"No. I leave it there all the time."

"You're kidding. Why?"

"So the housekeepers don't come in here."

"You don't want the housekeepers in your room?"

"No."

"Why not?"

"I don't want anything to get stolen. I go down and change out my towels at the front desk when I need to, but other than that, I'm only going to be here for a week. It's not like the room is getting filthy during that small amount of time."

"What makes you think they would steal your stuff? There's a safe in here for valuables, right?"

"Yes, but that only holds smaller things."

Beth started laughing and couldn't stop. She supposed she was getting to the point of being rude, but she just found it so funny. Finally, she caught herself, straightened up, and said, "Do you always do that when you travel?"

"Always. My father was a stickler about it."

"Really?" Beth giggled again and shook her head. "I, on the other hand, leave the door to our house unlocked about half the time. I guess different families have different ideas about things, huh?"

"I guess so." Kelli blinked and turned away. Beth had the distinct impression she wanted to cry.

On the drive home, she called Rand and told him about it. "I don't know what it is, but Kelli is nursing a great big hurt."

"I know what that means."

"What?"

"That you've found another one of your projects."

"Now that you mention it, yes, I think I have." Beth smiled as she pulled into the driveway.

After a long day, Alison looked forward to this evening of good food and relaxed conversation. She was only halfway up the driveway when the front door swung open and Shane hurried out to meet her. Before Alison even knew it happened, he had the casserole dish out of her hands and into his. "Oh, Shane, you don't have to do that."

"I know, but Pop told me you were bringing your famous squash casserole. I decided I wanted to be personally in charge of the safety of this dish. You can't be too careful with these things, you know." He grinned his usual mischievous grin.

"Yes, I'd heard there have been several casserole burglaries in this area recently."

"My point exactly." He led her through the house and out to the back porch. "I just heard from Rand that he and Beth are running a couple minutes late. Pop should be home any second." He poured her a glass of iced tea.

"Thank you." Alison looked at her watch. 7:40. "He's there late, is everything okay?"

"Now that Frieda's gone, it takes him a little longer to get closed up."

"Oh right. I'll bet he'll be glad to have Kelli there to help him out." She motioned toward the table. "Speaking of help, what can I do for you?"

"Kelli? You know her?" Shane dropped onto the bench seat of the picnic table.

"I met her at church last Sunday. Your father had asked me to keep an eye out for her because he thought she might be coming. Then he actually asked for my opinion before he hired her."

"You are kidding me." Shane folded his arms and leaned back. "Does he usually do that?"

"Ask my opinion about work? Never. I found it rather odd."

"There's a lot I find odd about this Kelli situation. None of it makes sense. Pop has never been one to act impulsively like this."

Alison nodded. "I agree, it is unusual. What do you think is going on?"

Shane stood up and shook his head. "I don't know. I've got to believe there's a con involved, but I can't see what it is she hopes to gain."

"If she was after money, there would definitely be more promising subjects in town than your father. Besides, Kenmore told me that all of her rent checks have cleared the bank already. If she doesn't do a good job at the store, he can fire her and you're no worse off than before. And since he's the one who always does the end-of-the-day bookkeeping, if she's skimming money anywhere in the store, he'll know about it soon enough."

"You're right, I know you are. For some reason, there's something about it that just gets me really worked up."

"You want to take care of your father, and there's nothing wrong with that." Alison placed her hand on his arm. "Speaking of con artists, did you hear Beth's latest?"

"Nothing since the china debacle."

"Who could forget that one?" Beth volunteered two days a week at the local thrift store. A young woman had come in, told Beth a long story about her abusive husband who had finally been arrested, but when he found out the police were on their way, he broke every last piece of china in the house—that china was the only thing the woman had left from her poor dead mother.

Now, the family was in such financial straits they were eating directly off the counter.

Beth had run home, packed up her beautiful set of Royal Doulton fine china, brought it in, and happily presented it to the woman. Two days later, Rand found it all for sale on Craigslist. Turned out the woman had never been married and did not have any kids, but she and her boyfriend had a whole houseful of stolen goods.

Alison shook her head. "You would think she would have learned something of a lesson from that, but she didn't. She handed over her car keys a couple of days ago to a woman who asked for cab fare so she could get her sick baby to the pediatrician's office."

"She didn't."

"Unfortunately, she did. Thankfully, the woman, who had a blood alcohol level of more than twice the legal limit, ran the thing into a ditch before she was ten miles out of town. It dinged up the car a little, but no one was hurt."

Shane shook his head and laughed. "That girl takes the word *gullible* to a whole new level."

"I know. It scares me to death to think of what she might get talked into next. There's a woman she works with at the thrift store that she keeps talking about now. She's determined to get her a merchandising job in a department store. I'm pretty sure the next issue will have something to do with her."

"Hello, hello." Rand and Beth came walking around the corner of the house, Rand pulling a rolling cooler behind him, Beth carrying a bag of rolls. "It smells really good back here."

"I'm getting the hang of using this smoker. This is my first attempt at Texas-style brisket, though, so consider yourselves forewarned."

"From the smell, I'm saying I'll take my chances. By the way, your dad pulled up right behind us."

"Hello there." Kenmore came ambling out of the house. "Looks like I arrived after all the food is ready. Perfect timing." His limp was getting more and more pronounced. Alison noticed Shane watching his father with a look of disapproval.

Kenmore walked over and smiled at her. "Last day of school, eh?"

"Yep. Until a week from Monday, anyway."

"Mom, you're doing that summer program? I thought we agreed that you weren't going to do that again this year."

"No, you agreed that you didn't want me to do it again this year, but I told you that I was planning to."

"Kenmore, tell her she needs to stop doing that. You know it's not a good thing."

"And why is that?"

"Well, she has to drive all the way to Nashville twice a week, and the kids in that enrichment program are not nice kids. I just think her time would be better spent here in town. You can teach more music lessons if you want to work more."

"That's what's wrong with your theory, darling. The summer is when my students go on vacation. My music lessons always drop off in the summer months, so I can either teach music two days a week at the Radison Academy summer program, or I can try to find work at Walmart. Since every high school and college student has already applied for all those jobs, the chances are not in my favor."

"What is it with kids that they think they can tell their parents what to do?" Kenmore grinned a challenge toward Beth. "I liked you all better when you were little and you didn't try to boss us around so much."

"Maybe you should try listening to us sometimes, right, Shane? I'm sure we'd all be a lot better off."

"Agreed. Especially when you're making decisions about who

you are hiring and who is going to be living in the rental house you *co-own* with one of those kids."

"Well, at least your father made a good decision there." Beth dropped into a lounge chair. "He's hiring Kelli, right?"

"You know her, too?" Shane bellowed.

"Oh yes. I met her at church, then went by to visit her earlier this week. She's a great girl, you don't have anything to worry about there. Trust me, I'm a great judge of character."

Alison exchanged a glance with Shane. His face was bright red, and she thought for a second he might explode. Somehow he managed to turn toward the smoker and get busy, but she could still see his hands shaking.

21

Kelli was bent into the back hatch of her car, lifting a load of clothes, when she heard a voice behind her. "Welcome to the neighborhood! Need help carrying anything?"

She turned around. "Beth?"

"Yep, we saw your car just now when we drove up. Rand's just putting away the groceries and then he'll be down. Here, give me a handful. I wish we'd known that today was moving day. We'd have been over to help you sooner. You got a lot more?"

"No, this is it, really. I didn't plan to stay here for more than a week when I first came. Kenmore and Shane rent the place furnished, so I just have a few clothes and nothing much else."

"That makes it nice for moving, then."

"Good afternoon, young ladies." Miss Birdyshaw came walking around the corner of the house. "I thought I heard voices over here, and I was hoping that it was move-in day. I'm so glad to see I was right."

"Yes, ma'am, it is." Kelli had been in town for just over a week, but that was plenty long to know that around here, you addressed a woman as old as Miss Birdyshaw as *ma'am*, whether you were southern or not. "Just getting settled in."

"Well, I've got something over at my place to add to your settling in."

"Oh?" Kelli pictured another plate of cookies. "Shall I come around and get it after I carry in this load?"

"Ho there! Have I stalled long enough to miss out on most of the work?" Rand walked up wearing an orange University of Tennessee T-shirt and khaki shorts, grinning at Beth.

"Looks like you've lucked out. No furniture involved." Beth swatted him. "But don't worry, we would have saved it for you if there had been anything heavy."

"Well, young man, you can come over to my place." Miss Birdyshaw waved him toward her front door. "The mailman delivered a box today that was intended for Kelli. He brought it to me and asked me if I'd watch over it. I promised him I would see that the rightful owner got it."

"A box, really?" Kelli stopped moving. "Are you sure it's for me? I'm not expecting anything."

"Yes. It was marked *Express Delivery*, and it's from an Opal Larson."

"Oh, that's my . . . grandmother." Kelli remembered Denice's stern talk about boundaries and realized she needed to steer this conversation elsewhere. "She must have sent me some of my summer clothes or something." That most certainly was not the case, but it was the quickest thing she could think up to diffuse any interest.

Miss Birdyshaw looked at Rand. "Would you mind being the beast of burden? It's a bit too much for me to carry."

"At your service, ma'am." Rand extended his elbow for the older lady and the two of them disappeared around the corner.

Kelli and Beth made their way inside Kelli's section of the

duplex, each carrying a load of clothes. As they walked through the small living room, Kelli saw the mound of paperwork on the coffee table. She had put all her information about her family there. The envelopes were sealed, but there were so many possible ways things could go wrong now. "Let's just carry these clothes on back to the bedroom."

"Sounds good."

"Hellooo. Where do you want this box?" Rand called through the apartment.

"Uh, back room, I guess. Knowing my grandmother, it is clothes."

"My kind of grandmother!" Beth set her load on the bed. "Lucky girl."

"Yeah." Kelli had to turn her attention to the closet. "I guess so."

Rand appeared at the doorway, carrying a medium-sized box. "Also, I brought another set of muscles along in case we need any help."

Shane followed him through the door, his eyes scanning the room as if expecting damage. He looked at her. "I was in the neighborhood and thought I'd make sure everything was going all right with the move-in."

"Just fine. I don't have a lot of stuff." Kelli turned her back toward him and continued arranging the closet. The sooner he left, the better.

Miss Birdyshaw followed the men inside. "Shane, you sure did a nice job fixing up this place after that last group. Those young men left the place a bit of a mess and you've done a really nice job." She looked around the room. "Where is that drum set of yours, Kelli?"

"Drum set?" Beth let out a squeal. "I knew it. When we were talking the other day, I could just feel that you weren't being completely truthful."

"Truthful?" A cold sweat broke out on Kelli's forehead. "What do you mean?" Shane was completely focused on their conversation now, looking like a tiger ready to pounce.

"About not being musical. You're just one of those really modest people, aren't you? Don't worry, I've already talked to Mom, and she said she would give you a singing lesson on the house any time you want it. But maybe you don't really need that either, huh? Maybe you were just playing that down just like you didn't tell me you play the drums."

"I . . . well . . . I was just kind of learning the drums back home. I decided I wouldn't bring them here, though. It's too expensive to ship them back and forth for just a few months."

"Really?" Shane said. "Judging from what you said when you were looking over the place, I thought you were quite a serious drummer. Didn't you say something about it calming your nerves at night?"

Beth looked toward him, wide-eyed. "Oh, then you definitely are going to want a set here, so you can relax. Don't you worry about that. I'll bet Mom can find you an old set to borrow while you're here. She knows every single musical person in town. A few calls, and we'll have you completely taken care of."

"I really don't—"

"It's settled. Now, what else do we need to do around here?"

Kelli could think of one answer and one answer only, but she thought it best not to say it aloud.

Run.

"Are you sure that you don't want me to help you with the clothes your grandmother sent you? They'll all likely need to be ironed after traveling cross country in a box. I'd be happy to stay behind and help you with that." Beth seemed more than a little determined not to take no for an answer.

Problem was, Kelli had no idea what was really in that box. Opal had never in her life sent Kelli a package—not for birthdays, Christmas, or otherwise. She always just showed up, extravagant gift in hand, any time there was a party to mark a special occasion. But when it came to spontaneous mailings, it never happened. Never.

"No, really. I think I'm just going to rest a bit before I dig into it. Moving was more work than I bargained for, and I want to be ready to start work on Monday—don't want to wear myself down at this point."

"All right, if you *absolutely* insist, but how about we agree now that we will pick you up for church tomorrow? We'll be by about 8:45."

"8:45? But church doesn't start until 10:30."

"That's big church, of course, but since you're going to be living here, don't you want to start coming to Sunday school, too? It's a great way to get to know everyone. Unfortunately, I'm in the class for young marrieds and you'll be in the women's class, so we won't be together." She offered this information with no indication that it had entered her mind that Kelli might be uncomfortable with any aspect of this.

"You know, I think I'll probably just meet you there for—what did you call it? Big church?" Kelli did plan to attend tomorrow. It was another excuse to talk to her mother, but she didn't want to listen to any more teaching or preaching than was absolutely necessary. A class full of strangers who'd probably memorized the Bible by the time they were teenagers didn't sound even remotely tempting.

"But you really—"

"Beth, she says she'll meet us at church, now back off." Rand gave her a pointed look.

She shook her head. "There I go again." She reached out to

touch Kelli's hand. "I am so sorry. I just get so carried away sometimes when I'm trying to be helpful. I know it drives people crazy."

Kelli squeezed her hand. "Don't worry about a thing. I'm touched by your concern." More than Beth knew, and for reasons she would never know. "How about if you save me a seat in church? That would be great."

Beth's face broke into a huge smile. "Of course I will." She nodded. "Yes, that's exactly what I'll do."

"We'll see you tomorrow, then." Beth and Rand made their way down the hallway, Shane following. He turned to Miss Birdyshaw. "Shall I walk you back home?"

"No thanks. I think I'll continue on down the street. There's a little girl who lives across the street from Beth and Rand that I've taken to visiting. Might as well keep moving that way." She walked outside with the others but then turned back toward Kelli. "I finally figured it out."

"Figured what out?"

"Who it is you look like. I knew the first time I saw you that you looked familiar, but I couldn't figure out why. You remind me of a girl I knew from high school, that's who it was. You don't have any family around these parts, do you?"

"No, ma'am."

"Thought not. It's a striking resemblance, though. I'll see if I can find an old picture and show it to you sometime."

Shane had stopped walking and was clearly listening to this exchange. Hopefully this would be the last time Kelli would see him, as he was far too intuitive. Did he hang around his father's store much?

Kelli held her breath until they all finally made their way down the sidewalk. She had no idea if one of her relatives had gone to school with Miss Birdyshaw, but this was dangerous territory.

She walked back inside and immediately picked up the box

from Opal. She brought it into the kitchen, but not before she locked and dead-bolted both the front and back door. She wasn't going to take any chances.

Inside the box, there were a couple stacks of letters, bound by rubber bands. On top of it all was a lone envelope on which Opal had printed *READ THIS FIRST.*

Kelli opened the envelope to see a long letter in Opal's handwriting.

Dear Kelli,

Given the fact that you have made the journey to Shoal Creek and decided to stay for a while, I can only assume that you have come across information in your father's things that has led you to do so. Ever since the crash, I have wrestled with whether or not I should say anything to you about all this, but I didn't want to do anything to hurt your fond memories. Apparently this decision has been taken out of my hands, because you are up to something.

I have included letters that your sweet Mimi sent to me over the past twenty years, and which I feel might help you understand why things happened the way they did. You know that I've always had a reputation for bluntness, saying what I think when I think it. Let me warn you, these letters are Suze's heartfelt letters to me, and there are some things in them that you will find painful. It may be that you would prefer not to know all this, that you would rather be left with some less painful questions than the sharp edges of the truth. If you choose not to read them, I honestly believe you will be doing yourself a favor, but I also know that if I were in your situation, I would want to know everything. I am sending these to you. Choose what you will do with them.

Please know that Mimi and your father loved you very much. None of what you may learn will change that.

Yours always,
Opal

The two stacks of letters both had a yellow sticky note on top, the first with a number 1, the other with a 2. Kelli assumed this meant they were in chronological order. She picked up stack 1 and pulled out the top envelope. The return address was from Suze Larson, Shoal Creek, TN. A place that, until her parents' accident, Kelli had never even heard of. Somewhere that, until this very second, Kelli had never known that her stepmother had resided.

Mom, you're not going to believe it. I can barely believe it myself, but I have finally met the man I have been waiting for all my life. Oh, Mom, he's just so amazing. He's considerate, and thoughtful, and he tells me all the time how beautiful I am and how much I mean to him. It's like nothing I've ever experienced before, because when he says it, I actually think that I might start to believe it. I never thought that would happen to me again.

He came into Jerry's Place one day during lunch, and even though he's quite a bit older than me, I just felt this instant connection—and I could tell by the way he kept watching me that he felt it, too. He started showing up every day for lunch, and it seemed like it would take forever, but he finally asked me on a date.

We drove up to Nashville and ate at one of the fanciest restaurants in town. Then we stayed out dancing until the early hours of the morning, just having a blast together. He's exactly the kind of man I've dreamed of finding some day.

Next week, he has business in New York and he asked me to go with him. I managed to get the time off and I can hardly wait to spend some quality time, just the two of us, because we're having to keep everything here on the down-low because he's married.

Not for long, though. He's in the process of filing for divorce. His wife doesn't give him the time of day, and I'm telling you that kind of woman doesn't deserve a man like him. He's working all these long hours as a stockbroker, you'd think she'd appreciate him a little more than she does. She doesn't even care about him anymore, she gives her attention to the kids and that's it.

As they say, her loss is my gain. I can't believe how happy I am.

Love,
Suze

So her father and Mimi had started their affair right here in this town while Kelli, her siblings, and her mother were all left in the dark? Or *was* Alison in the dark? Kelli found herself curious as to what her real mother did and did not know. The problem was, how was she going to find out answers and stay within her predefined boundaries?

She didn't know the answer yet, but she was going to keep pushing until she found a way. She reread the letter, and this time she focused in on *Jerry's Place*. She did a quick Internet search and found that it was a local diner, still open. Maybe someone there would remember something.

For now, she set the letters back in the box and slid the whole thing into the back of the bedroom closet. She didn't think she had the emotional strength to read Mimi's version of things all at once. Or the stomach for it.

Jerry's Place looked more or less like a stereotypical small-town diner, and Kelli enjoyed the ambiance. It was mostly deserted at dinnertime, so when Kelli took a seat on a stool at the bar, the waitress immediately walked over.

She pulled a menu from the stand on the counter and handed it to Kelli. "Can I get you something to drink?"

"Iced tea, please."

The woman nodded and was quickly back with a tall, red plastic tumbler. "You ready to order?" The waitress was young, younger than Kelli, so there was no way she would remember Mimi. Kelli really didn't have money to be spending on frivolous dinners, so she looked for the cheapest thing on the menu. "The chicken fingers, please."

"You got it." She wrote something on her pad of paper, then hollered back through the opening toward the kitchen. "Got a live one." And she hung the order on a line in the window.

The TV was on above the bar, a news story about an uprising in the Middle East. Kelli looked around the small restaurant.

There was a family at a round table to her left, and a young couple holding hands in one of the booths.

"I'm Siena, by the way. Give me a shout if you need anything and I don't notice, like that's going to happen. Not exactly a Saturday night hotspot, huh?" The waitress leaned on the counter across from her.

"Not exactly." Kelli smiled toward her. "Have you lived here long?"

"All my life. How about you?"

"Just moved to town."

"Really? Where from?"

"California."

"What brought you to this dump?" She smiled as she said it, making Kelli think she actually had quite a bit of affection for the place.

"Long story. But a woman I knew in California used to work here, a long time ago. I've heard so many stories about the place, I decided I better check it out while I was in town."

"Really? What's her name?"

"Suze Huddleston."

"Hey, Gramps"—she stuck her head through the order window—"do you remember a Suze Huddleston who used to work here?"

Kelli couldn't hear the reply, but she went into panic mode. Giving Mimi's real name made an Internet search to find her, and by association, Kelli's father, a rather easy task. Of course, Huddleston hadn't been Suze's name when she was here, nor was it her father's name when he was here.

Siena turned back toward her. "Jerry says he remembers a Suze, but he doesn't recognize the name Huddleston."

An older man appeared at the window and shoved a plate of chicken fingers and fries toward Siena. He had a head full of gray hair and bright blue eyes that seemed to twinkle. "You the one asking about Suze?"

Kelli nodded.

"There was a Suze Larson that worked here, before you were born, I imagine."

Time to come up with a cover and quick. "That's probably her maiden name, although I couldn't say for sure. I didn't know her that well. But she talked about working here."

"She was a looker, I remember that. We started getting in a lot more men in our daily lunch crowd." He grinned and shook his head.

"A looker, really?" Kelli tried to play dumb. "She must not have aged well, because that's not exactly how I would describe her. Kind of dumpy, I'd say." Mimi would be rolling over in her grave if she heard that comment.

"Too bad. She was a nice enough girl, just needed to find a decent man. Seemed like she always attracted the wrong kind, if you know what I mean."

"I know exactly what you mean." Kelli looked down at her plate of food and realized she was no longer hungry. "Could I maybe get a box for this? I just remembered somewhere I am supposed to be."

Kelli walked through the door to her duplex, her mind still working overtime from her visit to the diner. Had her father sat at that same bar? Or did he always sit in a booth so the two of them would have more privacy when he came in?

Knowing better than what she was about to do but needing to do it anyway, Kelli went back to the box of letters from Opal and pulled out the next one.

Great news, Mom! You know how I told you that David has all of these church-related guilt issues about our relationship? I found him the absolute BEST book, written by the pastor of a megachurch. It's called Putting the Happy Back in Your Life. *While the book has lots of good points about a lot of things, there is an entire chapter devoted to issues that make divorce acceptable. One of these issues is if the wife neglects the husband or makes him feel undesirable. Of course, that is exactly the case for David. David has been reading up on it all. I can see that he is finally coming to realize that just because he goes to church, it shouldn't mean that he has to spend the rest of his life in a miserable and unfulfilling marriage. He is finally starting to see the light. He told me last night that he is sure that God would want him to be happy.*

Now that he has started to understand the truth, maybe it'll be a happy ending for all of us.

I'll write again soon.

Love,
Suze

Kelli wondered who this megachurch pastor was. She couldn't remember any religious books in her parents' library. Maybe after they'd found enough information to justify what they wanted to do, they'd quit looking altogether. She pulled out the next letter.

Mom, I have the most awful news. David finally agreed that it was time to tell his wife about us. It shouldn't have been a big deal, I mean, they were planning to get divorced.

He went home tonight all prepared to tell her he was leaving and she hit him with her own news first. Mom, you're not going to believe this. That little witch is pregnant. I know she did this just because she must have found out about us and wanted to mess things up. Of course now David is torn with guilt and says he can't possibly leave his wife while she's pregnant, and blah, blah, blah. He didn't even tell her about us.

To be honest, I don't understand this at all. They've been staying in separate rooms for several years now, so she obviously tricked him into sleeping with her just to try to stage something like this. Why he doesn't see it is beyond me. I will try to make him come to see the truth. A man shouldn't be responsible for a woman he no longer loves and a baby he never wanted. Right?

Oh, Mom, I'm just devastated right now. I don't know what I'm going to do. How could she be so selfish?

Suze

A baby he never wanted? Is that what Kelli was? She picked up the phone. "You're not going to believe what I've found now." She read the entire letter to Denice.

"Kelli, I know that you know better than this. Everything about that letter tells me that Mimi was only seeing what she wanted to see. All that stuff about your father already planning to get a divorce, isn't that what married men always say to their younger girlfriends? 'My wife doesn't understand me, we sleep in separate rooms, I'm planning to leave her soon.'"

"Maybe, but it makes me wonder. Did my mother get pregnant on purpose so that Daddy couldn't leave her? Did Daddy really never want me?"

"If that were true, why would he have taken you along?"

"I don't know. But these are the kinds of answers I need to find before I leave here."

"Find 'em fast and get out of there before someone figures out who you are and what you're doing."

"Agreed. I'll call and check in tomorrow." Kelli lay back in her bed, but she didn't close her eyes in sleep for a long time. She kept rolling the scenarios over and over in her mind. No matter how she looked at it, she always ended up with the same three-word conclusion.

An unwanted child.

I'll be glad when I look truly pregnant." Beth turned sideways toward the full-length mirror.

"I think you are starting to. Don't you?" Rand cast a wary glance in her direction while he finished buttoning his shirt. He was no fool, and he obviously didn't want to say the wrong thing here and make her cry.

"Starting to, yes, but that's the problem. People who know me well enough to know that I am pregnant see a little baby bump. Most of the world looks at me like a woman who should lose a few pounds. Or even worse, the ones who know me a little think I've been eating a few too many bonbons lately."

Rand wrapped his arms around her, his hands coming to rest on her midsection. "I think you look lovely."

"Yes, but you have to say that—otherwise you'll have to spend the afternoon listening to the quiverings of your insecure and highly emotional wife."

He laughed. "I will agree that the pregnancy hormones seem to have dealt a blow to your self-confidence. I've never seen you this unsure of yourself."

"Do you think that's really what all this is? Just my hormones? I'm afraid it's me finally figuring out that I'm worse off than I believed. Like, all that stuff with Jennie when we were leaving Knoxville, maybe it's all true."

"Jennie was crazy."

"No she wasn't. She was high-strung maybe, but apparently I'm even worse. She called me a hovering control freak. Maybe she was right."

"Hormones. Definitely hormones. You get carried away in your attempts to be helpful sometimes, you've always known that, but how could anyone criticize the heart that would do that? You're just like Mary Poppins—practically perfect in every way." He released her and reached down for his shoes. "Now, let's get moving. You don't want to be late for church."

"Okay, I'm ready." Beth followed him out to the garage. "Maybe part of the problem is that I am overly focused on myself right now. I'm going to make a point of concentrating my energy on other people this morning, making sure everyone feels welcome and comfortable. It will take my mind off my own issues."

"That's the Beth I've come to know and love. I knew you were still in there somewhere." Rand walked around to hold open the door to the passenger side of the SUV. "After you."

"Since when do you open car doors for me?"

"What do you mean? I always have."

"Yeah, for about the first month we dated maybe, but once you realized you had me hooked, you haven't touched a door since."

"Really? I guess maybe you're right. Whatever are you doing married to a schmuck like me?"

"That's what I keep asking myself, but I haven't found a good answer yet." They both laughed. Beth said, "I'm looking forward to seeing Kelli. She will definitely be part of my others focus this morning."

"Well, I'd say that's a good thing. I don't remember the last time I saw someone who seemed less comfortable in our church."

"I suppose the churches are different back in California."

"Maybe, but it seemed like more than that to me."

"What else could it be?"

"Maybe she doesn't go to church back in California."

"But then it doesn't make sense that she should suddenly start coming to church when she's in a strange town where she knows no one, does it? Not unless she's really searching spiritually, and that doesn't seem like the case to me."

"No, you're probably right. But something about her being there really struck me. It was that deer-in-the-headlights look that you don't often see around here."

"Well, if she's there today, I'm not going to let her go until I am convinced she is comfortable." Beth started thinking through different ice-breaking activities she could do to help Kelli, ticking the ideas off on her fingers. Introduce her to the women's group? Take her up after the service to meet the pastor? There were all sorts of good possibilities, and she determined she wouldn't give up until she found one that worked.

Rand started laughing. "The old Beth is back. I like it. I like it a lot." He parked in their usual spot in the back row.

Beth kissed his cheek as they walked toward the door. "Maybe you better enjoy it while you can. You know how my moods are swinging these days. The old Beth might be gone again by the time church is over."

"Uh-oh." They were still laughing when they walked into their Sunday school class.

Kelli woke up later than she'd intended, and by the time she arrived at church the singing had already started. She took a seat in the back row and comforted herself with the thought that at least back here it would be easy enough to zone out during the sermon. It wasn't like she was coming here for the teaching, after all.

The song came to an end and everyone took a seat as a suited man came forward to make some announcements. Kelli scanned the audience, and it didn't take her long to spot the backs of their heads. Beth turned just then, looked at Kelli, and broke out in a smile. As soon as they stood to sing another song, Beth made her way down the aisle. She threw her arms around her and hugged tight as if they were old friends instead of almost strangers. "So glad you're here. I thought you'd ditched us there for a minute. Come on up. I saved you a seat."

"Well, I . . ." The people around them were mostly involved in singing a song Kelli had never heard, but those closest did glance in their direction, sending a silent rebuke for disrupting the appropriate mood. "Sure."

When the service ended, Beth reached over and grabbed Kelli's forearm. "I was telling Rand that I was going to be so sad if you weren't here today. I was hoping you were just running late, and now here you are."

Kelli couldn't help but smile at Beth's exuberance. "Yes, here I am."

"Say, I'm in a little women's Bible study group. We meet at various houses every Wednesday evening, and this week it is my turn to host. Do you want to come? Since you're new in town it would be a great way to get to know a few people, and they are just as nice as they can be. Come on, I'll introduce you to some of them now."

"Well, I'd like to, it's just that . . ." As much as she wanted to spend some time with Beth, being part of a group of women who studied their Bible and then spent one evening a week talking about it did not in any way appeal to Kelli. "I already have some plans for Wednesday evening, but thanks for thinking of me." She stood up, ready to make her escape, before Beth asked her what kind of plans she had. Kelli hadn't come up with a plausible answer for that one yet.

"Oh, that's too bad. I really think you would enjoy it. How about shopping, then? Or lunch? I'm planning on spending some time downtown this afternoon, do you want to come with me? I'm afraid I might bore you with shopping for baby furniture, so we could just eat lunch, if you'd rather."

Now, this sounded perfect. Time alone with her sister and an environment in which Kelli was not the main focus. "Sure, sounds good. I'd love to look at baby furniture, and I need to buy some supplies for the duplex, so a little shopping sounds great."

"Perfect. Just perfect." Beth grabbed Kelli's arm with one hand and reached out for her mother's with the other. Alison was engaged in a conversation with the woman in the row behind her, so it took just a moment before she turned. She smiled when she saw Kelli. "So nice to have you with us today. I hope Beth hasn't talked your ear off."

"No, I haven't talked her ear off. I've just been greeting her, is all, and making sure she knows she's welcome here. And we're making plans for some shopping and lunch this afternoon. And I found out Kelli has been holding out on us about her musical talent. Remember how she said last week that she wasn't musical? Well, she plays the drums."

"Really?" Alison smiled. "That's terrific. How long have you been playing?"

"Uh . . . just started really. Couldn't even call it playing, what I do."

"I bet you're just being modest. Mom, you could find her a

set of drums to borrow while she's in town, couldn't you? So she can keep practicing?"

"I'm sure I could. I think a couple of my students probably have old drum sets cluttering up their garages."

"I knew it. We'll look into it and let you know, and when you stop by to pick them up, then you can talk to Mom about those voice lessons."

Alison looked at Kelli and smiled. "I'm sorry. Beth has made more than a little assumption that you would even want to take singing lessons."

"No need to apologize, it was a nice thought." Kelli smiled at Beth, trying to let her know that she wasn't angry. It was a split second later that she realized her mistake, because this only encouraged her.

"See, Mom, she does. She's just too shy to ask, so I'm asking for her. When we come by to pick up the drums, we'll give her a lesson."

"We'll?"

"You. You know what I mean. But I absolutely insist. I want to do something nice for Kelli and let her know that she is welcome here."

At this point, Kelli thought her face must be deep purple. "I really don't sing in front of people."

"I know, that's what you said last time, but this won't be singing in front of people. Just my mother and me."

"And you?" Alison tilted her head to the left.

"Of course. You don't think I'd leave her behind, do you? Mom, we'll come by your house sometime this week and pick up her drums, okay?"

"Why don't you bring her by for a cup of tea? She can see the music room, and if she wants to do anything more than that it will be her idea, not yours."

There were all sorts of alarms clanging in Kelli's mind right now. But along with that came the idea that she was about to see the inside of the home of the woman who was her mother. When else might she get the chance? "I would love to see your music room and have some tea."

"It's all settled, then." Beth beamed with a combination of pregnancy glow and satisfaction that things had turned out like she'd apparently planned.

Kelli had to admit it. She liked the girl's spunk. She hoped that before she left here, Beth and Alison might think the same thing about her. Only time would tell.

You wanna have a Popsicle with us?" An adorable little red-haired girl stood on the porch, extending a Fudgsicle toward Kelli, Miss Birdyshaw right behind her.

"A Popsicle? Well, that does sound delicious." Except that Kelli was in the middle of looking through her research. She glanced back over her shoulder at the kitchen table, covered with the papers. "Let me just go clean us off a spot and you can come sit down."

"Great." The little girl shoved right past her and into the kitchen, turning a circle and looking around. "This is a nice place. Real nice. My name's Lacey, by the way, and I'm new here, too." She plopped down at the table as Kelli began to scoop up all her research.

"Nice to meet you, Lacey. Please, Miss Birdyshaw, have a seat and make yourself comfortable. I'll be right back." Kelli hurried down the hall, papers in hand. She slid everything under her bed, then rushed out to join the others, making a point to sound calm. "Sorry about that, I'm still sorting through some paperwork about my move." She took a deep breath and smiled toward Lacey. "What have you two ladies been up to this evening?"

"Just sharing some Popsicles." Lacey bit off the top of hers. "What about you?"

"I guess I'm just sharing some Popsicles, too."

"Was all them papers grown-up stuff?"

"Excuse me?"

"Them papers you put away. You hid 'em real quick when we came in. Mama is always extra sneaky when it's grown-up stuff—like when she's drinking that brown stuff or talking on the phone to one of her boyfriends."

"Well, I . . . yes, I guess that it was grown-up stuff."

"Know what I think?" Lacey took another bite.

"What do you think?" Kelli sat down and unwrapped her Fudgsicle.

"I think grown-ups only call it that when they're doing something they're not supposed to be doing. I'll be glad when I'm old enough to say that. Some day Mama'll come into my room when it's real messy and I'll tell her we can't talk about it because it's grown-up stuff."

Miss Birdyshaw leaned forward. "Lacey, that's enough of that kind of talk. Why don't you tell Miss Kelli about the afghan you're knitting?"

Lacey started jabbering about the "blanket that me and Miss Birdyshaw are making" and about the blue and orange thread that was "real special." She took the last bite of her Fudgsicle. "I'm guessing we need to go work on it some more, right, Miss Birdyshaw? Now that we're done with our ice cream and all. Glad to have met you, Miss Kelli." And Lacey was up and out the door without a backward glance. She did stop on the porch and wait for Miss Birdyshaw to catch up. "We'll see you next time we have a Popsicle to share."

"Thanks a lot, both of you."

"Don't mention it. It was a pleasure," Miss Birdyshaw said as she hurried to keep up. "I'm still looking for a picture of my friend that you look like. I'll bring it over when I find it."

"Great. I'd like to see it."

It could be anyone, Kelli knew that, but somewhere deep inside she had a gut instinct that the picture involved a member of her birth family. If that were the case, though, why would Miss Birdyshaw recognize her and not Beth or Alison? No, she must just be paranoid.

Lacey stopped at the corner, turned, and waved. "Have fun looking at all your grown-up stuff."

Kelli walked into the duplex and locked the door behind her. Keeping her secret in this town was going to be harder than she'd thought.

On Friday morning, after her first week of work at the store, Kelli was ready to start gleaning some useful information. She made a point of stocking the shelves close to the front so she could engage Kenmore in conversation. "So what did you do before you took over your parents' store?"

He looked over his glasses at her. "I was a financial planner."

"Oh, right. Did you work for a big investment company, like Smith Barney, or was it someplace smaller?"

"Considerably smaller. There were only two of us. My partner and me. My wife worked as our secretary until she got pregnant with Shane." He shook his head and looked away.

"I'm sorry. I know you still miss her."

"Yep." He didn't look up.

"Do you ever miss the job itself?"

"Not one bit. Ever." That was a stronger response than Kenmore gave about most anything. Kelli wondered about it but decided it might be time to back off for a few minutes until he'd relaxed his guard a bit.

"Sounds like you made the right choice, then."

"Yep." The subject was obviously closed, but Kelli had no intention of leaving it that way for long.

She went to the back and restocked various kinds of tape and car supplies. An hour later, when there were no customers in the store, she decided to try again. "I can't imagine you working in investments. It seems sort of, I don't know, uptight for you."

He smiled at that. "Yeah, it kind of was. I enjoyed it, though. I enjoyed helping people. I especially enjoyed the young couples who had enough foresight to come in and want to make a plan to provide college for their as-yet-unborn children or even their own very distant retirement. Young people with that kind of common sense, the ones with enough willpower to put off a little extra spending fun now for future security—those are the kind of people I like to invest my time in helping."

This was the longest nonstop string of conversation Kelli had ever heard from Kenmore. "Yeah, I could tell that by the way you hired some stranger you'd never met, who told you that she had just been fired from her job. You like the young people who are well disciplined, that much is for sure." She folded her arms across her chest and looked at him with a dare in her eyes. Thankfully, he took the bait.

He guffawed. "I guess that doesn't sound like it makes much sense, does it? But you volunteered that you had been fired, and if ever I want to hire someone it's because they are too honest for their old boss." He continued to smile at her. "And to be perfectly honest, there are a few other reasons I hired you."

"Like what?"

"I guess some people would call it déjà vu. I look at you and it's like I remember something I used to know—something that made me happy once."

Kelli's heart skipped a couple of beats. She tried to affect a playful tone in spite of what she felt. "Sounds mysterious." *And terrifying.*

The bell above the door jangled, and a family of six walked into the store, effectively ending conversation. Kelli carried her empty boxes to the stock room and hoped she would get a chance to ask more questions later.

It was almost closing time before the flow of people slowed enough to try again. "So you told me the best part about being in investments, what was the worst part?"

He squinted his eyes and looked at her. "Why all these questions today? You've talked more today than you have in the past week."

Kelli shrugged and attempted to look blasé. "Just curious."

He rubbed the bottom of his chin and looked at her, as if trying to decide how much he was going to say and how honest he was going to be. Finally, he nodded his head. "The worst part of that job was finding out that someone I would have trusted with my life was not worthy of that honor. I guess that's why your firing story appealed so much to me. Sometimes, looking back, I wish I could start all over again. I can think of so many things I would have done differently. So many times that I knew something was going on that wasn't quite right, but I didn't call him out on it."

"Someone you worked with?" Kelli held her breath, waiting for the answer.

He nodded slowly. "Yes." He reached up, lifted his glasses with his left hand, and rubbed between his eyes. When he finally looked back toward her, he had a firm set to his jaw. "He ended up leaving us unexpectedly, and the biggest blessing of that was that it happened early enough to spare his family from finding out the truth."

The words landed like a blow. Kelli leaned against the counter and took a deep breath.

Kenmore walked toward her. "Are you all right?"

"I'm fine. I guess I'm just tired."

"Why don't you go on home for the evening. The last hour is always slow anyway—no reason for both of us to stand around with nothing to do."

Kenmore never stood around doing nothing, and neither would Kelli. "No, I'm fine really, and I wanted to get that new snack food endcap done before I leave." She walked away without giving him a chance to argue.

"He left us unexpectedly . . ." Kenmore could have used that word combination just to avoid the unpleasantness of saying the word *died,* but somehow Kelli doubted it. He had used those specific words on purpose. He knew something. She needed to find out what and how much.

Kelli went home, ate a turkey sandwich, and began looking through her library research. At this point, she'd read through everything several times, but she was still compelled to keep digging. Finally, she made her way toward the box at the back of her closet—the place she both needed and dreaded.

Today's letter was written from Santa Barbara, and Mimi was referring to her father as Don, not David, so this was obviously after the "accident."

Mom,

I'm so upset. I don't know what to do. You're not going to believe this, because I sure can't. I found out that Don has been keeping a P.O. box. Not only that, but it's under a completely different name, and he was subscribing to the local Tennessee papers. You know he was doing that only so he could find out information about his family. He promised me that when we did this crazy thing that he would leave it all behind and never look back, and now this.

He has a safe at our house that he won't let me anywhere near. I'm pretty sure it has pictures and articles about all of them. I let him bring Kelli along so he could leave without a bunch of regret, and now he pulls something like this. I can't believe it.

You were right when you said that this was going to be harder than I thought. I'm so mad right now I can't see straight. I think I'll go out for the night and have some fun—let him know I am not going to just sit around at home when he acts like this.

I'll call you tomorrow.

Suze

Kelli looked for the postmark on the envelope, desperately wanting to know when this had happened. Was it not long after they'd left, or was it years later that her father had started looking for information about his past family? But the envelope was ripped and faded and the date impossible to make out.

She supposed it didn't matter. Whatever he'd found out, he didn't do anything about it.

Beth had called at nine on Saturday morning to ask Kelli to go on another shopping expedition. "I just can't decide what to do about the nursery. Please help me," she'd said. Six hours later, after a fun afternoon of lunch and shopping, Beth insisted they ride together over to her mother's house. "Just so you will know where it is for next time—in case you ever want to take music lessons."

"Beth, I really don't think—"

"You didn't sing a single word at church last week. Mom can take someone who is shy about singing in public and turn her into a soloist, you mark my words. I've seen her do it with a couple of people. At least she'll give you enough confidence to sing along in a group."

"It's not so much that my confidence is lacking," Kelli mumbled. This was not quite true—that mostly *was* the problem—but the other part was equally true. "It's just that I didn't know any of the songs."

"Really? None of them? What kind of songs do you sing in your church back home?"

Kelli thought about how honest she should be here, but she decided that any kind of bluffing could easily come back to haunt her in further conversations. Better to come clean. "I don't usually go to church. Not very often, anyway."

"Really? Well then, Mom can be sure to teach you some of the more common songs during your lesson." She nodded resolutely. "If you don't mind my asking, what is it that caused you to visit our church? Is there something in particular you're looking for, or are you just curious, or what? I mean, don't get me wrong, whatever the reason, I'm thrilled and happy that you're there. Just curious, that's all."

Kelli was pretty certain that if she pretended the reason was spiritual curiosity, it would someday come back to bite her in the form of pressure. Better to remain as truthful as possible without inviting an outpouring of well-meaning but misplaced evangelism. "None of the above, really. I mean, I believe in God and everything. My parents never really saw much reason to go to church because Dad always said organized religion was more a social network than anything and the important thing was to be as good a person as you can be." Something her father had not done as well as Kelli had once believed. "So I guess I mostly showed up at your church for the social aspect—to meet some people, get the feel of the area."

Beth turned her attention from the road to Kelli for just a split second, and there was no mistaking the look of alarm on her face. To her credit, she quickly regained her composure and went on like nothing had happened. "Hmm. Interesting." She said nothing else, and the silence in the car had grown rather awkward by the time they pulled up in front of a small brick house.

"This is your mother's home?" Kelli could not keep the shock out of her voice. The house was tiny—at least compared to the original place. Older and made of red brick, but the lawn was well tended, and baskets of ferns and flowers hung every few feet all along the front.

"Yes." Beth looked at her then, her eyes narrowed with concentration. "Were you expecting something different?"

"Oh, I . . ." Kelli's mouth went dry. "I don't know, I just sort of pictured her in a large old home full of antiques or something. Isn't that strange how you can get something like that in your mind about someone that you've only just met?"

"I'd say you've got a good sense of reading people, because that's the kind of house she used to live in. When I was a kid, we lived in a large house that was older than my grandmother. It was drafty and squeaky, but I loved that place. I know my mother did, too. It was a shame when we had to move."

"You had to move?"

"After my father died, Mom's salary as a teacher didn't come near to covering the expenses of the place, and my grandmother was sick and needing full-time care, which also cost a lot of money. It came down to a choice between selling and moving somewhere much smaller or declaring bankruptcy. It broke her heart to do it, though, for our sakes." She shook her head. "She always said that losing your father and sister is a traumatizing enough event for a kid, it was a shame we had to lose our home in the process. She tried working extra jobs and such, but the two of us were young, and she did a lot for Nana, too. To be honest, she's still paying off some of the debt from all that. My mother is truly the bravest and best woman I've ever known."

Those words struck Kelli hard. Surely her father would not have left his wife and children behind in such financial straits. "Did your father not have, you know, life insurance?"

"Yes, he did, but it took several years to collect. We had to have them declared legally dead in court, which was awful for Mom." They started walking up the driveway. "She resisted for a long time. I think it was because she really expected them to turn up on an island somewhere."

Kelli thought she might be sick. "I'm so sorry." These poor people had been left behind to lose everything while her father moved on with a new life and a new wife, never taking any responsibility for the mess he'd left them in. How was it possible that this was the same man she'd always known? It didn't seem like it could be. "But she finally got the insurance money, right?"

"Yes and no. She got the payout, but she didn't keep any of it."

"What'd she do with it?"

"Used it to keep my grandmother in a decent care facility. Nana's money had run out. And the only alternative was to put her in a nursing home where my mother did not believe the care was adequate."

"What was wrong with her?"

"She had a form of dementia. I'm not sure who I felt the most sorry for, my grandmother or my mother, who ran herself ragged trying to do anything she could to make her more comfortable and happy."

"So she used every bit of the life insurance money to take care of her mother?"

"Not *her* mother. She was my father's mother."

My father's mother? He left Alison to take care of everything, including his own sick mother? The thought was too horrible to comprehend. There had to be some sort of misunderstanding. "Your dad's mother was the grandmother you were talking about who was in a home? Who had been in a home for a while before the accident?"

"Yes. Nana was Daddy's mother. Why do you sound so surprised by that?"

He'd left all of them to fend for themselves while he took off for a new life with a sexy waitress who made him feel young again. The tiny brick house in front of Kelli seemed to sway back and forth, and then her world went black.

26

Beth ran to her mother's house and shoved the door open "Mom, come quick. Kelli just passed out." Even as she yelled these words, she already had out her cell phone and was dialing 9-1-1.

"9-1-1. What's your emergency?"

"My friend just fainted. She's lying in my mother's front yard." Beth ran back toward Kelli and saw that she was awake and trying to sit up.

"All right, I'll dispatch an ambulance. What is your mother's address?"

"875 North Fairfield." Beth hurried back to Kelli's side as she was beginning to move around. "Stay down. Help is on the way."

Kelli's eyes popped wide open. "No, I'm fine. Please tell them I'm fine." She sat up then, but her skin was pale. "Really, there is no need for an ambulance."

"Kelli, you passed out. Something is wrong."

"No, really, it's just my blood sugar. It happens sometimes. Listen, I truly can't afford the insurance co-pay of an ambulance ride, and I promise that I am okay."

Beth did call off the ambulance, but she didn't want to. Something was wrong, she was sure of it. Her mother stood on one side and Beth on the other, and together they helped Kelli walk inside. Mom had her lie down on the sofa, then brought a cold rag to put on her head. Beth sat on the edge of the couch beside Kelli, concern obvious in her eyes. "Do you need some orange juice? Or maybe a piece of hard candy?"

"No, I'm fine. Really, I don't need anything."

Beth didn't know much about medical things, but she'd had a friend in high school who was diabetic, and she knew that blood sugar didn't come back up on its own. When Mindy started getting loopy and dizzy, they had to get her some juice or hard candy fast. "But how are we going to get your blood sugar up? We've got to do something so you don't pass out again."

"Oh . . . right. Yes, maybe some orange juice."

"I'll get it." Beth walked into the kitchen to get the juice, but really she volunteered because she needed a moment to think. She poured a glassful, knowing that something was wrong with this picture. Kelli's story did not add up.

It wasn't until later that night that she finally realized what was bothering her. They had just come from having lunch. How was it possible for Kelli's blood sugar to be low at that point? Beth was more than sure that blood sugar was not the problem.

She wouldn't say anything to her mother, not yet, but she determined to figure out what was going on with Kelli. That girl was definitely trying to cover something up. But what?

Kelli was sitting in the middle of her mother's living room. Her real mother! The one she had spent the past twenty-four years believing to be dead. The one who had apparently loved her and grieved for her all these years. She looked around the room, wanting to memorize everything about this place. To know what kind of decorations would have filled the house where she grew up if things had happened like they should have.

Truth was, Alison had a knack for decorating. The tops of cabinets were covered with seashells, brightly colored glass, and boats, and all things summer. Everything in this small room felt homey and comfortable and as if it were placed there with a great amount of love. Kelli was more than a little certain that if she came back in the fall, she would find pinecones, pumpkins, and everything good about the season. Above the mantel, there was a framed cross-stitch with the words *Home Sweet Home* in blue and red.

Home Sweet Home. It really was. The house smelled of freshly baked muffins and stale coffee. The walls were full of framed photographs of the family, several including the baby version of Kelli, some teenage versions of Beth and her brother, wedding pictures, vacations at the coast. It was the kind of home most kids dreamed about, warm and welcoming and cluttered with memories of love and happiness. But, in the wall of pictures, there was a photo of Daddy, smiling at the camera, holding up a fish he had caught. The very sight of it sucked all that was good from the room, leaving behind only a cold emptiness inside Kelli. A void that could not be filled with any amount of warmth. He should have to pay for what he'd done.

"You need to set some boundaries and hold firm to them." Denice's words floated through her mind, but the urge to tell everything was raging a strong war against them.

Beth walked over to the wall, obviously having noticed where Kelli was looking. She smiled at one picture after another, then turned her attention toward some black-and-white photos at the far end. She looked toward her mother. "You know what? Kelli reminds me of Great Aunt Mary when she was young."

"Really?" Alison moved closer to the photograph in question. "Wow, in this picture from before the wreck, there is quite a resemblance, isn't there?" She looked toward Kelli. "My husband's aunt Mary was in a terrible car wreck in her early twenties. Plastic surgery wasn't nearly as advanced back then, so I never knew her when she looked this way." She smiled. "Quite amazing." She sat down beside Kelli and checked the cold rag on her forehead. "How are you feeling?"

"I'm fine now, just embarrassed. I think I should probably go home and rest a bit."

"Mom, don't you think we should call Kenmore and tell him—"

"No!" Kelli leapt to her feet. "No, you can't tell him about this. He needs me at work on Monday, and I am fine. Like I said, I need to get home and rest a little." Kelli started for the door, hoping Beth would get the hint and let it all go.

"You've got to promise me you'll call me if anything happens. If you feel sick. Anything."

Kelli air-gestured an X symbol. "Cross my heart." She turned to Alison then. "Thank you so much for the orange juice and the hospitality. Sorry to have been such a bother."

"You weren't a bother at all. I'm glad the two of you dropped by. Hey, while you're here, I did manage to track down an old drum set from one of my students. I spoke with his mother, and she said she could drop them off at the duplex for you."

Kelli shook her head. "Really, that's okay. I wouldn't want to disturb Miss Birdyshaw."

"She told me she'd love to hear it."

"Yeah, well, she's not thinking about my kind of drumming." Kelli took another step toward the door. "Beth, I really do need to be going."

"All right, but if you're not going to do drums this summer, we absolutely must settle on a music lesson right now. Sometime in late June?"

Alison shook her head, leaned toward Kelli, and whispered plenty loud for Beth to hear, too. "Why don't you come over for tea again sometime? We'll kick Beth out of the place, and if you don't want to sing, then we'll just chat, how about that?"

This was an offer Kelli could not refuse. It was guaranteed time alone with her mother. "Sounds like a deal."

"Great. You're gonna love it, just you wait and see." Beth cranked the door handle. "See you later, Mama."

"Good-bye, you two. Feel better, Kelli."

But Kelli didn't feel better. She wasn't sure she'd ever feel good again.

27

Shane walked through the back room of the store precisely at closing time. Strange, as much as he had nagged his father about hiring another person, now that Pop had done it, Shane wished he hadn't.

"Well, I'd say that was another good day. Thanks for your help. You catch on nice and quick." His father's voice carried from the front of the store.

Kelli answered immediately, "Thanks. I'm glad I could be a help."

I'm glad I could be a help? Could an answer be any more phony? Shane jumped over the two steps into the actual store from the back room to find Kelli sweeping near the cash register, where his father was counting the drawer.

She paused with the broom. "By the way, over the weekend I asked around and did some visits to other stores in the area that are similar to ours."

"Similar to *ours*? What, have you bought out a portion of my father's store, and I didn't even know it?" So much for Shane's plan to simply observe. He looked at his father, eyes opened wide, trying to impart to him exactly what it was this girl had just said to him. His father didn't look even one bit alarmed, which was in and of itself alarming.

"I meant *our* in a more figurative sense—the store we both work at." She glared at him, then turned back to Pop. "As I was saying, I've been checking out stores that are similar to"—she turned and glared at Shane—"this one . . ." She stared for a full ten seconds before she turned back to his father. "I found one called Mashburn's over at Five Points. Are you familiar with it?"

"Mashburn's? Of course. That's a great family-run store. Super people."

"So I'd heard. So I drove over there on Saturday afternoon. Did you know they have a deli counter? There was a line several people deep the entire time I was there, people waiting mostly for bologna sandwiches from what I could tell. The lady behind the counter cut it really thick, and everyone seemed to love it."

"Yes, I've had more than a few of Mashburn's bologna sandwiches over the years. They are terrific."

"Exactly. Which makes me think, why don't you put in a deli counter, too? It would bring in the lunch crowd every day, and it couldn't help but increase sales by having more people in here on a regular basis. Mashburn's is far enough away from here that they wouldn't be direct competition, but maybe their customers who have friends and family in this part of the county might help spread the word."

What was motivating this girl? Did she expect to worm her way into Pop's business if she made a few suggestions? She had another thing coming if she thought that was going to happen.

Pop waved his hand dismissively. "Don't need more sales. We're doing just fine. If I opened a deli counter I'd have to hire some help for the lunch rush, and that'd just be more people in my way. I like things the way they are."

He turned toward Shane. "More good news for you. You've been on my case about scheduling my surgery. This afternoon, I called Dr. Craviotto and agreed to one of those so-called 'minimally invasive' hip replacements. He said he could have me up and back at work in two weeks, and since Kelli is working out so well, I told him to book it. Keith said he'd come in extra, just like after Frieda left. So, I hope you're happy."

Kelli had gone to the far end of the store with the broom. Shane glanced over at her, but she didn't appear to be paying attention to their conversation, which he supposed was how she wanted it to appear.

"When?"

"Two weeks. Or more like one week from this Friday."

"One week? Are you sure you can . . . that Kelli will be ready to be left here alone that soon?" He glanced over his shoulder to find her still sweeping.

Pop nodded toward her. "Far as I can tell, she's ready now. She's got some merchandising and cash register experience, caught on real fast to my way of doing things. I just need to teach her the evening bookkeeping, and then she'll be good to go." He quirked his mouth up in a left-sided heap, like he did when he thought someone was being stupid. "You're the one who's been nagging me to do this for months. Now I'm finally breaking down to do it, and you're all worked up about it. What's your problem?"

"It just seems soon, that's all."

"Well, it's not, so relax. Hey, Kelli," he called through the store.

"Yeah?" She looked up from her broom.

"A couple of weeks from now, you'll be able to handle the store by yourself for a while, right?"

"Sure."

"For two weeks. Alone?" Shane glared toward her, daring her to say yes to a question that any fool had to understand was a no.

She glanced toward Pop, looking nervous, then leveled her gaze directly on Shane. "Of course I could. Do you need me to?"

"I'm thinking of getting my hip fixed. You wouldn't mind, right?"

Shane did note the expression of terror in her eyes with some degree of satisfaction. Unfortunately, it was quickly replaced with a look of something like determination. "Absolutely not. I'm happy to stand in for you."

"That's what I thought." Pop nodded triumphantly toward Shane, then turned back toward Kelli. "As a thank-you, would you want to go fishing Saturday morning?"

"Really?"

"Yep. Just got a call from Morris, and he's going to be out of town this weekend, and if you're going to see the Southern way of life, fishing's something you shouldn't miss."

The expression on her face looked every bit as stunned as Shane felt. Then she smiled broadly. "Sounds fun."

"Great. I'll pick you up at five."

"I'll be ready." She returned to her sweeping job, but she was still smiling. About fishing? Like Shane was going to believe that.

Kelli had an agenda. It was up to Shane to figure out what it was, and he needed to do it fast.

So much for my plan to make a quick getaway. Kenmore's having surgery a week from Friday, and he wants me to fill in for him for a couple of weeks. This traps me into being here for longer, even if things go wrong and someone starts figuring this all out. But it also gives me a way to help him out a little. I'm pretty sure Dad messed up some things for Kenmore by leaving the way he did. If by staying here a little longer than planned helps him, then maybe I'll feel a little less guilty.

Also, he invited me to go fishing on Saturday. I halfway think he did that just to annoy Shane—and quite frankly anything that annoys Shane is good by me—but it will be the perfect time to try to get some more information out of him.

Daddy used to take me fishing at Lake Cachuma every now and then. I wonder if Daddy and Kenmore were fishing buddies back in the day. Hopefully, this Saturday I'll find answers to some of that and more.

When Kelli pulled into her driveway on Wednesday night, there was a note taped to her door. She flipped open the folded paper.

> *Kelli—help! They've put me on bed rest. Can you believe that? I'm not allowed to get up at all except to go to the bathroom and ride in the car to doctor's appointments. Please come over and hang out for a while. It will save my sanity (probably Rand's, too).*
>
> *Beth*

Kelli looked toward Beth's house. By now, Rand was home from work, so he could at least let her in. Poor Beth. She hurried over, afraid of hearing bad news.

She knocked rather than rang, in case Beth was asleep. Rand opened the door, a smile on his face. "Kelli, so glad to see you. Beth told me she'd left you a note."

"Yes, how exactly was she down at my house leaving notes on the door if she was supposed to be in her own bed?"

"I asked her the same question. She said the doctor sent her home from his office with orders to go to bed as soon as she got home, but she stopped by your place first, so technically she says she wasn't disobeying."

"I wasn't!" her voice called from the bedroom.

Rand laughed and gestured Kelli toward the room. "You might as well go on back and hear the excuses from the perpetrator herself."

Beth was lying on the bed, a *Baby Talk* magazine open across her midsection. "Thank goodness you're here, Kelli. Rand can't sit still long enough to keep me company."

"I can't sit still because I'm trying to make your dinner."

"You mean *your* dinner."

"Well, yes, I do plan to eat, too. I think that would normally be allowed, don't you?" He looked toward Kelli. "I'm going to leave you two ladies to visit while I finish up. Would you like a grilled burger and salad? We've got more than enough."

"Oh, that's nice, but I'm—"

"Please stay," Beth interrupted. "Truly, we do have more than enough, and I know you just got home from work, so you must be hungry."

"If you're sure . . ."

"We're sure." Beth nodded with satisfaction.

"We most certainly are." Rand smiled as he left the room.

"So what's going on that you've been put in bed?"

Beth put both hands on her stomach. "It's something called a funneling cervix. Long story short, it would be really easy for me to go into early labor, so they're going to give me some hormones and such, but I'll probably be in bed for the foreseeable future." She shook her head. "I'll do whatever it takes to get Sprout here safely, but I'm afraid I might go insane in the meanwhile."

"Well, don't worry about anything. I'll come by every evening and check on you. And weekends, too."

"You are such a godsend. Mom is going to spend a lot of time over here helping, but she's teaching up in Nashville two days a week, and Rand is in and out of town with his work. I don't know what I would do without you."

"You won't have to find out, will you?"

Beth reached over and squeezed her hand. "I'm so happy God put you in my life."

And for just a second, Kelli thought Beth knew the truth.

Later that night, as she walked home, Kelli thought about the long months ahead for Beth. She was glad she could be here to help for at least part of them. Then an idea hit her. She ran home and called Denice.

"I know what it is I can do."

"What do you mean?"

"You know how I've said I have to stay here until I can leave in peace?"

"Yes, and I've told you that's not going to happen."

"But it is. My sister is on bed rest, and I've offered to help out at her house. Don't you see? In some small way, I'm doing something to pay her back for what she's lost. If I can stay around here and help Beth through the worst of it, then I will know that I have done what I could to right Daddy's wrongs in some small way. I'm working for Kenmore while he recovers from surgery. I'm making some amends. Next, I'll look for ways that I can do something for Alison, too."

"Kelli, you are treading on dangerous territory."

"Don't worry, I'll be careful. But this is something I've got to do. This is what is going to make me free in the end."

"I hope you're right."

"I am. I've got to be."

By a quarter to five Saturday morning, Kelli was staring out her front window, looking for any sign of Kenmore. It wasn't so much because she was excited to sit on the side of a pond and fish, but because she hoped it would be the perfect chance for some deeper conversation.

Headlights appeared in the distance, and she watched them approach with growing anticipation. Today was going to be a good day, she just knew it. She hurried out to meet the truck, carrying a water bottle in one hand and a couple of granola bars in the other. She pulled open the passenger door. "I brought you a granola bar too, in case . . ." It took the time for the door to come full open before she realized what she was seeing. More like, *who* she was seeing.

Shane. Sitting right there in the passenger seat.

Kenmore said, "Shane got a hankering to do some fishing this morning, so I guess there's going to be a third."

Kelli fought the urge to turn around and run back to the house. She simply stood there, absorbing this information, as Shane scooted toward the center of the seat. "I'd get out and let you in first, but believe me, it's much more comfortable on the end." Considering the way his knees were crammed up against the dashboard, Kelli did not doubt the truth of that.

"Should I . . . go get a granola bar for you, too?"

"Nope"—Kenmore leaned forward to look around his son—"just hop in. I always stop at Hardee's for a sausage biscuit on my way out of town. Now, let's get moving while the fish are still biting."

Kelli climbed in beside Shane. The truck was small enough that her shoulder was jammed up against his on one side, and her hip was shoved against the door handle on the other. What had she just gotten herself into? His being here was going to ruin everything.

"How's Beth doing?" Kenmore asked as he pulled out of the driveway.

"She seems to feel fine. She's going stir-crazy though, as I'm sure you can imagine."

Kenmore snorted. "Poor Rand. He's going to have his hands full, and his ears full too, by the time that girl is up and around again."

At Hardee's, Kenmore and Shane each ordered sausage biscuits, and Kelli got a chicken biscuit. She took a bite and blurted out, "This is delicious."

"You say that as if you're surprised," Shane said.

"Yes, I guess I am. I've never had a fast-food breakfast before. I just assumed it would taste more bland."

"You've never had a fast-food breakfast?" Shane was all-out staring at her now.

"My stepmother was always watching her weight, and my father enjoyed cooking his own breakfast. It was part of his morning routine."

"What did he make?" Shane took another bite of his biscuit.

"Depended. Sometimes pancakes, sometimes scrambled eggs and bacon. He even made his own biscuits from scratch, which were delicious." Memories of tastes and smells flooded back to her, making her homesick for what she used to have. Or at least, what she'd thought she had.

Half an hour later, the three of them had opened a rural gate, driven through it, and then locked it behind them. "Are we breaking and entering?" Kelli asked, only half kidding.

Kenmore smiled. "The fishing in this pond is good enough that it would be worth facing jail time, but no, this property belongs to a friend of mine. There's about ten of us who have a key and permission to come fish whenever we like." He parked the truck and pulled three rods out of the back, along with a Styrofoam bucket with air holes in it.

Kelli looked at it. "Night crawlers, huh? Somehow I had you figured for more a spoon type guy."

"You know lures?"

"My father used to take me fishing some."

"I thought lures might be too complicated for your first outing. Little did I know I was dealing with an experienced fisherwoman."

"I'm not that experienced, but I can bait my own hook."

"Thank goodness for that," Shane said.

They walked through a wooded area and came to a large pond. It was surrounded by lush grass and tall trees, with a steep wooded hillside running up the far bank. It was absolutely stunning. "This place is so beautiful."

"Yeah." Kenmore nodded. "One of the reasons I chose this place is because you told me you were looking for inspiration for your jewelry. I thought this place as about as inspiring as it comes."

"You make jewelry?" Shane looked down at her bracelet, the only piece of jewelry she was wearing. Thankfully, it was one she had made. She held it up for him to inspect. "Yes. Just a hobby, really, but who knows, someday it might be more. Everything I've made up until now has been inspired by the ocean." The bracelet she was wearing was braided nautical rope with freshwater pearls woven in.

He took her wrist in his hand and turned it over. "I have to say, I'm impressed."

Who knew Shane could even be impressed? "Thanks."

"If you'd like, you'd be welcome to put some of your pieces in the display case at the front of the store. We're not exactly a jewelry store, but it'd be worth a try."

"Not exactly a jewelry store?" Shane snorted and shook his head. "Now that's an understatement."

Kelli looked at Kenmore, purposely ignoring Shane. "What a good idea. Thanks. Maybe I will."

"I still don't know why you decided to come this morning." Kenmore glanced at Shane, then back at Kelli. "He's never been much for fishing, and not once in his life has he ever been accused of being a morning person."

Shane busied himself setting up three chairs at the pond's edge, ignoring the question altogether. Kelli knew why he wanted to come today, and it had nothing to do with fishing and everything to do with trying to uncover her secrets. His presence would completely destroy any hope she had of having a meaningful conversation with Kenmore.

Three hours later, Kenmore had caught six bass, Kelli three, and Shane one. Shane had spent most of the time looking at his phone and complaining about the lack of a cell signal.

"We're fishing. You don't need a phone for that." Kenmore didn't bother to look toward his son as he said it.

"Yeah, but I've got a showing this afternoon." He stood up. "I'm going to walk back toward the truck and see if I can find a signal anywhere."

Shane disappeared through the woods. Kelli listened until the sound of his footsteps crackling in the leaves was too far away to hear. Now was her only chance, and she knew it. "How long ago did you say you left the financial world?"

"Long time." He pulled in his hook to find it empty. "Thought I felt something down there messing with this." He pulled another night crawler out of the bucket.

"And you said it was just you and a partner? Is that right?"

"Yep." He cast his line toward the left bank.

"What was he like?"

Kenmore didn't say anything for so long, Kelli thought maybe she should repeat the question. She was just beginning to seriously consider it when he turned toward her. "You going to tell them?"

Kelli's mouth went dry. "Tell who?"

"Alison and Beth, you know who. Are you going to tell them?"

"I don't know what—" Kelli stopped the lie before it came out. "How did you know?"

"Can't quite put my finger on the exact moment I knew for sure. That first day you came in, I took one look at you and thought you resembled David. Then you told me you were from California, and I knew that was a place he'd always been interested in, so it made sense that he might have gone there."

"If you recognize me, how is it that Alison doesn't?"

"She thinks you're dead. I'm sure she's thought there was a resemblance, but she wouldn't have taken the thought any further than that."

"And all this time, you've known that my father and I were still alive?"

"Not for sure, but I've always suspected it. David was my business partner. For over a year before the . . . um . . . accident, I knew that he'd been seeing a waitress from the old diner downtown. I also knew that he'd started stowing money away someplace.

I didn't know where or why, but I knew he was moving funds around. Frankly, I assumed he was funneling it to his girlfriend so she could get a nicer apartment or something. Then she left town, and just a few weeks later he had this mysterious accident. I knew it, I knew the moment I heard the news report. I thought, 'He's gone and done it. Left everything behind and started a new life.'"

"Why didn't you tell anyone what you thought?"

Kenmore rubbed the back of his neck. "I did consider it, but I figured what was the use? I thought it would be better for Alison to believe that her husband had died, and better for Beth and Max, too. It seemed to me to be the kinder thing than for them to know what lengths he had gone to so he could dump them."

"Then you've answered the question for me, haven't you? The kinder thing is to keep them in the dark. That was my original plan, to just come here for a few days, meet them, and then get on with my life. But the more I've gotten to know them, well . . . my plan is to stay through the summer, help Beth while she's bed-bound, and see if I can't do something to help Alison in some way before I leave. Something that can help make up for what he did."

He looked over his shoulder, then leaned closer to her and lowered his voice. "Your father, he was killed in a car accident before you came here, right?"

"Yes. And I know what you're asking, and yes, he definitely died this time. He didn't pull another disappearing act."

"That wasn't what I was thinking, but it's a good point. What I was wondering is if it wouldn't be a better thing for Alison now, years after she's worked through all the grief, to get her baby back. Yes, I think she would be devastated to know what David did, but I also think she would be thrilled to have her Darcy back. Especially since she puts such a high store in you already. And I'm gathering that Beth loves you to pieces."

"Yes, but she also has memories of her father. In her mind, he is this flawless man who was never anything but the perfect father in every way. If she were to find out that he actually ran off and left her, I think it would be devastating."

"Perhaps."

"And we haven't even talked about the insurance money. I'm afraid that when the insurance companies find out they've paid out on my father twice, they'll come looking for some reimbursement, and we both know they would look right at Alison. I've already invested my entire payment into a restaurant that's opening in the fall, so it's not like I could give her my share. There is no way I could get that money back without financially ruining my friends."

"You might be right about that one. I'm sure we could ask Shane to look into it, since he knows a fair amount about insurance."

"You can't tell him."

Kenmore looked at her long and hard. "That's up to you."

Kelli leaned forward, putting her head between her knees. "I think it's better for everyone if I just go away at the end of the summer, with no one but you and me the wiser. I'll at least have memories of what my mother and sister are like, and they'll still have their happy memories of my father without knowing what a . . ." As much as she knew that most any word she inserted here had been proven true, Kelli still couldn't bring herself to say anything terrible about him. "Well, that he wasn't the man they all thought he was."

"It's a pretty pickle you find yourself in, that's for sure."

"Kenmore, why do you think he took me?"

"He loved you kids. He was always complaining that it was useless to be a father if he never had time to spend with his children. Between work and his mother and all his other obligations, he felt like he was missing everything about your growing up. Beth and Max were both too old for it to work, but you . . . with you he could start over and do it right."

"I'm not sure I'd call what he did 'doing it right,' but I understand what you mean." She paused, working up her nerve for the next question. "Were he and Alison planning to get divorced before everything happened?"

"Never came up, to my knowledge."

"My grand— Suze's mother gave me some of her old letters. She was under the impression they were getting divorced."

"Sounds like a married man telling his girlfriend what he thinks she wants to hear."

"That's kind of what I thought, too." Kelli wiped at her eyes, then looked Kenmore full in the face. "Do you think Alison had any clue?"

"I'm sure she knows things weren't as perfect as Beth remembers, but no, I don't think she had any inkling that David was thinking of doing what he did, or even capable of such a thing." He shook his head. "How long have you known?"

"A few weeks. I was going through Daddy's things after the wreck, and I found some old papers. I couldn't believe it."

"What were you told, as far as your past?"

"That my family was killed in a fire in Louisiana. A fire that destroyed all their pictures and everything. I've never known what they looked like."

Kenmore whistled. "I'm sorry for you, kiddo. I'd be lying if I didn't say it."

Kelli shook her head. "I'm sorry for all the damage he left behind. You included." She took a deep breath, and didn't continue until she was certain she could do so without getting choked up. "Is there anything I can do to help Alison while I'm here? Or more that I can do for Beth or you?"

"Still planning to make amends?"

"Yes, I guess so. I need to get some sort of peace out of all this before I go back."

"You're helping me now, just by being at the store. And you'll be helping me more than plenty after I have my surgery next week. But you might as well quit looking up this tree, it's one you'll never be able to climb."

"You mean Daddy did so much damage I can never make up for it?"

"I mean, there's only one person who can pay for someone else's sins, and you're not Him. He died on a cross a couple thousand years ago."

"Well, I've got to try."

"Can't fault you for that, just telling you that you're looking in the wrong place."

The crunching of leaves behind them told Kelli this conversation was over. At this point, she was glad.

Kelli arrived home at noon. The morning had not gone as she'd planned in many ways, yet there was some relief in Kenmore knowing the truth.

She pulled the box of letters from the back of the closet, in spite of the fact that she kept promising herself she was going to quit reading them. She chose a letter from the second stack, when things were a little further along. Maybe then she wouldn't have to read so much about how "in love" Mimi was with the married man who was also Kelli's father. The man who seemed so little concerned about the family he was leaving behind.

Dear Mom,

Well, I've done something so awful I just can't keep from

crying. It is truly the most terrible thing I've ever done, but I just don't know how I could have done it any differently.

The tryouts for the junior high musical were this week. They are doing Bye Bye Birdie, *and Kelli wanted the role of Kim so bad. She's been practicing and practicing. Mom, let me tell you that kid has an AMAZING voice. Don came home yesterday and heard her, turned about three shades of pale, and told her she was not allowed to audition, that theater was a waste of time and energy. He even went and called Mrs. Ross and told her to mark her off the tryout roster.*

A little later, I found Kelli crying in her room about it. She was so hurt, and she was confused because her friends had heard her practicing too, and they were all telling her how fabulous she was. I knew there was only one way to convince her to give it up.

I did it. I did what I had to do, but I am so ashamed of myself I can hardly stand it. I told her that her father thought she sounded terrible, and it embarrassed him. Oh Mom, you should have seen that poor girl's face. I crushed her. But it was the only thing I could do to keep us all safe.

I have never felt so awful in my entire life.

Suze

Kelli crumpled the letter and threw it across the room. She, too, had vivid memories of that day—the last time she'd ever sung in public.

She remembered seeing her father at her bedroom door, and she remembered the rough edge to his voice. "Enough of this musical stuff. You need to be focusing on your schoolwork."

"Daddy, I've got A's in every single class." She hadn't thought he was serious at first.

"And it needs to stay that way. You are entirely too preoccupied with all this show stuff. You need to be focusing on things that matter, not wasting all your time on silly things like plays."

The tears ran down her face in earnest. She had wanted to be in that show so badly, and all her friends had told her she was good enough. She had believed them. Until an hour later, when Mimi came into her room and said—

Now that Kelli knew why it had all happened, it only made it hurt that much more. She went to her journal, thinking she'd maybe pour out some of her pain. Instead she looked at the title, *Finding Kelli*, she'd written across the cover. Kelli wasn't even her real name. She picked up a Sharpie and marked a big X across it. Just above it, she wrote the word *Me*.

Finding Me. "That's what I've got to do." She said the words aloud to no one, then picked up the phone and called Denice. "I think I hate my father."

Wow. That is awful. In your father's defense, he likely had no idea Mimi said that to you. He probably thought his own words were enough, and that you'd get over them."

Kelli didn't care about what details her father did or didn't know. "Maybe, maybe not, but it was still his idea to shut me down." Kelli wiped at her eyes. "I have spent my entire adult life too embarrassed to sing around people. It has been a wound and a feeling that I wasn't good enough, and now I find out that maybe I actually am good enough—was in fact, a little *too* good, so my father and his wife decided to kill every bit of my self-esteem to keep themselves safe."

Denice was silent for a moment, and Kelli knew some kind of psychoanalysis was about to be bestowed. "I think we both know that I think—and have thought all along—that you are not ready to deal with all of this right now. Why don't you come home?"

"No! If I come home now, then he wins. And Mimi wins. I've got to stay here until . . . I'm not sure until what, exactly, but until I can leave here feeling as if I've done enough."

"Okay, if that's how you feel, we're going to have to work our way through it as best we can. Let's try to focus on some positive, shall we?"

"I'd love to hear this one."

"Your father, like every other human on the planet, is like a giant gemstone—there are many facets to each of us, and when we are focused on a particular facet in a person, many others are hidden on the back side of the gem. Thankfully for you, the facet of your father you saw most was his love for you and his kindness. However, there was another side, dark and hidden, that he did his best to protect you from. That doesn't make him a completely bad man, it just makes him human."

"Facets maybe, but this is more like complete forgery."

"Admittedly, there are some very dark facets to your father, some that we've never seen before now. We all have some dark facets of our own—that is not to say I excuse your father one bit, or Mimi either, although in Mimi's defense, she was fighting for her life, or at least she believed she was."

"Yeah, she was fighting to keep the fact that she'd run away with a married man and his daughter a secret, so she decided to say something so hurtful to that daughter that she would never be the same again, all in the name of protecting herself."

"Mimi has always had more than her share of self-interested facets, and we both know it. We also both know that Opal wasn't exactly the warmest of mothers, and Mimi never had a father. Wounded people tend to create more wounded people. Baby, you're wounded to the point of wrecked now, so you're going to have to make conscious decisions with everything you do and say from here on out not to continue the cycle on those around you."

"You mean my mother and sister?"

"Partly. And anyone you might love in the future."

"Assuming that's even possible for me now. How can I trust anyone ever again?"

Mimi woke me up on Saturday, which was something she'd never done before. Mimi appreciated sleeping late on weekends. She was positively giddy about the whole thing, though. She kept saying "Out of bed, sleepyhead," and then she'd giggle at her little rhyme and say something to the effect of, "It's going to be a big day. We've got to get moving."

Today was the day she was taking me shopping for prom dresses. It was my senior year, and Ken Bastion had already asked me to prom. There were a couple of stores in Santa Barbara and then another couple about thirty miles away that carried nice dresses, but Mimi had been insistent from the beginning. "This is one of your most important high school memories, and we are going to do this right."

I rolled out of bed and took a quick shower. I stumbled downstairs to the kitchen and found that she'd scrambled some egg whites and cooked some meatless "sausage" patties. She was so excited, and kept talking about us needing our protein to keep our energy up.

It was pouring rain, so the usual two-hour drive to Los Angeles ended up taking more like three. I can still remember how fast her windshield wipers were moving, trying to keep up with one of the heaviest downpours I've ever seen. I told her that we could turn back, but she wouldn't even talk about it.

We finally arrived at this place. Mimi had apparently made an appointment several weeks ago (I'd had no idea until we arrived). They hurried me back to this really nice dressing room and put Mimi in a chair in the area just outside—complete with a pedestal and full-length three-way mirror. The sales lady asked me all about colors and styles, and then she brought me dress after dress.

"I want to see, I want to see," Mimi would say with each new arrival.

There was one dress that was this absolutely beautiful ice-blue satin thing. As soon as I saw it, I just flipped. But when I put it on, it clung to my thighs just a little too tight, making them look bigger than they are, then sort of hung loosely at my chest, making me look even flatter than I am. It was an obvious no-go so I hollered out the door that it was a dud. Mimi insisted on seeing it anyway, and I can still remember how embarrassed I was as I walked out in it. Especially in front of Mimi. Everything about her was so perfectly proportioned (part of that was surgically induced, but that doesn't really matter when you're looking in the mirror, does it?). I braced myself for whatever she would say, because Mimi was famous for not-quite-filtered comments, even when she meant no harm. She learned that from Opal, who took bluntness to a whole new level.

She took one look and shook her head. "Now that's a downright shame." I have never forgotten one single word of her answer, not one single inflection in her voice, not one single movement as she spoke. She flipped her perfectly highlighted blond hair over her shoulder, still shaking her head. "You are hands down the prettiest girl who will ever put on that dress, and the idea of that dress is so perfect, it's just a shame that the designer didn't pay a little more attention to detail in the way that it is cut. It's his loss, but it's a shame he'll never know it."

I was stunned. It was perhaps the most direct compliment I'd ever heard from Mimi, or ever have since, I suppose. But she was completely serious, it wasn't that silly little flattering thing that she and her friends would sometimes get into. "You look beautiful." "Oh no, you look so much better." None of that nonsense.

She did love me. I know that she did, in her own way, and this memory is one that I will always cherish. We ate lunch in Malibu that day, and then walked through some shops before driving home. We laughed and chatted the whole way. I remember thinking at the time that she maybe was my best friend.

Now, in retrospect, I see that even though the two of us didn't get along all that great, and Dad and I were always such pals, it appears that in actuality she may have been the better person. At least she didn't leave a spouse and children behind to take care of her invalid mother. She was a part of it, no doubt, but they weren't people that she knew and loved—they were people that HE knew and supposedly loved. What kind of monster does that?

Surely there is more to the story. Something that I'm missing. I've got to find it, if I'm ever going to feel even remotely okay about my father again.

Kelli had spent the week learning and relearning Kenmore's system for doing things around the store. She'd finally achieved a level of competence to his satisfaction just in time for his surgery yesterday.

On Saturday morning, she drove over to the hospital to visit him. He had been moved from the surgical wing and was now on a floor for rehab. The doctor had said he would be there at least a week, but when Kelli arrived, he was already talking about going home. "I'm plenty able to take care of myself. No reason to sit around here when I could be at home sitting around in my own comfortable chair and sleeping in my own comfortable bed."

"Yes, but don't you need someone to help you for a bit?" Kelli asked.

"I've got Shane, that's all I need."

"I wish I had a dime for every time I've heard that." Shane walked into the room carrying an armload of books.

"Heard what?" Kenmore asked.

"'Shane is all I need.' It seems that a lot of people feel that way."

Kelli and Kenmore both laughed, but Kelli found herself

wondering about the words. Shane was good-looking—beyond good-looking, really. He walked around with plenty of confidence that led Kelli to believe he probably had plenty of admirers in his life, but as far as she could tell, he didn't have a girlfriend. He seemed to spend all his time either at his job, at home, or in the store harassing her. How many women had fallen head over heels for him? Too many, most likely, which perhaps accounted for some of his arrogance.

"So, tell me," Kenmore said, shifting in his bed, "how did things go with the store yesterday?"

"Pretty well. We were busy, but nothing overwhelming." Kelli didn't tell him that she had stayed well past closing, and in fact planned to go out to the store as soon as she spent a couple hours with Beth, in spite of the fact that this was her day off.

"Mr. Moore, it's time for your physical therapy." A man who looked to be in his mid-thirties walked into the room, pushing a wheelchair in front of him.

"You can put that thing away. I'm walking."

"Yes, sir, we just bring this to follow you around in case you get tired and need to sit."

"Well, I won't. Leave it here. I'm going to walk every bit of it, because I need to get out of here and back to work, and sitting on my duff is not going to make that happen."

Kelli and Shane exchanged a grin. Kelli said, "Well, I better hit the road so you can do your thing, boss man. Have a nice workout."

"I'll walk you to your car. Something tells me I don't want to be around here for the next little while."

As soon as the two of them made it out of Kenmore's room, Shane said, "I was planning on coming to find you today, so this was a bit of good timing. I drove by the store last night. What exactly are you doing in there?" He didn't sound angry, just curious, but Kelli knew that could easily change. Besides, Shane lived thirty minutes away from the store, so there was no accident in his "driving by."

"Ever since I've been here, I've thought there is a better way to arrange the merchandise. Right now, a lot of the plumbing and car supplies are toward the front. It tends to make the store look a little junky. Plus, those items sell a fair amount, so if we moved them to the back, then the customers would have to walk past several aisles of other things that they might also need but don't know that we carry. I just thought that if I can make the store look a little neater and increase our sales at the same time, it would be a good thing."

"Did you tell Pop you are doing that?"

She braced herself. "Not exactly." Kelli looked at Shane, trying to gauge how he was taking it. "Your father isn't particularly open to suggestions where the store is concerned."

Shane laughed outright. "Don't I know that."

"I thought if I make the changes while he's gone, once he gets back and sees how much better it works, he'll be happy about it."

"You are a shrewd woman." He cocked an eyebrow in what could only be a flirtatious manner.

"So you seem to believe."

Shane stopped beside her car. "I still don't understand what you are up to. You show up from across the country, take a job at a little market in the middle of nowhere, and you're putting in all of these extra hours like you own the place. Something doesn't add up."

"I'm sorry if I'm doing too good of a job for your liking." Kelli opened the car door. "I'm leaving in a couple of months, and you can make certain to replace me with someone who won't work as hard, okay?" She climbed in and drove away without looking back. She also made a mental note to continue avoiding Shane as much as possible. Problem was, he wasn't making that easy.

"Any sign of Kelli yet?"

"I'll go check." Alison walked across the hall, drew back the curtain, and looked down the sidewalk. "Not yet. But it's only nine-thirty. She isn't supposed to be here for another fifteen minutes." She went back into Beth's room, where her daughter was making an attempt at knitting a baby blanket.

"I know. I'm just anxious to hear about how her day went yesterday. She worked by herself, you know."

"I don't think she was by herself, exactly. Kenmore said Keith was going to work extra hours to help her out."

"Still . . . he's just a kid." She pulled the knit square up for a closer examination, shook her head, and pulled out a row of stitches. "It was her first day in charge of the place. I asked Rand to drive me out there to check on her, but he wouldn't."

Alison laughed. "I'll just bet."

The doorbell rang, and Beth practically squealed. "I knew she'd be early."

Alison met Kelli at the door. "Good morning."

"How's our patient today?"

"Not very patient, I'm afraid."

Kelli laughed. "Somehow that doesn't surprise me."

"Thank you so much for hanging out with her while Rand and I are working."

"I'm happy to. I only wish I could do it more during the week, when you're teaching in Nashville."

"She's fine by herself, for the most part. Besides, Kenmore needs you more than we do right now. You've become quite the helper in your short time in our city. You better get out of here before we decide we can't let you go."

Kelli blinked fast, as if fighting tears. "Glad I can help."

Alison made her way out the door, wondering if she'd somehow upset Kelli. There was something about the girl that made Alison uneasy—not in a bad way, but it just felt as if Alison were missing something about her. Something important.

Still, she was glad Beth had befriended her. It seemed as if both of the girls needed a friend right now. This was a friendship she would continue to encourage.

Shane waited until midday Wednesday before he executed a surprise inspection of his father's store. He'd waited long enough to give Kelli a false sense of security that she was not being watched. By now, her true colors were likely beginning to show. He was going to double-check the receipts for the last few days and find out exactly what was going on.

When he pulled into the parking lot, there were several other cars there, as well. Rather a lot of cars for this time of day. Shane went inside and couldn't believe what he was seeing.

It had only been four days since he had last been there, but in that time, shelves had been rearranged, the dusty old displays of life-sized Dale Earnhardt cardboard cutouts and such had been removed, and there was a fresh coat of paint on the wall behind the register. The whole front counter had been reorganized and actually looked neat and clean.

He looked toward the register, where Kelli was ringing up Mabel Smith and her passel of grandkids for the afternoon's Milk Dud fix. "I love what you've done with this place," Mabel was saying. "The kids' play area over in the corner is genius.

Just genius. I've told Marion and Bernice about it, too. I expect they'll be bringing their grandkids in to check it out in the next day or two."

"Thanks," Kelli answered. "I thought that would make for a nice convenience for families with small children. I'm glad you think so, too."

Shane walked over to the play area. He found a little fenced-off corner with a very small slide, a box of stuffed animals, and a kitchen play set, complete with plastic dishes and cookware. He turned back toward the register and saw Kelli smiling at the next customer in line, who was also making some sort of comment about how good the place looked.

After the woman left, he walked over to the front. "Who authorized you to spend the money to do all this?"

"Last I remember, I don't need to be authorized to spend my own money."

"By 'your own money,' you mean money you took from the store's earnings."

"I think I know the difference between my own money and the store's money, Shane. I said I spent my own money, and that's what I meant."

"Are you telling me you paid for this yourself?"

"It wasn't that much, and yes, that is what I'm saying. Your father has been more than generous to me. I thought I could return the favor."

"Does he know about all this?"

"No, I was planning for it to be a surprise."

"What am I supposed to tell him, then?"

"You can tell him that everything here is going just fine. I know he was worried about the motor oil that was on back order, but I talked to them yesterday and it has shipped. You can tell him that."

Shane looked around again, then back at her. "I have to say,

I'm amazed at what you've done with the place. You must have Keith putting in a ton of overtime."

"Not at all. He's been working extra, of course, like your father asked him to. But he comes in just after lunch and stays until around five. I believe that's exactly your father's plan, so you can stop insinuating that I'm busting the budget on unauthorized overtime. I'm not."

"If Keith isn't working extra, who is doing all this?"

"The good fairies." She rolled her eyes. "Now if you don't mind, I've got customers to take care of."

Shane looked behind him, and there were indeed a couple of teenage boys standing there with sodas in their hands. Shane headed for the door, but not before he heard one of the boys say, "Woo-wee. Kenmore's fixed this place up in more ways than one. What ya doing after work tonight, pretty woman?" The kid was wearing a John Deere cap over his long stringy hair.

Kelli laughed and made some reply that had both of the boys laughing. They took their change and made their way toward the door. Shane slipped outside and waited for them. "You shouldn't speak like that to a lady."

"Speak like what? Last I heard, most girls like to be told they're pretty."

"She's not a *girl*, she's a lady, and you should show more respect. Didn't your parents teach you anything about manners?"

"I didn't say nothing that was disrespectful, nothing I wouldn't say to my own sister." He glanced toward his friend and snickered. "Except I wouldn't ask my own sister out."

"Yeah, well, that makes two of us." They both laughed.

The green-cap kid took a sip of his soda. "Relax. She didn't get worked up over it, so I don't know why you are. Maybe it's just 'cause you haven't had the nerve to tell her that yourself, huh?"

"Bet you're right," his friend said.

"You like her, don't you? But you're too much of a coward to say it." The boys did a fist bump and laughed all the way out to the beat-up red pickup they climbed into. As they pulled away, the one in the cap leaned out the window. "Better hurry up and tell her, 'cause we'll be back tomorrow." The sound of laughter followed behind the truck as it pulled away.

Complete idiots, that's what they were.

On Friday afternoon, Kenmore settled into his easy chair. "It feels good to be home." He nodded at his son. "Real good. Didn't know how much I liked this place until I wasn't here for a while."

"It's nice to have you back, Pop. Things weren't the same without you." Shane set the phone and the TV remote on the table beside him, then made sure his cane was in easy reach. "Okay, I think you've got everything you need. I have to show a house, but you have my cell number, so call me if you need anything."

"I'm perfectly capable of getting around myself and getting things done—as I kept telling them in the rehab center for the last week."

"Yes, you told them plenty, I dare say." Shane laughed. "You've always been a bit of a curmudgeon, Pop, but I'd say you've taken that up a few levels to downright grumpy during your recovery."

"Don't know what you're talking about."

"Refusing pain meds, demanding to be released before the doctor and physical therapist thought you were ready, complaining about the food—which was actually pretty good, by the way.

All I'm saying is, now that you're back home, I hope you'll be a little less cranky."

When had his son gotten so insolent? "Hmph. Don't count on it. Not until I get back to work on Monday."

"Monday after next, you mean."

"Says who? I'm home now. They can't tell me what I can and can't do." Kenmore had every intention of being back in his store on Monday morning.

"The doctor told you to take it slow for the next week, and I can promise you that I'm not going to be driving you to work during that time."

"I'll drive myself. Don't need your permission."

"You don't need my permission, maybe, but you do need the keys. Unfortunately for you, I have taken the liberty of putting them away."

"I'm going to drive if I darn well feel like driving. They just don't want me driving while I'm under the influence of painkillers, which I am not. Haven't taken anything but Motrin since yesterday."

"Dad, you know that if you get in a wreck while you are under your doctor's direct orders not to drive, you could be sued for anything and everything, including your precious store. So it's your choice. Go back to the store week after next, or risk losing your store forever and always. And your retirement fund, too. How about that?"

Kenmore waved his hand dismissively "Ridiculous to hold a man hostage. It sure is." He picked up the TV remote and started channel-surfing. He'd figure out a way to get to work this week, one way or another.

Even though she rarely slept in, after a full week of extreme overtime, everything inside of Kelli rebelled at getting up on

Sunday and getting ready for church. Still, it was her best time to see Alison, so even though it was her one day off, she got up, showered, and dressed in nice clothes. Her cell phone rang, and she saw Beth's name on the caller ID. "Hello?"

"Do you want to come spend the day with us? Rand is planning to stay home, and we're just going to lay low—especially me—but we'd love to have you over if you'd rather not be alone today."

"I'm okay, but does Rand want to go on to church? I was just thinking I was too tired to manage it, but I'm happy to come sit with you while he goes."

"I told him he should go, but ever since we started dating, he's always stayed with me on Father's Day."

Father's Day?

It was as if the air had been knocked from her body. Kelli couldn't breathe, she couldn't speak, she simply stood there and felt the pain. Denice was right: this was something she was not equipped to deal with. "Oh," she said to Beth, "I've been so busy, I had completely forgotten that was today."

"I'm sorry I reminded you, then. I was afraid you were alone and upset, and I didn't want that. Come hang out with us. Mom will be over after church, and Rand is going to make his one and only specialty: grilled burgers."

"I'll be right there."

Father's Day.

Without Daddy.

With the mother and sister she'd never known.

Can my life get any more mixed up?

Rand met her at the door. "Hey, I did want to warn you about something."

"What?"

"It's always been Beth's sort of Father's Day tradition that after we eat lunch, she gets her mother to tell a bunch of stories about her father. We all know what you've just been through, so if this will upset you, then please don't feel obligated to stick around and listen."

"Thanks. I think I'll be all right, but I will leave if I need to." Kelli knew she wouldn't leave even one second early. How could she resist this chance to hear stories about what Daddy had been like in his former life?

"One more thing." He looked over his shoulder, although they both knew Beth was back in the bedroom and out of earshot. "Beth has decided that it would be good for you to talk about your father, too. She thinks it would be helpful for you. Just catch my eye if you need me to get her off your case."

"Thanks, Rand." Even as she said the words, Kelli struggled to remember what she had—and what she hadn't—told Beth about her father. She couldn't exactly remember.

Turns out things really can get more mixed up than they already are.

Alison tried to watch Kelli's reaction as she started on the obligatory story about how David once shimmied up a tree to save a frightened Beth, who had made it about eight feet up, panicked, and grabbed hold of the tree trunk, crying. After soothing talk, lots of instructions, and simply waiting her out for over an hour, David had decided he had no choice but to mount a rescue. Problem was, he'd just had surgery on his shoulder, had his arm in a sling, and was already in pain.

"But he managed to climb up one-handed. By the time I arrived home a couple of hours later, you were happily playing with a doll in the living room, and David was practically passed out on the couch. He'd already met his surgeon at the hospital, gotten a shot for pain, and scheduled the second surgery that would be necessary to repair the damage done during the rescue."

As usual, Beth shook her head and wiped away tears at this story. To her, the story was all about her perfect and self-sacrificing father. And truly, that was what the story was about, but if Beth had been old enough to remember how mad he was—at Beth for getting stuck, and particularly at Alison for leaving him home while she'd gone to the women's ministries meeting—well, it was just as well Beth didn't remember any of that.

Kelli nodded a few times during the story. She didn't seem particularly upset, but it was as if the story made sense to her in some way. Maybe her father had been the same way? "How about you, Kelli? Do you want to tell us something about your father?"

Her face went pale as she looked at them. "Uh . . . no. No, thanks." She looked toward Beth. "You know who I would like to hear a story about though, if you don't mind, is your brother. I know he lives in Kentucky and is married with a couple of kids. But why don't you tell me a story about the two of you?"

Alison and Rand shared a glance across the room, both grateful for Kelli's change of subject. Beth always became so depressed on Father's Day, but once she started in on the stories about Max's and her childhood, she had everyone rolling with laughter. She told story after story, and Kelli kept prodding her with more questions.

By the end of the evening, Alison walked out with Kelli. She turned to her. "Thank you. It was nice of you to keep Beth distracted by questions about her brother today. What made you think to do that? It was brilliant."

Kelli shrugged. "I'm interested, I guess." She paused for just a second. "Being an only child, I've always wondered what it would have been like to have siblings. This gave me a glimpse. It sounds . . . wonderful." She looked almost teary as she said that. Alison wondered what kind of hurts the poor girl was harboring.

Early Monday afternoon, Beth heard her mother return from a quick run to the store. She was speaking to someone, a man. Seconds later, Kenmore came walking into the room. "I conned your mom into a ride over. It's only right that I drop by and check on the other patient. How you doing?"

"I feel fine. How about you?"

He hobbled in, using a cane, his face scrunched in concentration. "Just fine, just fine." He took a seat in the wingback chair across from the bed. "Tell me what kind of hoops you have poor Rand jumping through trying to get the house ready for a baby."

Beth laughed. "To tell you the truth, he is jumping through a few. You know, making the porch safe, covering electric plug-ins, getting rid of cords that are a choking hazard, all those kinds of things you don't think much about when you're just a couple."

"Yes, having a kid changes the way you look at just about everything. And that's not all bad. You never realize how selfish a being you were until there is a little bundle of joy in your life."

"I can't wait to hold her . . . or him. I don't know why, but I just think Sprout's going to be a girl."

"Wishful thinking, perhaps?"

"I don't really think so. I would be completely happy either way."

"That's going to be one lucky kid, I'll tell you that much."

"I'm glad we have the role models that we do. Mom is amazing, as you know, and Rand's parents are awesome, so we at least have that to help guide us."

"And of course, they will make terrific grandparents, ensuring that baby is adequately spoiled, and effectively thwarting every effort you two make at discipline." He smiled as he said it.

"In case you've forgotten, Mom was pretty strict." She reached back and plumped the pillow behind her head.

"As a mother, yes. As a grandmother, I wouldn't really count on that so much." Again he had that smile.

"It will be interesting to see how it all plays out," Beth said. "How are you feeling about the changes Kelli's done at the store? Are you thrilled?"

"What do you mean? What changes?"

Beth realized too late that he didn't know, and that she shouldn't have said anything. The only thing she could do now was try to play it down. "Oh, you know, I heard she's rearranged some things."

"Rearranged?"

"She has a knack for organization. I'm sure you'll like it." *Change the subject. Change the subject. What's another subject?*

"She is rearranging my store while I'm stuck at home?" His voice was getting louder.

Okay, the time for changing subjects was past—what was needed now was damage control. "I think it might have been my fault, really."

"Your fault?"

"You see, I talked Kelli into going baby shopping with me before they put me in bed, and we were looking at all the little toddler slides and play sets, and she made a comment about all the little kids who come into the store with their parents and all the havoc they wreak. I said something to the effect that it really wasn't their fault—if they didn't have a safe place to move around, what were they supposed to do? I'm pretty sure that's what planted the idea of setting up a toddler corner over in the area where the hardware used to be."

"Hardware *used* to be?" His face was growing red.

My damage control may have backfired. "Well, you know, she moved it farther to the back, over where the plumbing supplies are. There's sort of a home improvement section now, with everything together in one place. I haven't seen any of that, but it sounds awesome."

"What?!" His eyes went wide as soon as the word boomed across the room. "Sorry about that. I didn't mean to shout at you, Beth. It's not your doing. It's just that I can't believe she's changing the store around without talking to me about it."

"She probably wanted to surprise you, and now I've gone and blown it. Please don't tell her I told you. I really didn't mean to say anything I shouldn't have." Why couldn't she ever just keep her mouth shut?

"Of course I won't. When Shane comes home tonight, I'll tell him I want to go for a drive and check out the store. I'll pretend like I had no idea anything was going on."

"Don't be mad at her. She really is doing a good job."

"Well, I guess I'll be the judge of that tonight after Shane gets home."

Oh no. She'd done it again. Why couldn't she ever keep her mouth shut?

Kenmore punched number two on his speed dial. Shane picked up on the other end before Kenmore even heard a ring.

"Dad, what's wrong?"

"Nothing's wrong." That kid needed to learn to lighten up just a little. "I want to go to the store. You've finished with your important work by now, right? Since I am *not allowed* to drive, I need a ride."

"Since when do you call me at work? Ever? I thought you must have fallen or gotten hurt or gotten a blood clot in your lung or something."

"What's the big deal? You've been telling me to call you if I need anything, so that's what I'm doing. I need something, and I'm calling."

"Maybe it has something to do with the fact that if I had a dollar for every time you've gone off about people who make personal phone calls during work hours . . . Oh, never mind. Why, exactly, do you want to go out to the store right now? You know I've been checking in there. It's running just fine without you."

What was it about this generation that they needed an explanation for everything? “Can you take me or not?”

“Yes, I can. I just want to know why we’re going.”

“I’ve heard an alarming report that I need to check out right away.” He rubbed the back of his neck, only now realizing that Shane would likely be delighted to hear of this. It would thrill him to no end to say, “I told you so. Kelli was a bad choice.”

“Ah.” Shane coughed, or was he laughing? He said, “Someone’s told you that she’s been rearranging, huh?”

Kenmore held the phone away from the side of his head and stared at it, trying to decide whether it was worth throwing. He finally decided against it and put it back to his ear. “Yes, and my own son knew it and didn’t bother to say anything?”

“Dad, she’s—”

“When were you planning on telling me about it?”

“I don’t know. I wasn’t sure how’d you take it, and I didn’t want to upset you.”

“Since it’s my store, I would say that I have that right, wouldn’t you?” The more this conversation went on, the more Kenmore realized that Shane was—in his own way—defending Kelli. Hmm.

“You know that going over there and getting all fired up because she has moved a few things around is not going to do anything to speed your healing. Besides, I think she’s done a pretty fair job of it, much as I hate to admit it.” He was speaking in his extra-calm voice. Yep, he was definitely taking Kelli’s side here, but trying not to be too obvious about it.

“Go ahead, then. You can at least give me the satisfaction of hearing you say the words.”

“What words?”

“I was right, and you were wrong. Tell me your old man did a good job of finding someone to hire on his own.”

“Nothing doing. I’ll admit she seems to be doing a pretty fair job so far, but if you ask me, there's still something entirely fishy about the way she turned up and talked you into giving her that job."

"Oh really? Apparently you've been checking up on her. Tell me, what nefarious deeds have you uncovered so far?"

"Well, for one, she rearranged the store. You're the one who is, or was until ten seconds ago, so worked up about that."

"Yet you're defending her. Very interesting." His anger at Kelli had melded with anger at Shane for defending her and downright amusement at the current conversation. It wasn't very often he got Shane on the ropes like this. "Fact is, you have not found a single thing to complain about. You just admitted that she's doing a good job moving things around without my permission and against my will. We both know this can only mean one thing."

"What?"

"That her charms are not totally lost on you."

"Get real."

"I'm real. And since we both know that you think she's pretty and you're looking for excuses to spend time with her, I don't see that there's any reason for you not to stop by the house and take me with you out there to check on the place. Do you?"

"All right. Let me finish up some paperwork. I'll be by in half an hour."

By the time Shane arrived, Kenmore had worked himself back up into anger. How dare Kelli move things around in his store?

He made his way across the parking lot with his cane while Shane hovered behind him. "Will you go on? I'm not a little old lady. I'm perfectly capable of making it to the door without falling."

"I don't know why you insisted on using a cane instead of a walker. It seems a much safer choice."

"Walkers are for old people. Besides, like I've told you a hundred times before, I had the new 'minimally invasive' procedure. Much faster recovery time, that's the whole point."

Shane pulled open the front door and held it for him. "Yes, sir. Got it."

Kenmore reached out with his cane and whacked his son on the backside before entering the store. Once inside, he stopped dead and looked around. "What happened here?"

Kelli was at the register with a customer, while two more were shopping in the store. Kim Smithfield was standing over in the corner watching something. Kenmore walked closer to get a better view, and as he approached, Kim looked up and smiled. "Kenmore. I can't tell you how much we love what you're doing with this place. We've all been talking about it."

"Really?" He rounded the corner to see the little play area where Kim's daughter was currently climbing the three steps to the top of a slide. She was grinning from ear to ear, and so was Kim. "And what are you all saying?"

"You know, just how much we like the updates you're doing. And of course the kids' area makes stopping by here with the little ones so much easier. For the first time in a long time, I don't have to worry about Ariel knocking down a display while I'm trying to decide which kind of antibiotic ointment we need this week."

Kenmore hobbled around the store to take a closer look. Several of the areas in the back remained unchanged, but three of the shelves up front had been completely redone. He waited until Kim and the other two customers left the store before he approached Kelli. She was looking at him with a mix of hope and fear.

As much as he wanted to grouse at her for making all these changes, he just couldn't bring himself to do it. He took a deep breath, trying to breathe out some of his annoyance before he managed to say, "I like what you've done with the place."

Kenmore wasn't certain who looked more shocked: Kelli or

Shane, who stared at him, mouth open, pencil in hand, looking over the receipts. He'd have to think of a way to explain this one on the ride home. Then he thought of a better plan. "Kelli, why don't you come over for dinner after you close up? I may be hobbled up, but I can still grill a mean steak."

This would take the pressure off Kenmore and put it right back where it belonged. On Shane.

"Do you mind telling me what that was all about?" Shane waited only until his father had closed the car door behind him before he pounced with questions.

"What all what was about?" His father was the picture of innocence. Yeah, right, like Shane was naïve enough to buy that.

"You wanted me to drive you out here because you were all fired up about the changes. Anyone who knows you knows that there was a pending explosion that someone has dared to move your stuff. You were obviously agitated all the way here. I was trying to think of ways to keep Kelli from quitting after you unleashed on her. And then, out of nowhere, comes this kinder, gentler Kenmore who thanks her for making these changes and invites her to dinner."

"I have no idea what you're talking about. I said I wanted to come see the changes. I liked them and said so. And she looks tired—and she's bound to be tired after doing all that extra work—so I thought the least I owed her was dinner. Seems to me that it's the right thing to do."

"Right thing to do, maybe, but the thing you'd usually do? Not so much." Shane glanced toward his father, whose face was turned toward the window as if he were enthralled with the landscape—the same landscape he'd passed every day for the past fifty years.

"I have no idea what you're talking about."

"So you said." Shane shook his head.

"How are the receipts looking, by the way? I know you've been double-checking her since I've been gone. What are you finding?"

"I've only been checking her for a little over a week."

"And she's only been working alone and doing the books for a little over a week. What are you finding?"

Shane shrugged. There was no choice but to admit the truth, as much as he knew his father was going to yuck it up. "She's a better bookkeeper than you are."

Pop snorted. "Not the greedy little money grabber you thought she was?"

As much as Shane wanted to keep arguing back with his father, he was on the losing side and knew it. Better to just cave in now and get it over with. "Okay, okay. I was apparently wrong about her. She seems honest. She's one of the hardest workers I've ever seen, and she's done an amazing job getting the store spiffed up." As he said the words, he realized just how true they were. "Grandma would be proud of her, I think." He said it before he had time to think better of it. He looked toward his father, waiting for a reaction.

"Yes, I think she would." He was silent for a moment. "Her mother would be proud of her, too, if she only knew what an amazing young woman she is."

"Her mother was killed in a wreck a few months ago, right?"

"That was her stepmother."

"Oh. Where's her mother, then?"

Pop sighed and looked out the window. "I guess I couldn't really say for sure."

Yet another mystery about Kelli. Shane decided it was time to do some looking around on Google. He wasn't sure why he hadn't thought of that before.

I realized something tonight. It was so obvious and right in front of my face I don't know why I didn't see it before.

Shane brought Kenmore by the store. I'm pretty sure he did it because he thought his father would be mad about all the changes I've made. To tell the truth, I thought he might be mad, too. He did seem to have his feathers just a little ruffled at first, but then he calmed right down and seemed happy about it. Excited even. It felt so good to have his approval, and that's when I realized the truth. I've been doing all this, working so hard, because I want Kenmore's approval, not just for amends.

It's sort of like he is the closest thing to Dad that I have left, and he is a representative of the honest side of Dad, if such a side even existed. Somehow, though, I feel like if I can get Kenmore to approve of me, then I've done enough. I suppose I should call Denice and tell her all this so she can analyze exactly what it all means.

He invited me to dinner tonight. There is a weird vibe with Shane. It's like he half resents me and is half glad that I am helping his father. He doesn't seem to know which way to lean, and I'm never sure from one minute to the next which side of the blade I'm going to get. Sometimes he's flirtatious and quite charming, and other times it's like he's mad that I'm in the universe. It's just as well, because getting too close to him would make it too easy to slip up and give myself away. He is suspicious of me—he's just not certain why, which makes him dangerous.

Kenmore starts back to work next week, so I'm going to try to get the rest of the place spiffed up before then. I think I will be able to leave at the end of the summer satisfied with my time here. Especially if I continue to help Beth, maybe get to know Alison a little better, and earn Kenmore's approval. Those are the three things I am shooting for.

Kelli had just finished her most recent journal entry when the doorbell rang. It was after nine—she couldn't imagine who would stop by this late. She turned on the porch light and peeked through the window.

Miss Birdyshaw stood there, wearing her robe over a long nightgown. She had what appeared to be a book in her hand.

Kelli opened the door. "Hello, Miss Birdyshaw, is everything all right?"

"Right as rain, dear. It's just that—remember when you first moved in here, I told you that you looked like someone I used to know? Well, I finally found her picture, and it looked so much like you I just had to come and show you." She held up a white book with the words *Wildcats 1945* printed on the cover. "It's right in here." She flipped open the cover of what appeared to be a high school yearbook.

"Would you like to come inside? It might be more comfortable at the kitchen table."

"No, thank you, dear. It's past my bedtime, but I really wanted to show you this." She flipped open the book to somewhere in the middle. At the top, *Senior Class* was printed in bold black letters, and each page held about eight photographs. Miss Birdyshaw pointed a shaky finger at one particular girl. "Mary Albright was her name. She was the most popular girl in our class. Such a beautiful girl, but then she moved away to North Carolina and I heard a rumor that she was in a terrible car accident and never looked quite the same." She shook her head. "Such a tragedy."

Kelli looked closely at the picture. Like all the other girls, Mary had mounds of curly bangs all around her face, and long hair down to her shoulders, neatly curled under. Even with those differences, there was no denying that, other than her hairstyle, she looked almost identical to Kelli. "Wow, she does look a lot like me. I wonder if she has family in California."

Miss Birdyshaw shrugged. "I have no idea, but you know who she is related to? Your friend Beth. It only occurred to me when I was looking through this old album. She was her grandmother's older sister."

Kelli's mouth went dry. Great Aunt Mary? The one Beth had already commented about Kelli looking like?

Red flags were waving everywhere. If two people were already making a connection about who she looked like, how much more dangerous would things get?

Thursday night, the lighted clock above the front door of the store glowed behind the words *Royal Crown Cola, so bubbly fresh* and told Kelli it was 6:55. Only five more minutes until closing. She was grateful for this, as the last couple of days had been draining.

Since no one was there, she figured she might as well get a head start. She walked over to the aisle that had all of what Kenmore called the "bents and dents." This section was full of items that were dented, missing packaging, or had for some reason been deemed unsalable by the chain stores. The store got a delivery of new items once a week, and it was always a mystery as to what might arrive. Kelli looked at the shelf—porcelain dolls, a couple of lamps shaped like dolphins, a set of toddler dinnerware, stuffed animals, a ceramic Santa and his reindeer, a box of pencils. How could she even begin to go about organizing this in any sort of meaningful way? And wouldn't it just have to be redone every week when the new shipment arrived?

The bell above the door jangled and Kelli looked over her shoulder to see who might be coming in for a last-minute item.

It was Shane. “Since when do you come in the front door?” She turned back to examining her shelf, knowing he would make his way to the back office, where he came every night to look over the books.

She was surprised when he walked over to stand beside her and asked, “What are you looking at?”

“This mishmash of junk. I’m trying to think of a logical way to organize it, which is hard enough. But considering that a new unknown shipment comes in every week or so, I’m trying to think of some sort of system that your dad can maintain when he’s back here on his own.”

Shane reached out and pressed the button on one of the monkeys, causing it to start banging its cymbals together. He flipped it off and smiled. “Why are you doing this?” He turned to look at her, not angry or accusing, simply questioning.

She straightened a doll that had fallen over. “Don’t you think it needs to be tidied up a bit?”

“Obviously, but that’s not what I meant, exactly. I mean, why are you putting in all this extra work? Dad hired you to help out, to stand behind the cash register, and just keep things running. Yet the approach you are taking here is as if you own the place and desperately need it to succeed. You’re putting in more hours than my dad does, and that’s saying something. Yet you’re barely making more than minimum wage, and to the best of my knowledge, you’re planning on leaving town as soon as the summer is over. There must be something you think you’ll get out of it.”

Kelli started to give him a flippant answer, but then stopped herself. Better to be vague, yet truthful. “For one thing, he needed some organizing, and I enjoy trying to think of ways to do things better. I was a business major in college but I’ve never really had a job where I could apply much of what I learned.”

“There’s got to be more to it.”

"To be perfectly honest, I haven't really slept well since . . . well, for several months. So I try to work myself into enough exhaustion that I can fall asleep."

He was still watching her, standing just a little closer than was comfortable. "Does it work?"

She shrugged, thinking of how often she jerked awake after a nightmare, or more likely, another slam of guilt over everything she'd recently discovered. "Sometimes."

"What are you running from, Kelli?"

"Why do you always—"

He reached out his hand and put it on her arm. "I didn't mean it in an accusing way. What I meant was, there is obviously something that is eating you up. Something that bothers you enough to keep you awake at night."

"I think it's called grief. Try losing your father and stepmother in a car wreck and see how well you sleep at night."

"Is that really what it is?" His voice was soft, concerned. "Sometimes when I watch you, it's like you're listening to everyone around you talking, and you're trying your best to understand what is going on. Like you're trying to solve a great mystery in every single conversation."

"I have no idea what you're talking about."

"Don't you?" He looked at her evenly for the space of several heartbeats, then glanced toward the front door. "Shall I lock up?"

Relieved for the change in subject, Kelli said, "I guess it's time."

Shane walked over and locked the door, then went behind the counter and began the process of zeroing out the cash register. Kelli walked over to him. "You've been double-checking my books every single night, and now you don't even trust me to do it the first time?"

"No, tonight I was thinking if I did it for you while you're doing whatever else it is you need to do, then maybe you'd have enough time that we could go downtown, grab a quick bite, and maybe go for a walk around the square. It's Thursday Night Lights, which means there'll be a live band and probably a few vendors. Have you ever gone down and checked it out?"

"No."

"How about it?"

Dinner and a live band. Relaxation and fun . . . with Shane. There were several things about that which sounded really appealing.

Boundaries. Boundaries. Boundaries. Denice's voice echoed through her head. "I really was planning on moving this shelf around tonight."

"It'll wait until tomorrow." Shane came to stand in front of it, effectively blocking the shelf. "I'll even come by and help. But my father is highly convinced that you are working too hard and is insisting that I see to it that you take a break. Truth is, I happen to know that Highway 35 is the band playing downtown tonight, and I'd really like to go see them. I figure if I take you along, then I get Dad off my back and get to see my favorite band at the same time."

"Heaven forbid that I should get in the way of your multitasking."

"Exactly. Now, if you'd prefer to do the register yourself, then tell me what else needs doing around here and I'll get it done so we can get out of here."

"Yes, in fact I would like to do the register myself. And if you insist, then feel free to sweep the floors and check the glass door to see if it needs a cleaning."

Kelli started counting the money, but she looked up every now and then to see what Shane was doing. Like his father, he was a hard worker, but almost every time she looked up, she found him watching her. Was he really sorry about being suspicious for so long, or was he just trying to make it appear that way because he believed he would then be able to watch her without her being aware of it? Surely he didn't think she was that gullible.

The register was a nickel off tonight, which although considered perfectly acceptable, still bothered her. She always counted the money carefully, and she didn't like the idea that somewhere along the way she had made a mistake. She shook her head.

"How's it look?" He was leaning over, looking at the report.

"You want to double-check it?"

He held up both hands. "No, just making conversation, that's all."

"It's five cents off. How's that for conversation?"

"Not very interesting. The reason I came up here is to find out where you keep the Windex. Dad always had it behind the front counter, but I don't see it."

"Really? It should be— Oh wait, I had it over at the knife case earlier today, and I got interrupted. I bet I left it over there."

"I'll go look." He walked over to the case way too casually. He still didn't trust her, she could tell.

"Found it," he called from across the store.

"You know, I really should stay here and—"

"Nothing doing. You promised you'd go with me, and I'm holding you to it."

Kelli sighed and locked the money in the safe. "All right. Are you ready?"

An hour later, Kelli and Shane sat in lawn chairs, eating the last of their sub sandwiches and chips, and listening to Highway 35—a quite good young band. Over the course of the evening, Kelli had come to the alarming conclusion that she was enjoying herself. Perhaps a little too much. Denice's voice was practically screaming inside her head.

"So . . . do you enjoy real estate?" Dull conversation was an effective and proactive way to keep things safe.

He shrugged. "It's not my dream job, but it was time that I started acting like an adult and took a big-boy job. I've never really wanted to work at the store. Pop said it wasn't really a good time for it, anyway. So real estate seems to fit the bill pretty well."

"Shane? Shane Moore, is that you? I can't believe it, I haven't seen you in forever." A beautiful blonde bounced over in front of Shane's chair. Her hair was shoulder length and perfectly curled, her makeup was expertly applied to make her blue eyes shine bright even in the streetlights, and the pale blue sundress she wore showed off the perfect tan. She was followed by two others who were also very pretty, both of whom seemed equally excited to see Shane.

"Well, hello there." Shane stood up and hugged all three of them as they chattered excitedly.

"How is baseball?" "Dad said you got hurt, are you better?" "You should come over to Sandy's tomorrow night. We're having a cookout." The words flowed so quickly from all three girls that Kelli couldn't begin to keep up.

Shane turned toward Kelli. "May I introduce Kelli Huddleston? She's helping at my dad's store this summer, especially now while he is recovering from hip surgery."

Kelli stood up to shake hands, but all three girls hugged her instead. "I'm Amy," the blonde said. "Shane and I go waaaay back, don't we, Shane?" She smiled coyly toward him.

He nodded and turned toward Kelli. "Amy and I grew up just a few blocks away from each other. We've been friends for as long as I can remember."

"I think almost every good memory I have from junior high

or high school involves Shane in some way or another. We were the absolute best of friends, you might say."

Something about Amy made Kelli wish she'd spent a little more time fixing herself up this morning—and gave her the slight urge to reach out and wipe the grin off Amy's face. She had such an air of superiority about her, and the way she was obviously trying to lay a claim on Shane right now . . . which was fine, because Shane and Kelli weren't really even friends, but Amy didn't know that. What if this had been a date?

In spite of knowing better, Kelli reached over and put her hand on the back of Shane's arm. "I'm glad to know that Shane had such good friends when he was growing up. That's why he turned out to be such a wonderful man now, I suppose."

Amy looked from Kelli's hand on Shane's arm to Shane's face and back again. "Oh . . . well, we've kept you long enough. But remember, tomorrow night at Sandy's. We expect to see you there." She turned to go, then looked over her shoulder. "Kelli, obviously you'd be invited to, if you want to come." She offered a finger-only wave and then walked off into the crowd, followed by her two friends.

Kelli dropped her hand and looked at Shane. He was grinning like he'd just read her mind—the part about smacking Amy. She shrugged. "Sorry about that. Somehow that girl just got my ire up. I mean, for all she knew we were here on a date, and she's all but stating that you are hers. It just irritated me."

"Glad to know you care." He bumped his elbow against her arm.

"Ha. Like that would ever happen." She shoved back.

They both laughed and sat back down. Kelli took a moment to process all that had just happened. "Baseball?"

"Yeah, what about it?"

"She asked you how baseball was. What did she mean by that?"

He flexed his right arm up, then slowly stretched it out in front of him. "I used to play."

"For your high school, you mean?"

"Yeah." He continued to work his arm up and down, rubbing the back of his elbow as he did.

"College, too?"

He nodded. "College, too." He looked up toward the stage. "I like this song, don't you?"

"I like it fine. Did you play baseball after college?"

He turned toward her then. "I was in the Braves' organization for a few years. Last year I played for their Triple-A team and was expected to get called up for the end of the season when they add to their roster. Unfortunately, I messed up my elbow about two weeks before that time. Since then, I've had a couple of surgeries and done lots of rehab, but it just never regained its former strength. The doctors finally came to the conclusion that it likely never would, so the decision was made that it was time for me to move on with my life."

Kelli blew air out slowly. "How is it that I never knew this about you?"

"It's not like I go around talking about it all the time. What am I supposed to say, 'Hey, did you know I almost made it in the major leagues'?"

"Maybe not, but still, you'd think it would have come up in conversation."

"I generally try to avoid talking about my failures. It's a strange little habit I have."

"You consider making it to Triple-A baseball a failure? I think most men in America would be thrilled to be able to say that."

"Yeah, well, not me."

"What if you'd made it to the big show, then? Would you have been a failure unless you were a starter? Or the best player on the team? Or the best player in the National League? Where is the line that separates success from failure?"

He looked at her long and hard. Finally he said, "I guess I have no idea. I just know I haven't crossed it yet." He paused for a moment. "That sounds like I'm feeling sorry for myself, and maybe on some level I am, but not really. It's just that I had a picture in my mind of where my life would be right now, and that's not where I am at all. It's hard to explain, really."

"Oh, you'd be surprised how well I can understand that concept."

"Right. I hadn't thought of that. Sorry."

Of course Shane thought she meant the death of her parents—he had no idea how much her life had veered off the course she'd always assumed. At least he still knew who his parents were. She blinked hard against anything that might threaten to spill out of her eyes. Shane reached over and grabbed her hand. She looked up at him in surprise. "Amy's heading back this way. I just thought we ought to make it look good."

Kelli turned toward the crowd and did indeed see Amy looking their way. "Well, I suppose we can't be too careful." She scooted her chair a little closer to his.

35

Kelli rolled out of bed on Saturday morning, thankful for a day off. She still planned to spend some time at the store, but for now, she needed a little break. She got a text message from Beth, who'd spent the past couple of days at Alison's house while Rand was out of town. *Still at Mom's until this evening. Please come over. Mom says she'll make you some tea.*

This was an offer Kelli would not refuse. *Sounds good. I'll be over soon.*

A little later, she walked up the driveway, trying not to think about the last time she was here. She looked up to see Alison standing at the front door. "So good to see you again, Kelli. How are you doing?"

"I'm fine, other than being embarrassed about passing out the last time I was here." She felt the heat creep up her neck and cheeks.

"Nothing to be embarrassed about. I'm glad to have you back here. And, unlike my daughter"—she glanced back toward her house—"I will not put any pressure on you to sing while you're here." She held the door open wide. "Please, come in."

Alison led her back to the guest room, where Beth was staying. "About time you got here," Beth said as soon as Kelli walked in. "Hey, since you're here, and since Mom is here, what do you say—"

"Beth, enough." Alison's voice was as firm as Kelli had ever heard it. Is this what she'd sounded like when Beth and Max and even Kelli were little and doing something they weren't supposed to? It was a far cry from Mimi's shrill reprimands, that much was sure.

"Would you like some sweet tea?" Alison glanced at Beth, then back at Kelli.

"Tea sounds great, thank you." When Alison headed to the kitchen, Kelli sat on the edge of Beth's bed. "How are you feeling?"

"I feel fine, just bored as usual. I'm not complaining though. If I have to lay around in bed for a few months to make sure Sprout gets here full grown and healthy, then that's what I'll do."

"Are you getting excited? About being a mother, I mean?"

"You have no idea. The doctors had told me I probably wouldn't be able to get pregnant, and for several years they seemed to be right. I definitely appreciate being pregnant more than most people."

Alison arrived with the tea. "According to Beth, you are working your fingers to the bone at Kenmore's store these days."

"I wouldn't quite say that, but it's definitely keeping me busy."

"I'm sure you're doing a good job, but do remember to take care of yourself, too."

"They say that music is a good way to relax." Beth grinned at them.

Kelli smirked at Alison. "Is she always this stubborn?"

"She gets an idea in her head, and just beats you down until you do what she wants you to do. At this point in my life, I've decided it's usually just easier to give in sooner rather than later, and then I can get on with my life." She tilted her head down and peered at her daughter over the top of her reading glasses, a mock-stern expression on her face.

Beth quirked one eyebrow and looked at Kelli. "A lesson you would do well to learn, as well. Oh come on, you're here already."

Kelli laughed. "I don't quite understand why the fact that I do not sing in church has made you so determined that I need to take a singing lesson."

"I get the feeling that somewhere along the line, someone in your life has hurt you and it has to do with music. This is something that is worth fighting through, and Mom and I are right here to help you."

"Yes, we're here to help you—not harass you or bully you." Alison cast a stern glance toward Beth.

Beth's face turned pink. "Sorry. I just can't seem to stop myself sometimes." She looked at Kelli. "I really am sorry. I'll stop."

"To tell you the truth, it scares me to death, the idea of singing in front of people, or even near them. It's fairly crippling to feel this way."

"Sometimes if someone is uncomfortable singing alone, I sing with them. That way, it's a little less in-the-spotlight. But there's no pressure here to do anything. In fact, we can change the subject altogether."

"I . . . uh . . . I can try it." Kelli's mouth had gone cotton dry, and the words came out a little croaky.

"Really? Oh, really? You're gonna love this, I just know you are." Beth was bouncing her head against the pillow.

Alison glanced toward the door. "Why don't we go into the den? The sound is better, and we won't have an audience in there."

"Wait. But I want to hear . . ."

Alison ruffled Beth's hair, then led Kelli out into the small den-turned-music-room. "Take a few deep breaths and just relax. Don't worry, I'll work you into this slowly—that is, if you're sure you want to."

The deep breaths actually did help Kelli relax a little. Now that she'd finally agreed to do it, she looked forward to working through some of her past fear, and soaking in the closest thing to love she would ever receive from the woman who had once been her mother.

"Your voice is truly something special. Do you think you want to try something on your own?"

Kelli shook her head. "I don't think I'm ready."

"Not a problem. Here, I'll teach you one of the songs I happen to know we are singing at church tomorrow. We'll practice it together."

It took a few run-throughs before Kelli got comfortable with the tune, but then she began to really feel the music. When they finished, Alison said, "Beautiful."

When they finally returned to Beth's room, she had tears in her eyes. "Wow" was the only thing she said.

"I don't really understand some of the lyrics," Kelli told them. "'Not because of who I am, but because of what you've done. Not because of what I've done, but because of who you are.' That doesn't seem appropriate for church."

Beth was in Kelli's peripheral vision, but Kelli could see her mouth fall open. Alison, however, didn't seem the least bit shocked. "What the lyrics mean is that nothing we do or don't do makes us right before God. Only because of what God did for us, offering His Son to die for our sins, can make us right with God."

"But that's not right. It is what we do—living a good life and doing our best. Because a lot of good people don't believe in Jesus, but that's not their fault. God wouldn't punish them for that, as long as they are good people."

Alison paused for a moment and took a breath. Kelli had the distinct impression she was trying to collect her thoughts. When she spoke, her voice was calm and soft. "Kelli, what it comes down to is whether you believe God is God and whether you believe that He sent Jesus. Because if the answer to both of those questions is yes, then you have to ask yourself, if all it takes for us to live close to God is to be the best person we can be, why would God send Jesus to suffer the terrible death that He did? That's not the kind of thing you would do unless it was absolutely necessary—unless there was no other way. It certainly wouldn't make God a God of love, now, would it?"

"But that's not fair, if God limits himself to only people who believe one way."

"There is a great unfairness in all this, you are right, but every bit of that unfairness was carried by Jesus when He died for sins He did not commit."

Kelli shook her head. This conversation did not make sense to her, but the last thing she wanted to do was to get into a theological argument on perhaps the closest day she would ever spend with her mother. "Well, thanks for the singing lesson." There was still tension in the room and Kelli could not allow things to end this way. She glanced toward Beth and smiled. "I enjoyed it a lot more than I thought I would. I'm glad I let Beth bully me into doing this."

"I did not bully. And I knew you'd like it if you just gave it a try. I believe that an 'I told you so' could be in order here."

"Maybe so." Kelli was grateful that Beth had quickly taken the change in conversation. "Okay, you win. You were right."

"Of course I am. That's exactly what I said, isn't it?" Beth folded her arms across her chest and grinned.

Kelli turned back toward Alison. "Truly, though, thanks again."

"It was my pleasure. You have an amazing voice, and your tone and pitch are almost spot on. For someone who's never done much singing, it's amazing. Here, let me give you something." She opened a drawer and pulled out a CD. "This has some practice scales on it. You can take it home and work on it whenever you feel like it."

"You know what?" Beth turned to fluff her pillows. "You two sound really good together. I think you should do a duet or something."

"I'm not ready for that yet." Kelli choked on the last few words. There were a lot of things about this she wasn't ready for.

She walked out of Alison's house, got in her car, and drove back to the duplex. She somehow made it inside before she burst into tears. She wasn't certain what the emotional outburst was all about. She just . . . felt. A lot. And a lot of everything.

"Dad, look at this." Shane came and knelt beside Kenmore's recliner, his laptop in hand.

When Kenmore saw what was on the screen, he turned back toward the TV, pretending to be absorbed in the current smartphone commercial. "What?" He tried to sound more grumpy than cornered, but Shane knew him too well. He'd see right through it.

"This is an article about Kelli's parents and the car wreck."

"Oh right. Sad story."

"Sad story, right, but look at his picture." Shane pushed the computer into Kenmore's lap.

"Yeah, she told me all about it. I don't have to read the details." He tried to look away, but he couldn't. His gaze was fixed on the person he used to know.

"Doesn't he look a whole lot like David Waters? I mean,

obviously I was little when David was around, but this guy looks a *whole lot* like the photos I've seen of him."

Kenmore shrugged. "I guess I see a little resemblance."

"A little resemblance? Are you kidding me? He looks older, of course, but David would have been older. I think it's downright spooky."

"Do me a favor, don't mention this to anyone else, okay? It would just upset everyone—Kelli, Beth, Alison."

"I'm not stupid. I wouldn't bring up someone's dead father or husband because I saw a picture of someone who looks like them. I just thought it was interesting, that's all."

"Yeah, I guess so." Kenmore nodded toward the screen. "This is a good game."

When Shane stood up, he stared down at his father for a long time, and that's when Kenmore knew he'd played it off a little too much. Shane's wheels were spinning, there was no doubt about it. That couldn't mean anything good for any of them.

Kelli walked into City Center Church on Sunday morning, wondering why she continued to come here, now that she had another excuse to see Beth and Alison. It had become something of a habit, she supposed, and it had the potential to raise too many questions if she suddenly stopped. Best to keep going through the motions.

Alison was nowhere to be seen, so Kelli took a seat near the back. She stuffed her purse up under the seat in front of her, crossed her legs, then uncrossed them, and tried to leaf through the bulletin a middle-aged woman had handed her when she'd entered. Someone stirred to her left, and she turned in time to see Alison sliding in beside her. Since this was quite a bit further back than Alison normally sat, there could be no question that she was sitting here to be with Kelli. Her mother was choosing to be with her, even having no idea who she was.

Kelli managed a quick hello.

Alison squeezed her arm. "Good morning."

The first song was "Amazing Grace." Although Kelli and Alison had not sung this one yesterday, Kelli figured anyone who had grown up in America knew at least a little bit of this song. Kelli took a deep breath and steeled her nerves but found that she couldn't open her mouth. At all. Maybe she should just listen to the first verse, get the rhythm, and then she could join in with the second.

"'Twas grace that taught my heart to fear, and grace my fear relieved . . ." Once again Kelli took a deep breath, but based on the nerves that had built up inside her chest, she could have been singing a solo in front of the entire church. This was crazy. She was simply trying to join in with a large group singing the same song—a group where her voice would not even be differentiated from anyone else's. Her mouth would not open.

Two songs later, they began singing the song Kelli and Alison had practiced yesterday. By this point, tears had started spilling down her cheeks, and she had given up all hope of actually participating. She looked sideways toward Alison, who was facing the front and singing. Kelli knew that she was being discreet, but that she was listening and watching expectantly, waiting to see the results from yesterday. Except there were none.

She took another breath, opened her mouth, and . . . failed. Again. She could not force out a single sound. She sat through the rest of the service with one thought and one thought only in her mind.

I think I hate my dad.

Beth drank the last of her milk and looked at the clock on the bedside table for what seemed like the thousandth time. What was taking so long? Rand came into the room. "How's my favorite patient?"

"Not very patient. Shouldn't church be out by now?"

He didn't bother to look at the clock. "I imagine so." He picked up the empty glass, then sat down on the side of the bed. "I wish I knew why you are obsessing about this so much. I know Kelli told you she would stop by on her way home, but you've been watching the clock all morning."

Beth shook her head. "I wish I could tell you. I don't understand it myself. I just have the strangest sense that there is some deep, dark hurt in Kelli, and somehow that beginning to sing again will be the beginning of her healing. I know"—she adjusted the sheet around her legs—"it's weird, even for me."

He brushed the hair back from her forehead and smiled. "Nothing you do surprises me, but it does seem that you get especially worked up about Kelli."

"I know, and I can't seem to help myself. I think she showed up exactly when my hormones were at their wildest, plus I was lonely, and I don't know . . . Oh, Rand, I'm going to shove her away by being so pushy, aren't I? That's what I always seem to do. I just can't seem to stop myself sometimes." She felt tears well up in her eyes but blinked them back, determined to maintain something like control.

"If someone can be driven away because you're trying so hard to be such a good friend, then it's just as well. Most people would kill for a friend who loves them that much." He leaned forward and kissed her forehead.

"I'm glad I have you to be my mega-best-friend for life." She wrapped her arms around his neck and realized just how much she meant that.

The doorbell rang. "Aha." Rand stood up and smiled. "Bet I know who that is."

Beth heard Kelli's voice, and she waited expectantly to hear all about her first foray into public singing. "How'd it go? Did you belt it out?" She hollered the question down the hall before Kelli even made it to her room. When she saw Kelli's face, she would have given anything if she could take back the words.

"Hey." She came to sit on the edge of the bed, having the good grace to pretend she hadn't heard Beth's questions. "How you feeling?"

"I'm all right. How about you?"

Kelli shrugged. "Okay." She looked at the ceiling for a minute. She swallowed hard, as if she was about to say something she didn't want to say, but then shook her head and reached down for a small gift bag she had set beside her purse. "I brought you something." She handed the bag to Beth.

Beth pulled out the tissue paper and couldn't believe what she was seeing. "It's amazing." She lifted it out of the bag and turned the wooden horse figurine around in her hands. The mane was so detailed that she could see individual strands of hair, and the dark brown wood was polished and gleaming. "I've never seen anything like it."

"I thought it would work for your nursery, whether you use carousel or rocking horses."

"Where did you get it?"

"It's something I've had for a long time. My father carved it for me when I was a little girl. I had my friend ship it to me so I could give it to you."

"Your father did this? By hand?"

"Yes. That's what he did. He was a carpenter and artist—he could do anything with wood."

"Wow. That is so amazing, but I can't take this. Your father made it for you." Beth held it out.

"I have other things he made." Kelli pushed it back toward her. "He would be glad if he knew I was giving it to a friend like you. It would make him really happy for you to have it."

Beth couldn't help but notice that Kelli's voice caught on the last few words, but she pretended that she didn't. She held the figurine to her chest. "I will treasure this. Always."

"Thanks." Kelli stood up. "I'm going to run by the store for a little while. I'll text you when I get home, and maybe stop by again."

"Okay." Beth watched her walk out the door, her heart sick that she couldn't do more to help her friend. She waited until she heard the door close before she picked up the phone. "Mom, what happened with Kelli in church today?"

"I'm not sure," her mom answered, "but I'd say you are more right than I first believed. There are some deep hurts between that girl and her singing. I could see her standing over there, taking deep breaths, trying to get started, but she just didn't seem to be able to do it."

"Mom, we've got to figure out a way to help her."

Kelli pulled into the driveway, wondering why she'd accepted this invitation. She was dead tired after a long Tuesday at work, and all she wanted to do was to go home, grab a gallon of chocolate ice cream and a spoon, and maybe watch some mindless action movie on TV. Still, Kenmore had been so upset when the doctor insisted he take it easy for another week before returning to work, she couldn't have refused him anything. If it would make him feel better to cook her dinner again, then she was going to enjoy it. The steak she'd had with the two men last week had certainly been delicious. She wondered if Shane would be here this time, or did he even know that his father had invited her?

She climbed out of the car and moved toward the house just as the door opened. Shane yelled back over his shoulder, "Okay, Dad, she's here." He turned toward Kelli and grinned. "He wanted to put the steaks on as soon as you arrived, so he's had me watching the driveway for the past half hour. I feel like one of those snoopy neighbors that's always peeking out of their curtains." He jumped over the porch steps and landed beside her, offering an elbow. "Help you up the stairs, ma'am?" Shane knew how to use his boyish charm to full advantage, there was no doubt about that.

"Thank you, kind sir. I don't think I could possibly manage without your assistance." Kelli took his arm as they started up the three small steps. "Tell me, did you see anything interesting while you were watching for me? Some sort of neighborhood crime ring or anything?"

"Not unless Mrs. Jones walking her dog, and the Carmichael twins riding their bikes without training wheels would qualify as interesting. I'm pretty sure neither activity was of a criminal nature." He opened the front door and held it for her.

"You're not much of a detective, are you?"

"Apparently not." He looked at her for a few seconds longer than necessary, then reached up and rubbed his stubbled chin with his free hand.

Kelli walked all the way through to the kitchen before she trusted her voice. "Your dad's lucky he has you."

He reached for the back door but turned before opening it. "You okay?"

She nodded but didn't look at his face. "Just tired."

"Well, come on out back. I'll fix you something cool to drink, and you can sit and watch us men wait on you." He pushed the back door open.

"Ah, the world as it was intended. Women sitting, men waiting on us."

"Ha." Shane continued to study her as she walked past him toward the backyard. "You're a strong woman—much more so than I would have given you credit for when we first met."

Kelli hurried out the door to find Kenmore standing beside his grill, cane leaning against a nearby patio chair.

"There you are. I hope you've worked up a good appetite,

because as you already know, my steaks are second to none, if I do say so myself."

"And believe me, he will say so himself. Over. And over. And over." Shane gestured toward a padded chair. "What can I get you to drink?"

"Just some cold water sounds great."

"You got it." He made for the house, and Kelli was glad for his absence.

"How you holding up?" Kenmore came to sit beside her.

"Good. I mean, I'm tired, don't get me wrong. It's amazing to me that you work this many hours, on your feet, and have done so for years—especially with a bad hip. I'm surprised you waited as long as you did to find Frieda's replacement."

"I like doing things my own way in my own time."

"Speaking of which, I hope you're not too upset about me moving things around while you were gone."

"Truth is, you've done a nice job with the place."

"Thanks. I'm surprised how much I enjoy it. I never really pictured myself working in retail, but the people are so friendly, and I don't know, something about figuring out the best way to arrange things for full effect is sort of like working a giant puzzle."

"Never been much good at puzzles myself. Maybe that's why I never move things." He stood up and limped over to the grill. When he flipped a steak, it sent out a loud sizzling sound and a puff of steam.

"Here you go." Shane handed her the glass of water and took the seat beside her.

"So, Shane, last week you told me that real estate was your grown-up job—what made you choose it?"

He shrugged. "I like the people, and it's interesting work. Originally, I was thinking of insurance."

"Insurance?"

"I got interested in it back when a family friend—well, Beth's mom, Alison, you've met her . . ."

"Yes."

"Well, after her husband and daughter died, the coroner wouldn't issue a death certificate without a body, and life insurance wouldn't pay without a death certificate. Dad got involved in trying to help her, and I found all the red tape frustrating. When I started looking for a real career, I thought maybe if I went into insurance, I could be that person who could help people wade through all the red tape and get the help they need. What I discovered is, I find that all too frustrating to do it day in and day out. Life insurance is a complicated business."

"Sounds like it." Kelli sat silent, thinking about her father and stepmother living in comfort, after leaving his wife, kids, and mother to face devastating financial consequences. She wanted to change the subject, to move on to something else, but a thought began to niggle at the back of her mind and would not let go. She knew she could ask the question in the guise of this conversation and no one would think anything of it. If she asked at a later time, that would not be the case. She pulled up some courage from somewhere deep inside, forced a nonchalant look on her face, and said, "Okay, so from your previous training, let me ask you a hypothetical question—just because."

"Shoot."

"Suppose that after Alison had her husband and daughter declared dead, suppose they turned up somewhere. Maybe in a hospital with amnesia after their accident, something like that. What would happen to the insurance money?"

Shane looked over at his father, stared hard for a few seconds, then took a sip of tea and shook his head. "That's a good question. I'm pretty sure they would have to give it back. Seems pretty cut and dried."

"Okay, let's say this amnesia lasted for a long time, and they didn't discover him for several years—long after she'd spent the money. What would happen then?"

"Your hypothetical questions are farfetched, aren't they?" Again he looked at his father, and Kelli looked at him, too, wondering if Kenmore had said something. From the look on his face, he had no idea what they were talking about. Hopefully, Shane thought so, too. "To tell you the truth I don't know the answer for sure."

Kelli took a sip of water, then changed the conversation to Mrs. Chandler. She came into the store every single Friday, bought six cans of tuna, and complained bitterly about the price and how it was much cheaper in town at Kroger. And yet, every single Friday, there she was again. Thankfully, Kenmore jumped right in on this change of subject.

When Kelli got in her car to drive home later that night, she pondered the insurance situation and the threat to Alison, who had used her insurance money to support the sick mother Daddy had left behind. Revealing the truth could ruin her financially. Kelli couldn't allow that to happen.

Kelli was alone in the store when she heard the back door open. She was certain she had locked it behind her, so she took a nervous step toward the storeroom. Kenmore walked through the doorway, using his cane but moving pretty well. “What are you doing here?” she asked him immediately.

“Last time I checked I owned this place.” He grinned as he moved toward her.

“I thought you weren’t coming back until Monday.”

“Stopped by the doc’s office and convinced him I was ready.” He paused at the checkout counter. “Actually, I went to his office and told him I wasn’t leaving until he put it in writing that I was good to go.”

Kelli burst out laughing, having no doubt that’s exactly what he’d done. “Well, good for you. How are you feeling?”

“Honestly, I feel better now—even still sore from the incision and all—than I did for a couple of years before the surgery. I wish I’d done it sooner.” He made a show of looking around. “Don’t you dare tell my son I said that.”

She leaned forward and whispered, “Your secret is safe with me.”

"Speaking of my son, I gather he has made quite a pest of himself since I've been away."

"Let's just say Shane has your back in a major way." She rolled her eyes, but then grew serious. "Actually, I think you should be glad to have that."

"Something you wish you had more of?"

Kelli shrugged. She couldn't bring herself to make any sort of reply, serious or joking. It hit too close to home.

"I know I've asked you this before, but are you really not planning on telling them?" His expression was completely neutral, not accusing, not questioning, just as matter-of-fact as if he'd asked her if she'd swept the floor yet.

Kelli stared at the counter in front of her. It was beige, but there were a couple of places that had worn white over the years. They really needed to think about replacing it soon. She rubbed at an ink spot with her thumb; it didn't rub out. When she looked up, Kenmore was still watching her, head tilted slightly to the side, waiting for an answer.

"I don't think I can."

The front door flew open, and a group of teenagers entered the store and headed for the sodas and candy. Kenmore nodded at Kelli. "Any time you want to talk about it, you know where to find me. You'll make the right choice, I'm sure of it."

Later that night, as they were closing up, Kenmore asked her, "Why don't you plan to make an early evening of it tomorrow? I'll be back all day, and you've more than earned it. We'll be plenty busy the day after, so you'll need the rest."

"Busy on the Fourth of July?"

"Mostly ice and last-minute sodas and such—things that people don't want to drive back into town for."

"Makes sense."

"Speaking of the Fourth of July"—Shane emerged from the

back room—"how about I take you both to the high school to watch the fireworks after you close up? It's supposed to be a really good show this year."

"Not me," Kenmore said. "I'm too old for the crowds."

"How about it, Kelli? It'll be like Thursday Night Lights times ten." He paused for just a moment. "Besides, rumor has it that I might need a little protection."

Kelli looked at him, questioning, for just a second. Then she realized what he meant. "Amy is going to be there?"

Shane shrugged. "A man can't be too careful these days."

Kelli giggled like a teenager. "Sounds good." And it did sound good—and more than a little reckless.

Kenmore sat on his back porch swing, thinking through the events that had happened twenty-four years ago. Should he have stepped in when he saw the trouble brewing? Could he have stopped it? It had never entered his mind that David would dream of doing what he did—not until it was too late.

He thought back to one day in particular. It had been a long day at the office. They had just received a warning that the Fairfield Fund was about to be downgraded to "highly risky." David had made the comment, "Now, that's a shame. Fairfield has one of the best-paying commissions in the industry. I just signed up Mrs. Gish for a block of it."

"Why would you put her in that, anyway? Even before it was downgraded, it was far too aggressive an investment for a seventy-year-old."

"She's got more money than she'll spend in three lifetimes. If she goes aggressive with some of it and she loses, no real harm has been done. If she wins, that just makes it all that much better."

Kenmore looked over at David, hoping to see some sign on his face that he was joking. He didn't see any. It seemed that more and more lately he was speaking with a David he didn't really know. Gone was the best man at his wedding, the most stand-up guy around. In his place was a shifty kind of guy, who didn't trust anyone anymore and didn't seem particularly trustworthy himself. He'd made enough remarks about Alison that Kenmore knew he wasn't happy at home. Fool. Alison was the kind of woman any man should be glad to have as a wife.

"Did you explain the risk to Mrs. Gish? About Fairfield?"

"Of course I did. You know that all of our clients sign a paper that they are aware that investments are not secure."

"I mean, did you tell her there was even more risk with this particular investment right now?"

David simply looked at Kenmore for a minute, then leaned forward and put his elbows on his desk. "I did everything I needed to do. All right?"

Just then his direct line rang. "David Waters." He looked up at Kenmore. "Do you mind? This is personal."

Kenmore walked from the room, but not before he overheard David say, "I can't wait to see you tonight."

That evening Kenmore had called his parents and told them he thought it was time for him to think about returning to work at the store.

39

Since it was only three blocks away, Shane and Kelli decided to walk from her duplex to the high school stadium. Each carried a portable chair looped across the shoulder. The track was lined with all sorts of booths selling snacks, drinks, glow sticks, and glow necklaces galore. It was still hot and humid at almost eight, but it didn't seem to slow anyone down. "This is really nice," Kelli said, and she meant it. The small-town carnival atmosphere made her wonder anew about the life she had been meant to live.

"Here comes Amy. Come on, I'll secure your undying devotion with some fine jewelry, and then I'm counting on your protection." He stopped and purchased a braided blue, yellow, and green glow necklace, then slipped it over Kelli's head, grinning. "Fabulous." He glanced over her shoulder, then leaned forward and whispered, "Now earn your keep."

"I'll do what I can." Kelli reached out and took Shane's extended arm, thinking even as she did so that it was a mistake.

Amy bounded over. "Happy Fourth of July!" Her face was overly bright when she said it, especially when she turned to smile sweetly at Kelli. "Remind me of your name again. I'm simply terrible with names and faces."

"Kelli."

"Right, Kelli. You're the new cash register girl at the store, isn't that what I remember?"

"That's me." Kelli knew the question was meant to be demeaning, but she had no plans to take the bait. The sooner the conversation ended, the sooner Amy would move on to speak with someone else.

"That is hard work. I can remember back when I was in high school, I worked a cash register at Leitha's dress shop—as well as doing some merchandising, of course. That is one of the things that motivated me to keep my grades up and get into a good college so I could get a decent job." She paused then and put her hand over her mouth. "I mean . . . I'm so sorry, I didn't mean to imply anything by that."

Of course she did, but once again Kelli didn't want to say anything that would prolong this conversation. "I'm sure you didn't. No offense taken." She squeezed Shane's arm. "Shane and I were just about to go set up our chairs on the field. It was nice to see you again."

"Oh, you've simply got to come sit with us. We've got the very best seats in the house all staked out. Come on, you two, I'll show you." She pulled at the chair strap across Shane's shoulder, as if to lead him with it.

He shook his head. "That's okay. We were—"

"I insist. Come on now." She tugged with enough force that Shane started walking with her. He tightened his arm against his side, ensuring that Kelli couldn't let go. "Amy, we really were planning—"

"We want Kelsey to get the best possible view of her first Tennessee fireworks show, don't we?"

"I think the end zone is just fine." Shane planted his feet. "Thanks anyway." He pulled his arm away from her grip and took a step backward.

"Shane-dog, I didn't know you were back here." A male voice boomed over the drone of the crowd.

Shane's face broke into a huge grin. "Bear-man, so good to see you. What are you doing here?"

A tall, thin, rather scruffy-looking young man came to stand beside them, smiling every bit as big as Shane. "Visiting the folks for the weekend, and I thought I'd catch up with the old gang. Did Amy tell you we've got a big section out in the middle for the class of 2006?" He looked at Kelli. "Hello there, pretty lady. The name's Barry, and I'm looking forward to hearing all about you."

"Paws off, Bear-man." Shane bumped his arm "You think I'd bring Kelli into the middle of you piranhas?"

"Of course you will. Here, I'll take that." He reached over and took the chair off Kelli's shoulder. "Right this way, you two."

Before either of them had a choice, they were seated right in the middle of Shane's old high school crowd, which was a friendly but somewhat boisterous group. Barry plopped down right beside Kelli and remained there. Although he flirted with most everyone who came by, his nearness seemed to have the effect of keeping Shane a little extra close—or was it simply because Amy was also nearby? Kelli couldn't be sure.

When it finally grew dark, the fireworks started, accompanied by patriotic music blaring from loudspeakers throughout the stadium. Kelli couldn't help but believe it was the best fireworks show she'd ever been to—in spite of the fact that there were sometimes long pauses between explosions, and that none of it synced quite right to the music. The homey, small-town feel of it made everything so much more meaningful. Had her parents once sat in this very stadium, watching a similar show?

"Are you all right?" Shane leaned a little closer.

Only when he'd asked the question did she realize a tear was rolling down her cheek. She reached up and wiped it away. "Fine. I'm just really enjoying myself."

He looked at her, deep into her eyes, for the space of several heartbeats. He leaned a little closer, paused, then slowly brought his lips to hers. The kiss was soft, and gentle, and wonderful. When he pulled away, he still kept his face very close to hers and reached out and rubbed her cheek where the tear had been.

"Okay, you two, break it up, break it up." Barry leaned over and shoved Shane's shoulder. "You're getting way too mushy over here. Fireworks are in the sky, not *in each other's eyes.*" He said the last few words in a high-pitched, joking voice.

Shane continued to look at Kelli for another couple of seconds before he turned to his friend. "You sure know how to kill a moment."

"Why, thank you. Thank you very much." The guys laughed, and that was the end of it.

Kelli realized later she truly owed Barry a round of thanks. The last thing she needed was to get into one more emotional entanglement that would have to be severed at the end of the summer.

On Sunday morning, Kelli combed out her just-washed hair, reliving scenes from the night before. The atmosphere, the fireworks, the kiss. What was she going to do? She couldn't continue on the path she was on—there were danger signs flashing everywhere. Denice had been right. Utterly and completely.

Kenmore was back at work part time, so in just a week or so, she could stick to her original plan to invent an emergency back home and get out of here before things got any more complicated.

But that would have her bugging out on Beth before the summer was over. She would have to spend the rest of her life knowing she had not fulfilled her one and only promise to the one and only sister she'd ever have.

Her cell phone rang, and Kelli grabbed it. "Hello."

"You wanna come over and hang out for a while? I can promise you lunch in the deal."

"Beth?"

"Yes, of course it's Beth, and Rand has gotten this burr in his saddle that he needs to stay home from church with me today, and he's refusing to leave me home alone even though I told him I was fine for a couple of hours, and his men's group is right in the middle of planning their retreat, and he's supposed to be heading that all up and he's being a complete ninny about the whole thing."

"Beth, take a deep breath, you crazy woman. That was the longest sentence I've ever heard in my life. Are you always this feisty, even when you're not pregnant?"

"Feisty all the time, fortunately for all you lucky folks around me."

"Speaking of the lucky folks around you, how about letting me speak to Rand?"

"Rand? Why would you want to—" There was a scuffling sound, and then Beth's voice, sounding faint and distant, demanded, "Give me back that phone."

"Good morning, Kelli." Rand's voice was as pleasant and casual as if he'd just called to talk about the weather. "And how are you this fine morning?"

Kelli burst out laughing. "Better than you are, I'm guessing. What's up?" The fact that he didn't want to leave Beth home alone for even a couple of hours told Kelli that something was wrong.

"Beth has been sick to her stomach this morning, which isn't all that uncommon for her with this pregnancy, but I'm not going to leave her home and helpless in bed while she's green around the gills."

Another scuffling, then Beth's voice back on the phone. "I have no need for a 24/7 babysitter. I told him to just leave me a bucket beside the bed and I'd be fine, but he's just being so . . . so . . ."

"Considerate of his sick and pregnant wife?"

"You might call it that, but I call it being a bully. That's what everyone tells me when I'm trying to be strongly helpful. Anyway, I told him to get out of here, that I would be fine, and he won't, and now I'm kind of mad at him because he's being such a . . . Well . . . so anyway, I wondered if you would come over and sit with me while he goes to church. Maybe he'll learn something about being nicer to his wife while he's there, and you and I can talk girl talk. Rumor has it, you might have some information to share."

"I don't know what you mean." How could she possibly have found out?

"You can try selling that somewhere that's buying. You're in Shoal Creek, Tennessee, now, so you might as well accept the fact that I know we have things to talk about, like the extra fireworks exploding at the stadium last night."

Wow. Word really did travel fast around here. Kelli was going to have to be extra careful—about everything. "Tell Rand I'll be there in ten minutes."

"Great, I'll see you then."

Kelli hung up, glad she wouldn't feel the pressure to sing at church today. Unfortunately, though, she was missing her one and only chance of the week to see Alison.

Beth was glad she'd had the idea to invite Kelli over to "watch her." If Kelli saw it as an act of being helpful, she would feel useful and be happy to be here and never know that Beth had actually brought her over with something very different in mind. She reached out and took Kelli's hand. "You are such a good friend to me. I feel like we've known each other forever—much longer than we have."

"I feel that way, too." Kelli squeezed her hand and smiled back.

Perfect. "Do you really mean that? Because I know you were originally planning on leaving at the end of the summer, but I hope maybe you'll stay for a while. I really want you to be here when the baby is born. I was hoping you would maybe be Sprout's godmother."

"Do Protestants do that?"

"Not officially, but still." Beth shrugged in her way that let everyone know she didn't care what was considered the normal way of doing things.

Something warm and soft seemed to curl around Kelli and hug tight. Such an amazing feeling of inclusion and love. How she had missed that feeling. "You have no idea how much I wish I could stay, but there's the grand opening of our restaurant in a couple of months, and to tell you the truth, I know absolutely nothing about babies. I don't think I'd be much help."

"The two of us could figure out things together. Somehow I just feel stronger when you're around. That sounds silly, doesn't it?"

Rand had said the same thing to Kelli just last week, making some remark about how Kelli's friendship had been good for Beth. How could either of them possibly see anything good in her? She knew the answer—it was because they didn't know the truth. "Not silly, of course not. But I do think you're giving me credit when it's your own strength that you're truly seeing. Maybe the hormones of pregnancy helped bring them out."

"No, they just make me mad, and sad, and happy, and crazy. There's nothing confidence-boosting in any of that mix, trust me."

"Just feisty."

"Yes, feisty. And that feisty part of me says the whole restaurant thing sounds more like an excuse. If it came down to it, I'm sure your friends could find another manager to help them open the place, and you could just stay here. I overheard Kenmore telling my mother earlier in the week that you have really made some great changes at the store, and he wished you were planning to stick around."

"Really?"

"Yep. He told her that yesterday evening when he dropped by to bring some tomatoes from his garden."

"I'm sure he was just being nice. He'll be able to replace me, no problem."

"No he won't. He told her he thinks he'll shut down the store come November. He said it has just gotten to be too much work to keep up, and once you leave he doesn't think he can keep doing it anymore."

"You're kidding."

"Nope. See, we need you here. Now, quit telling people things that aren't true to make it easier for you to leave, when none of us want you to leave anyway."

Beth had no idea how close her words hit to the heart of the matter. But she couldn't stay. Between this small town that seemed to know everything everybody was doing, the time Kelli was spending with Beth, and her growing attraction to Shane, there were too many ways she could trip up and ruin everything.

Besides, Denice and Jones really were counting on her to open Homestead, and they were the only thing like family she had left. At least she'd thought so until now.

40

Dad and I were unloading all our camping gear on the front lawn. Dad always liked to wash things down and organize them before he stuffed them up in the garage rafters. We were exhausted and filthy, but it had been so worth it. A three-day weekend at the beach, just the two of us. We'd hiked cliffs, played in the ocean, roasted marshmallows over a campfire, and met some really nice families, too.

Mimi came sauntering out the door, dressed in a short sundress and sandals, carrying a red drink in her hand. She smiled at Daddy. "And how was your trip?"

"It was great, great, great, great!" I jumped up and down. "Daddy says we can start camping at least one weekend a month. He says it's his very favorite thing to do, and that we're super campers. Right, Daddy?"

My father cast a quick glance toward Mimi before he grinned at me. "I do believe you're right, Princess. We are super campers."

"The best in the whole world. All the other kids were jealous because my dad was the most fun of any of them. He built a shelter out of driftwood right there on the beach and everything. I helped

carry over the palm fronds for our roof. We make a great team, the two of us. Don't we, Daddy?"

"Yes we do, hon, the very best." He picked me up and swung me in a circle.

When he set me down, I wobbled a little as I looked toward Mimi. She was blinking kind of fast, and she took a big sip out of her cup. Then she sort of smiled toward me. "Well, I'm just so glad to hear it. So glad." She took another big swallow of her drink and walked back into the house.

Kenmore had arrived at the store extra early on Monday morning, so he was surprised when he heard the back door open only minutes after he'd entered. Kelli came walking up to the office. "Kenmore, I want to know what you know about my dad's decision to leave."

"Like I said, I didn't really know anything for sure. I just had my suspicions."

"What made you have your suspicions? Please tell me everything, no matter whether you think it will be painful for me to hear or not. I'm at the point now where I don't believe anything good about Daddy anymore, and I'd rather just know the truth."

"I really don't think it's going to do you any good to hear all this."

"You may not, but I do. I've been reading through the old letters Mimi wrote to her mother. Believe me, there's nothing that you thought might be happening that I haven't read about in glorious detail."

He looked at her evenly, then nodded. "If you're sure you want to know."

"Please."

"All right, but this is against my better judgment." Kenmore made his mind travel back down the road it had gone down so many times over the past twenty-something years. He'd always had doubts about what really happened—until Kelli's arrival had proven his suspicion correct. "I can still remember the look on David's face when he came into the office and told me his mother's money would run out by the end of the next year. He was a man defeated, overburdened, worn down. He told me he was going to have to move her out of Brighton Manor to somewhere more affordable.

"Brighton Manor was the best place in town for someone with cognitive impairment. I knew that, and so did he, and it was killing him to think of moving her. It was also by far the most expensive place in the area. He told me he'd looked at a couple of other local places, and a place called Bivens Haven the next county over. That place got written up for health code violations on a regular basis, and I reminded him of that."

"What'd he say?"

"He asked what he was supposed to do, because his money could only go so far. I told him it had been a good couple of years for our business, and the outlook for the next couple was good, as well. If he started setting aside more money each month, he should be able to eke through, I was sure of it.

"He said he was sick of eking through, sick of never having time to do anything but work, sick of the guilt that goes along with working long hours and leaving your family home alone, and your mother in a nursing home. He was just plain burned out."

"Maybe that's why he was attracted to Mimi, huh? She was young and pretty, and there weren't any other obligations attached."

"Exactly. And that's exactly what I told him. I said, 'Not to add to your misery, but to tell you the truth, I believe you would feel a significant lowering of guilt if you would quit spending so much time at Jerry's Place.' Over the past year, I'd known David was spending more and more time there, and it wasn't because of the food or the convenience."

"What did he say?"

"He said it wasn't any of my business where he ate his lunch. He jumped up from his chair, his face purple, and for a minute I thought he actually might take a swing at me. He yelled, 'How dare you insinuate . . .' But he stopped himself midsentence, stood there and looked at me, and then he exhaled long and slow and sat back down, shaking his head.

"Later that afternoon, like clockwork, he looked down at his watch and then back at me. 'I've got a meeting. I'll be back in a little while.' He walked out the door and down the street to the diner, just like always. It was only a few weeks after this conversation that he came in one morning and told me that your mother was pregnant." Kenmore pushed himself up from his chair and walked over to the coffee pot, poured himself another cup. "You want one?"

"No, thanks. So, Mom's pregnant, he can't leave right away, then what?"

"David had always been a solid guy, family man, church, the whole bit. I noticed it was about that time he started reading books that were by most any account non-biblical—books stressing how God wants us to make the decisions that will make us the most happy, not so much the hard decisions that involve doing the right thing."

"God doesn't want us to be happy?"

"Kelli, I have a deep faith. I don't spend a lot of time talking about it, don't know the answer to a lot of the great theological debates, but one thing I'm convinced of—we have to make the decision that we're going to do the right thing no matter what it costs us before we get pressed in tight between the hard place and the easier place. If things get difficult and you start looking for an easier way out than what you know is right, chances are you're going to find it, but it won't be the best long-term decision. Take Joseph, for example."

"Joseph?"

"From the Old Testament—coat of many colors, all that. His own brothers sold him into slavery in Egypt, right?"

"Yeah, I remember that."

"But God's favor was upon him, so soon he became the second in command of Potiphar's household. Seems like the best he could hope for in a bad situation—until Potiphar's wife decided Joseph looked pretty good and she'd like to have him for her own. If you think about it, this could only have made his life easier. She'd likely take special care of him, give him more things, not to mention he'd get a mistress out of the deal. Joseph could easily have said that God abandoned him and that there was no reason for him to continue to live the harder way, the way he knew to be right. But he didn't. He made the hard choice, and it got him thrown in a dungeon for ten years.

"But he kept trusting, kept moving forward, and from that dungeon he eventually ended up where he was supposed to be—in Pharaoh's palace, saving humanity from starvation and becoming second-in-command of the entire kingdom. See, something better was waiting, something that made him much happier in the long run, but if he'd decided to make the easier choice earlier on, he never would have known it."

Kelli bit her lower lip and nodded. "I guess I see what you mean. So you're saying if my father had stuck it out at home, in spite of the fact that there were some rough years ahead of him, he would have eventually been glad he'd done the right thing."

"I absolutely believe that. But, unfortunately for all involved, that's not the choice he made. I started noticing that he was moving money around in his accounts. I assumed he was funneling his money to Suze. I didn't have any idea he was actually setting up other accounts under a different name. This is all assumption on my part, but I think he had planned to leave your mother much sooner, then found out she was pregnant, and while he might have been a cheater, he wasn't going to walk out on his pregnant wife."

"Why didn't he just divorce my mother?"

Kenmore shook his head. "I think he knew that she would get custody of you kids, and by the time he paid child support and alimony, there wasn't going to be much left for him to live on and he would get to see even less of y'all. He was so entrenched in those so-called religious self-help books by then he must have convinced himself that by setting up an insurance policy he was taking care of your mother and siblings, and then by keeping you it was a bit like having his cake and eating a slice of it, too."

"I guess that's pretty much the way it happened, as far as he was concerned. He lived happily ever after and left everyone else to pick up the shards of the broken lives he left scattered."

"Maybe so." Kenmore rubbed the back of his neck. "But I'm betting he got plenty of cuts from all those shards himself."

Kelli was shaking her head. "Whatever wounds he might have received along the way, they were far less than he deserved. The worst part of it is that I can't even tell him how angry I am. He gets away with everything, without a single repercussion."

"Regardless of how things may appear on the outside, I'm guessing he paid a much higher price than you will ever know."

"I certainly hope so."

Kenmore watched Kelli turn slowly and walk into the storeroom without another word.

Kenmore, are you planning to shut down the store?" It was early afternoon before Kelli worked up the nerve to ask the next question on her mind.

He sighed, then nodded. "Yeah. Just between you and me, that has been my plan for a while now. Business had dropped off enough that I was losing too much money to keep it going. Things changed for the better after you got here, but I can't keep it up by myself."

"You can hire someone to replace me."

"I can hire someone else to help me out in the store, but it was your vision for running things that made us profitable again. That's not the kind of thing you can just find off the street. Besides, if you remember correctly, I hadn't even planned to replace Frieda until you came along, because I knew the store would be closing."

"You might find someone you like better. You'll never know if you don't try."

"Nah. To tell you the truth, I just don't think I have the heart for it anymore. This was my family's store, and I kept it going a long time for that reason. And then when you came, it all got exciting again—not just because business had picked up, but also because I was thankful both of us had a chance to work through some of what had happened. After you leave, though, I think I'm just done."

"But Kenmore . . ." She couldn't decide how she wanted to finish that sentence, only knew that it was important that she say the right thing to convince him to change his mind.

"The fiftieth anniversary of the store is in October. I plan to keep it open until then, and then it's time for me to move into the world of retirement."

"That makes me sad, to think of this place closed."

"To tell you the truth, it makes me sad, too. But there's not that much we can do about it." He stopped what he was doing to look her directly in the eyes. "Unless, that is, you want to stay."

"I can't." She twirled a pack of Life Savers around on the counter, watching the reds, oranges, and yellows spin before her. "You know I can't." She picked up the pack and put it back in its place.

"A couple of months ago, I would have agreed with you. Probably even a few weeks ago. But Kelli, I've got to tell you, I've been watching what is happening, and let me tell you, girl, you belong here. You belong with them."

"I wish that were true." She shook her head. "I can't stay, you know I can't."

"You're wrong. Dead wrong. Spend a little time thinking about it, and I believe you will come to agree with me." He rubbed the back of his neck. "You can stay and work at the store, build it up into something you can take over. You've got a natural gift for it. You can stay in the duplex as long as you need to, put down some roots."

"I can't talk about this anymore." Kelli knew deep down that Kenmore was right. If she kept listening, she would change her mind and stay, and that would make things very hard. For everyone she loved.

Shane took Kelli's hand as they walked downtown together, and she moved closer out of instinct. Another perfect Thursday Night Lights evening—this time without a glimpse of Amy, making it that much better. *This is wrong. You can't do this.* Her inner voice was soon countered with *It's no big deal. You just had sandwiches and watched a band. It's not like you're getting serious or anything.*

The two sides went back and forth, back and forth.

Kelli took a deep breath. "There's something I need to tell you."

"Yeah?" He smiled down at her. "Tell me everything."

Oh, how I wish I could, but I can't, so this will have to do. "Well, it's just that . . . I . . ." She had no choice but to continue. She had to put a stop to this. "I have a boyfriend back in California. He's really more like an unofficial fiancé."

Shane dropped her hand. "What? Why didn't you tell me?"

She looked down at the ground as they kept walking. Everything inside her wanted to confess the lie and then fall into his arms. But that was a choice that could not be allowed. "I, well, I mean, for the first month or so I was here, you pretty much hated me, so it wasn't an issue. After that, it just never seemed like the right time."

"What about that kiss? And our time together tonight? You weren't exactly fighting me off."

"No. No, I wasn't, but I should have. I . . ." This was harder than she'd expected it to be. "It was a mistake."

By now, they had made it to where his car was parked. He opened the trunk and put the chairs inside. "I make it a point of pride to avoid being other people's mistakes. I can assure you that I will not be your problem again."

"Shane, it's not like that. You don't understand—"

"I understand enough to know that it's time to get out of here." He drove her home in silence.

When they pulled into her driveway, she opened the door but turned to him. "I'm really sorry."

"Good-bye, Kelli." He didn't look her direction.

"Good-bye, Shane." She went inside and cried. Something that had become all too familiar as of late.

"Knock, knock." Kelli used the key she'd been given to let herself into Beth's house.

"Come on back," Beth called from the bedroom.

Kelli lugged her canvas bag into Beth's room. "Okay, I brought supplies. Let's see, a couple of chick flicks on DVD, nail polish, microwave popcorn, and a deck of cards, just in case."

Beth looked through the loot Kelli had just dropped on the bed. "I haven't had a girls' sleepover in about ten years."

"Well, then it's about time. Good thing Rand got called out of town on business."

"This isn't just a sympathy sleepover, right? Because I'm on bed rest and you're feeling sorry for me?"

"No, but let's be honest, if you weren't on bed rest, we'd be out on the town—well, at least dinner and a movie. So, no, the event itself is not about your bed rest, but the activities have been toned down to suit it."

Beth took a big gulp out of the liter-sized water bottle she always had at her bedside and nodded. "Good, then. Let's proceed with the modified girl fun."

When Rand had been called out of town for a trip that would take almost a week, Kelli had volunteered to stay with Beth on Friday and Saturday night, so that Alison could teach her classes and work on the kids' musical at church. She would come back in on Sunday night and take over until Rand got home on Tuesday.

"First on our agenda is telling me what happened between you and Shane."

"What do you mean?"

"I mean, you two were all grins and giggles, then suddenly you're both moping around like you've lost your best friend. I know you both like each other, but obviously something happened. What was it?"

Kelli thought about how to answer this and decided there wasn't a lot of harm in mostly telling the truth. She shrugged. "I told him that I couldn't see him anymore because I have a boyfriend back home."

"Wait, what? You have a boyfriend back home? How come I've never heard about him? Are you holding out on me?"

"No." Kelli picked up a bottle of nail polish and twirled it around. "I mean, I did have a boyfriend, but we broke up a few months ago."

Beth folded her arms across her rapidly expanding midsection. "Spill."

"I caught him cheating, end of story. It wasn't like I was in love with the guy. We hadn't been dating that long."

"I didn't mean about him, although we'll get to him later. I mean, spill about why you would make up an excuse not to see Shane anymore, when it's so obvious you enjoy being around him."

Kelli shrugged. "That's exactly it. I came to realize that I was liking to spend time with Shane a lot—quite a lot, actually. Since I'm going to be leaving here at the end of next month, I just thought it was best that I put some distance between us before things got too serious. I don't want to leave here with a bunch of regret."

"Haven't you ever heard of long-distance relationships? People do it all the time. Between texting, Skype, and airplanes, it's not like it's not doable." Oh how Kelli wished that were true in her case. But she knew that keeping a relationship going with Shane would also keep a relationship going with Beth and Alison. By now, she knew it was going to be excruciating to leave here and not tell them who she was. If the relationship continued long-term after that, it would be impossible. There had to be a clean break.

"For most people that would work fine, but I'm just not one of them."

"And why not for you, exactly?"

"It's just not something I can do, okay? Besides, I told you, after I get back to California, I'll be in the thick of opening up a restaurant with my friends. I'll need to invest every spare minute I have into making sure that it works."

"Sounds like an excuse to me, but it's your life."

If that's what Beth believed, Kelli was glad for it. Little did she know that it wasn't just Kelli's life—it was her life, too. And her mother's. And the brother Kelli had never met. If letting Beth believe she was afraid of commitment was what it took to give some peaceful closure, then so be it. Kelli was glad for the easier excuse.

"Now, let's put in one of these movies, okay?"

42

Early Monday morning, Beth pressed both hands against her stomach. "Come on, kick. Kick." It wasn't long after her mother left to teach a music lesson that it occurred to her that she hadn't felt Sprout move recently. It hadn't been that long really, only a little while, but these days he moved almost constantly.

She called her doctor's office, knowing she was probably overreacting, but needing some reassurance. Sandy, the nurse, spoke in a calm voice and didn't seem the least bit ruffled. "The little one is probably asleep or in a position where you just don't feel the movement. However, it is always better to double-check these things, so this is what I want you to do. I want you to pour yourself an ice-cold glass of juice—we want it extra cold and make sure it's juice and not water, because we want the sugar. Drink it, then lie down on your left side and remain very still until you feel movement. If you still don't feel anything after about half an hour, I want you to come into the office and we'll do some fetal monitoring and just make certain everything is okay."

"Thank you so much." Beth had walked to the fridge, thankful to be up and around for a minute, and pulled out some orange juice. She'd filled the glass to the top with ice and then poured the juice over it. She carried it with her to her room, drank quickly, then remained perfectly still on her side. Waiting.

Ten minutes into the process, she still felt nothing, and she was starting to panic. She had promised herself that she would not call Rand and worry him about this—he was in Atlanta until tomorrow. Her mother would be back in a couple of hours to make lunch, and she hated to pull her away from her lessons. Just then, her doorbell rang, followed by a knock and the unmistakable sound of a key in the front door.

"Beth? It's me. Stopping by to see how it's going." Kelli's voice moved closer through the house. She stopped in the doorway. "Beth?"

Beth remained still. "Hey."

Kelli ran over to her. "What's wrong? Are you hurt?"

"No, I'm fine." Beth explained what was happening, and Kelli took a seat on the edge of the bed. "Well, I'm going to sit right here until Sprout kicks the stew out of you. Have you called Rand and your mother?"

"Rand's out of town, and Mom would totally freak. She'll be back to fix me lunch, and I'm sure everything will be fine by then." She put her hands on her belly, willing the baby to move. "What if Sprout doesn't kick?"

"If Sprout doesn't start beating up on you soon, I'll drive you to the doctor's office and wait with you while they wake that baby up so he or she can do some inner karate."

Kelli was trying to keep her spirits up, so Beth tried just as hard to smile. She didn't think she pulled it off all that well. "Don't you have work today?"

"Yes, I was just about to go in, but Kenmore is there now. Under these circumstances, he would rather me be late, and I will give him a quick call, but there's no way I'm leaving you alone right now."

The clock seemed to move backward, it was so slow. Beth tried to remain still and keep herself calm. At the end of the thirty minutes, the baby hadn't budged at all as far as Beth could tell. "I suppose we should go in and get me checked."

"I'll drive while you make some calls."

"No calls yet. I really don't want to worry them for no reason." What seemed like an eternity later, Beth was sliding into Kelli's little green car and heading toward her doctor. "Please God, please God, let her be okay." Beth whispered the prayer as they drove through town.

"He's going to be fine. She has to be." Kelli kept saying those words over and over again.

"Will you come back with me?" Beth reached out for Kelli's hand.

"Of course." Everything inside of Kelli wanted to call Alison and Rand, but Beth was insisting that she not. Being a perpetual optimist, even when she was scared to death, Beth was more afraid of unnecessarily alarming other people than assembling her own support system.

The nurses took Beth straight back into the ultrasound room, and soon they were putting gel on her extended abdomen. Kelli was stunned at the perfect little head and arms she saw on the screen. She was so taken with this wonder, it took her a moment to realize what everyone else in the room had already figured out.

The baby wasn't moving. Nothing was moving. At all.

"Where's the heartbeat? Why can't I see the heartbeat?" Beth clutched at the ultrasound tech, whose mouth was clinched in a tight line.

"I need to have the doctor come in and take a look." But they knew. They all knew.

"Dear God, no, please God, no." Beth was mostly holding herself together, but tears were spilling down her cheeks. "This can't be. The baby was just fine at my checkup last week. This can't be. Maybe I didn't lie flat enough, maybe I . . ." She covered her mouth with her hand. "No, please no."

Kelli held tight to Beth's hand, refusing to allow her own tears to fall. She would be strong for Beth, no matter how hard it was. "Should I call your mother? Or Rand?"

"Call my mother, please." Beth wiped at her eyes. "Please tell her to hurry. I'll call Rand."

Kelli slipped out of the room and found a corner where she could make a phone call more or less in privacy. When Alison answered the phone, she could hear a piano playing in the background. "Alison, it's Kelli." She swallowed, focusing on maintaining control for Alison and Beth's sake. "Listen, I'm with Beth at her doctor's office. It appears that the baby may have . . . that she . . . isn't . . . Alison, his heart's not beating. Beth needs you here."

"Dear Father, no!" The pause lasted less than a second before her voice came back across the line, strong and determined. "Tell her I'm on my way."

When Kelli went back into the examining room, the doctor was there and Beth was on the phone. She was sobbing. "They are going to induce labor in the morning or maybe early afternoon tomorrow. They're working on getting it scheduled. You go ahead and finish up your meetings. You rushing home now isn't going to change anything, and it will just put you behind at work." She nodded at the phone. "Okay. I'll see you in the morning." She nodded a couple more times. "I love you, too."

She pressed a button and looked up at Kelli. "Rand will be here early tomorrow morning."

"Your mother is on her way."

She nodded. "Thank you."

Kelli turned toward the doctor. "What happened?"

"I can't say for sure. Maybe tomorrow we'll get a more definitive answer, but it's possible we won't ever know. My guess is that it's a cord accident. These things are extremely rare, but sometimes the baby flips around enough to tie the umbilical cord into knots. There's nothing anyone could have done."

"So it doesn't have anything to do with Beth's bed rest?"

He shook his head. "No. There's nothing that could have prevented this."

Beth bit at her bottom lip and tried to nod, her chin quivering. Kelli sat down at her other side and took her hand. "I'm so sorry."

"Thank you . . . for being here with me. I'm so glad I didn't have to get this news alone."

"I'm glad I could be here." Kelli choked up as she said the words. A tear slipped down her cheek, and she pretended to turn and look out the window so she could wipe it away.

"Oh, Beth!" Alison rushed into the room and threw her arms around her daughter. "I am so sorry, baby, so sorry."

The two of them cried on each other's shoulders for several minutes. Kelli wondered if she should slip quietly from the room but somehow felt compelled to stay.

The nurse came back. "I've talked to the folks over at General. They will be ready for you first thing in the morning. Make sure not to eat or drink anything after midnight."

"Okay." Beth nodded and sat up. "I guess it's time to go home."

"Why don't you come back to my house for tonight?" Alison still held her daughter's hand. "It's closer to the hospital, and I have everything you need."

"Okay." It was as if she didn't have the energy to say one more word.

"Is there anything I can do for you, Beth?" There had to be

something Kelli could do, and she would do whatever it was, anything that would ease Beth's pain.

Beth shook her head. "You've already done it. Thanks again for being here."

Kelli watched the two wounded women make their way to Alison's car. She waited only until she was in the privacy of her own car before she pulled out her cell phone. She wondered if the call she was about to make should fall under the realm of minding her own business, but she couldn't help herself. She dialed Rand's cell phone. "Hi, Rand, I'm just leaving the doctor's office, and I wanted to talk to you real quick."

"I'm so glad you called, because I'm going crazy here. How is she doing?"

"She is trying to be brave. Alison is taking her to her house for the night."

"Good. I'm actually on my way back right now. I told her I'd finish my meetings today because I didn't want her worrying about me driving, but I need to get there."

"I'm glad, because to tell you the truth, she needs you. I do have a question."

"What is it?"

"Do you want me to go over to your place and put away all the baby stuff? That way, at least she won't have to face it when she gets home from the hospital."

"That's a good idea. Maybe just get the things from the living room and kitchen and put them all in the baby's room. We can at least close the door and deal with those things when we're ready."

"Got it. I'll go do that right now."

"Kelli?"

"Yeah?"

"Thanks for calling, and thanks for taking such good care of her lately. She loves you like a sister. We both do."

Kelli watched Beth cling to Rand, her face so pale the skin was almost translucent. Rand's eyes were bloodshot, standing in stark contrast to the dark circles beneath. Alison wiped her eyes with a tissue. Max, Beth's brother—Kelli's brother—had arrived from Kentucky and now stood on the other side of Beth, his arm around her for support. His hair was red, his face freckled, and his pale green eyes glistened with tears for his sister's loss. His wife, Valerie, stood beside him, her arm around his waist. Other than these people, only the minister, Kenmore, and Kelli were present.

She felt out of place here. This was family only, but Beth had insisted that she come. She'd declared that Kelli had been the one to stand beside her when she found out, and she wanted her here at the end.

The cemetery was empty except for their little crew. Thankfully, the minister had enough sense to avoid most of the trite and cliché phrases Kelli had dreaded hearing. He had said a few words, read some Scripture, and reassured them all that Beth and Rand would see their daughter again in heaven, in perfect health and completely happy. Other than that, he mostly offered support and love. The man seemed to have a deeper understanding than most people of grief, and she was grateful for that—for Beth's sake as well as her own. The casket was tiny, solid white with brass trim. It looked so perfect and innocent. Just like little Rose. Rose Ann Waters they had named the precious little girl.

Right on the edge of the family plot was a small rectangular memorial with a cross at the top. *Darcy Waters, beloved daughter and sister. In the arms of Christ. 1990–1991.* Kelli stared at the piece of granite numbly. It was beyond comprehension that this had been placed here over twenty years ago, by a family out of their minds with grief, when there was no tragedy at all. What must it have been like? Beth would have been only five years old, and Max just seven. Alison was suddenly widowed and had lost a child, as well. The grief must have been unimaginable.

Kelli looked then to the similar marker for her father. *David Waters. Beloved husband and father. Home in heaven. 1950–1991.*

Kelli tried to look elsewhere but couldn't. The injustice of what had transpired here hit Kelli afresh. She simply couldn't fathom her father doing what he had done to these people. How could anyone even contemplate such an act? Much less the man who had delighted in taking her fishing, in spending hours a day teaching her everything from how to tie a shoe to advanced calculus? It did not make sense. Not at all.

After the minister had said the last of his words, Beth walked over to a container of white roses, pulled one out, and set it atop the casket. Rand followed, then the rest of them. Kelli couldn't help but cry. This poor baby was her niece, even if she would never have known it. When they were all finished, there were two roses left. Beth shuffled forward, took them in her hand, then carried them over and placed them at the memorial markers for her father and Darcy Waters. She looked up at her mother then. "Let's sing it. For all of them."

Alison nodded. She looked at Kelli and the minister. "There is a silly little song we used to sing for Darcy. We've made a tradition of coming here and singing it to her on her birthday. It's about a little stuffed doggy she loved." Alison took a deep breath and began singing in a shaky voice. "'Little Scruffy is very roughy. He barks and he growls and sleeps all day. He sure loves his mommy, he lays on her tummy, and frightens all the rest of us away.'"

Kelli's knees gave way, and she fell to the ground in a heap. This was the song she heard in her dreams—in her nightmares about the car wreck. It was a real song, with real words, sung by her real family. She buried her face in her hands and sobbed, forgetting for just a moment the reason she was here today.

Eventually she realized that everyone had gathered around her. Beth knelt down and threw her arms around Kelli, and the two of them sobbed together, each dealing with her own grief. It took a while before Kelli became coherent enough to realize how inappropriate her meltdown had been. This was about Beth and Rand's great sadness. She should not be the one people had gathered around to comfort.

She finally pulled herself together. She looked at Beth through blurry eyes. "I'm so sorry. I . . . don't know what happened. It just hit me really hard all at once. Forgive me—I should be the one comforting you. This is so embarrassing." She pushed herself off the ground and stood. She couldn't bring herself to look around at the others. She had crossed a line—really, really crossed it—and she knew it as well as anyone. She finally glanced toward Kenmore and saw concern in his eyes—he alone knew exactly what was happening.

Alison put her arm around Kelli's waist. "I'm so glad you are here with us, Kelli. It's a truly tender heart that can grieve so keenly for the loss of a friend. You are a special friend to Beth. To all of us."

Kelli shook her head. "I'm really sorry." She needed to get in her car and never see these people again. There was absolutely nothing so horrifying as what she'd just done.

"We're going over to Mom's house for a while. Can you come?" Beth squeezed her arm.

"I . . . uh . . . I really need to get to work. I promised Keith I'd get there as soon as I could. He needs my help." Kelli pulled herself away from the group and practically ran to her car. She needed to get out of here. She needed to leave this town. Now.

Kelli made it back to the duplex, ran to her room, and started packing her things as fast as she could. She piled it all into her car, grateful that Beth and Rand were several miles away at Alison's. She needed to be gone before they got back.

She picked up load after load and simply tossed everything in her car. There would be time to organize later. For now, she had to get out of here as quickly as possible. She was in her bedroom, getting the last of her clothes, when the doorbell rang. *Oh no.*

She went to the door and peeked through the window. It was Miss Birdyshaw. Kelli opened the door just a crack. "Good evening, Miss Birdyshaw. I can't talk just now. I'm really busy."

"You're not leaving yet, are you? I saw all those things piled in your car and it worried me. I thought maybe you'd had some kind of emergency or something, because you're staying through September, right?" She simply looked at Kelli, blinking slowly, waiting for an explanation with all the time in the world. Time Kelli did not have.

"A couple of things have come up and I need to get back to California. I've got to leave tonight, actually. Right away."

"Oh, what a shame. A real shame. I hate to hear that, I do. I'm going to miss you. Little Miss Lacey and I looked forward to our visits with you."

"Lacey's a sweet kid. You two have some Popsicles for me sometime, okay?" Kelli glanced back into the house.

Miss Birdyshaw stood unmoving, not seeming to get the hint that it was time to move on. "I'm not very good with people, never have been. Not good with kids either, really, but I think I've been a bright spot in Lacey's life. I'm really glad that God doesn't look at me for my failings, but He looks at me for what He can do through me in spite of them. That's great news for all of us, isn't it?"

Kelli did not have time for a sermon right now. "That's really great news, but I'm really in a hurry, so I've got to get back to my packing." She closed the door, slowly enough that she hoped it didn't appear as if she were slamming it in Miss Birdyshaw's face, though she knew for a fact that was exactly what she was doing. She hurried back down the hall and toward her room, but the guilt caught up with her and overwhelmed her. That sweet elderly woman had been nothing but a dear to her, and to leave her in such a rude manner was not okay, no matter what. She carried the last load out to her car, then walked around to Miss Birdyshaw's front door and rang the bell.

"Kelli, you're still here." Miss Birdyshaw's eyes were moist—was this because she was old or was she teary? Kelli had a good idea it was the latter, and she knew it was her fault.

"Miss Birdyshaw, I came over to say I'm sorry. I know that I was short with you at my door just now. I was stressed out and in a hurry, and I was rude. You are the last person I would ever want to treat that way. Please accept my apologies."

"Of course I do. Don't think another thing about it. Like I said, I know I'm not good with people sometimes. I sure am glad God doesn't just use the people who are good enough."

Kelli didn't have time to stand and talk, but she wasn't going to repeat the same mistake again. "Isn't that who He does use, though? The ones who are good enough? That's what I've always been taught."

"Do you think the people who taught you that were *good enough*?"

"No. I used to think so, but now I know, in a lot of ways, they weren't very good at all."

"Nobody is if you really know him deep down. That's why we have God."

"I really do have to leave now. I'm sorry I can't stay and talk more."

"Maybe someday you'll come back through town. You knock on my door any time. I'm always here for you."

"Thanks, Miss Birdyshaw."

"You're welcome, dear."

Kelli started down the stairs, but then she turned. "You're wrong about one thing."

"What's that?"

"You said you're not very good with people. You may not be good with crowds. I've never seen you in one so I couldn't say, but one on one, you're better with people than just about anyone else I know. Just ask Lacey, or me, or anyone else who has felt lonely and afraid around here. I'm glad I got to know you."

Kelli walked around to her car, got in, and started the engine. Time to get out of here.

Kenmore drove toward the store, telling himself he just wanted to check and make sure everything was running smoothly. He knew better, though. He was going to check on Kelli. Her breakdown today, followed by her hasty exit, had him more than a little worried about her.

He'd been concerned ever since Shane had come home all mopey after Thursday Night Lights. He hadn't said anything about what had happened, but Kenmore had a pretty good idea what was going on. Kelli was trying to build some walls. He couldn't blame her for it. He had tried to talk to her about it earlier in the week, to no avail.

"Shane hates me now," she'd told him.

"He doesn't hate you. He's hurt, just like you've been hurt by people who weren't honest with you. I'm not sure what story you concocted to put some distance between the two of you, but I'm sure you can find a way to smooth it out—if you want to."

Kelli looked at him. "You know I had no choice—"

"You really think so? Because I can think of a couple of other choices you had."

"Well, I can't," she'd said as she'd walked away. And that had been the end of their discussion. Now, as he pulled into the parking lot of the store, he didn't see Kelli's car anywhere. It had only been a couple of hours since she'd left to come out here, so he was surprised she'd gone already. She usually worked late. Maybe she'd just been too upset to stay, though, and he couldn't blame her for that. He walked in and found Keith at the cash register, looking disheveled and more than a little stressed. "Busy afternoon, I take it?"

"Crazy busy." He shook his head. "I don't think I've ever seen so many people here all at the same time, and they just kept coming."

"I'm surprised Kelli didn't stay to help you out, then."

"I'm sure she would have if she'd been here. She was at the funeral, too. Remember?"

"I remember, I was there. It's just that she left early to come out here and help you."

Keith shook his head. "She must have changed her mind, because I haven't seen her all day."

"Really?" Kenmore looked around the store, his mind racing with different scenarios of what might have happened and where his first obligation might lie right now. As much as he wanted to go check on Kelli, he knew he needed to stay at the store until Keith got things buttoned up. The poor kid looked like he was ready to have a breakdown.

An hour later, Kenmore drove from the store toward the duplex. As much as he didn't want to admit it, he knew what he'd find when he got there, so it wasn't a surprise when he pulled into the empty driveway of a dark house.

Alison sat in Beth's kitchen, watching her daughter pick at the warm banana bread she'd just brought over. Rand was at least making an attempt to eat his, but the usual gusto was missing. The poor kids. She wished she could do something to ease their pain, but it wasn't possible. She knew this from her own experience. Some burdens could not be borne by other people.

"Why don't you two go for a drive? Or go to a matinee or something? Get out of here and get your mind off things."

Beth shook her head. "I was going to spend the day cleaning out the nursery—the guest room. The sooner I get all those things boxed and put away, the sooner I can quit avoiding that closed door."

Alison reached out and took her daughter's hand. "I'll help you while I can. My first lesson isn't for a couple of hours, and you're still weak physically, so you shouldn't be doing too much."

"Let's get started, then. I'm ready to get this over with."

"I'll disassemble the baby bed and put it and the changing table up in attic storage." Rand stood up and pushed away from the table. "Then I'll carry up whatever boxes you ladies get ready for me." He came behind Beth's chair and kissed her on the top of the head. "I look forward to the day we take this all down again. And there *will* be a next time. I believe it with all my heart."

Beth nodded and reached behind her to give him a small hug. "You're going to make a wonderful father someday." Something about the flatness in her tone said she didn't quite believe this.

They all headed to the spare bedroom, hearts heavy. "I'll start with the clothes in the closet," Beth said.

Alison went to the bookcase filled with board books, stuffed animals, and knickknacks. She pulled out a piece of newspaper and wrapped a ceramic rocking horse.

"I'm a little worried about Kelli." Beth carefully folded a matching blanket and onesie ensemble together. "She really got upset yesterday, and I haven't heard a peep out of her since then. When Rand and I came home last night, she was out—working late, I imagine, but I'm really surprised she hasn't called to check on things this morning."

"Her car was gone when I went for my run, so she was up and out early. She must be putting in some extra hours," Rand said as he removed the side rails from the crib.

"Strange that she wouldn't check in."

Alison shifted from her sitting position onto her knees in order to get the items from the top of the bookshelf. She couldn't believe what she saw right at eye level. "Where did you get this?" She held up the carved wooden horse.

"Kelli gave it to me. Don't pack that away, okay, Mom? I want to keep it near me because it's so special. Maybe I'll move it into my room."

"How have I not seen this before?" Alison turned the figurine over in her hands.

"She just gave it to me a couple weeks ago."

"Where did she get it, do you know?"

"Her father made it for her when she was young, isn't it beautiful? She insisted I take it. Maybe I should offer to give it back now, huh?"

"Her father? Made this, you say?" Alison turned it over and over in her hands, which were trembling just the slightest amount. "What was his name again?"

Beth shrugged. "Mr. Huddleston. I don't know his first name. Why do you ask?"

"No reason." She flipped it over to look at the bottom. *DH '94* was carved into the base. Alison simply stared at it.

Her imagination was running wild, that's all this was. Lots of people carved horses out of wood, and lots of those people put their initials and date into the base. Lots of people.

She set the horse aside and got on with her work. Time to quit thinking nonsense.

About half an hour later, the doorbell rang. Beth looked over her shoulder. "That's most likely Kelli."

"I'll go let her in." Alison hurried down the hall, thinking through what she knew about Kelli. Thinking of some of the subtle similarities she'd been seeing for the last few months, yet not seeing. She shook her head just before she opened the door, to clear all of those silly thoughts obviously caused by the fresh grief stirring up memories of the old one.

She opened the door to find Kenmore, his face pale and heavy with grief. He didn't move to enter but glanced toward the inside. "Is Beth . . ."

"We're all in the nursery, putting everything away."

He nodded. "Good. Listen, there's something that's happened, something that is going to make this harder on her. I'm not sure how, or if, or when to tell her. But it's about Kelli. I went by her place last night, and then called her, and you see—"

"She's gone." Alison said it as a statement she knew to be true. Just as she knew that there was much more to this story than she'd ever imagined. "I'm guessing she won't be coming back."

Kenmore shook his head. "I don't think so, no."

Alison pinned him with the stare she usually reserved for her students. "Kenmore, what's going on, and how long have you known?"

Kelli was just pulling out of Memphis on her trip west when her phone rang for the umpteenth time. She looked and saw Beth's name on the caller ID. As much as she didn't want to face this, she knew that, for Beth's sake, the sooner the better. "Hello, Beth. How are you doing?"

"The question is, *what* are *you* doing? Kenmore was just here, and he said you've left town. Is that true?" Her voice carried a high-pitched hysterical quality.

Kenmore told her? Kelli hadn't answered his calls yet. "What else did he tell you?"

"He said you had an emergency, that you were on your way to California, and that you wouldn't be back."

"That about sums it up." Good old Kenmore. She should have known she could count on him to smooth things out as best as possible.

"Then why didn't you tell me about it? Maybe I could have helped you, too, you know. Did you ever think about that?"

"Beth, you've got enough troubles right now without me adding one more thing to the list." Beth had no idea how true that was.

"Weren't you even going to tell me good-bye?" Her voice was thick from crying. "How could you do this? To any of us?"

"I'm sorry. You're right, I should have come over to say good-bye, but things came up so suddenly and I had to hurry, and like I said, I didn't want to bother you."

"Bother me?" There was no mistaking the hurt in her voice. "The person who has been my best friend for the past three months, the one who stood by me while I found out that my precious daughter had died, the one who cried with me at my daughter's grave. How could that same person be so cruel as to just leave town without a single word to me?"

The four-lane highway was packed with summer weekend travelers—minivans loaded with families going on vacations, convertibles with young couples heading toward a romantic weekend, and Kelli. "I'm sorry." It was all she could say. There were no excuses she could offer that would mean anything, and she knew it. "I'm going to miss you—you'll never know how much. I hate that I have to leave you right now. I know it's a really hard time, but believe me, there isn't any other choice."

"I'm sorry. I'm being selfish, aren't I? Please tell me what's going on with you and how I can help. I'll do anything for you, you know that."

"It's something I can't talk about, not to anyone. I hate to be that way, but that's truly how it has to be."

"If that's what you say, then that's what I'm going to try to believe." Beth sighed. "You must have a really good reason to do this, even if you won't tell me what it is."

"I do. Thanks for trying to understand." Kelli took one last deep breath. "Good-bye, Beth." *I love you.*

"Good-bye, Kelli. Keep in touch."

"Of course I will." Even as the words came out of her mouth, Kelli knew they were a lie.

I am a terrible person. Just like my father was a terrible person. We both go around hurting the people who love us. We deserve whatever punishment we get.

I just keep pondering Miss Birdyshaw's words right before I left. She kept saying that she's not good enough—not in God's eyes anyway—but I think she is plenty good. Dad used to tell me there wasn't any need to go to church or do much in the way of learning about God if I was just a good enough person. He always implied that he was one of those people who was good enough not to need more—I think we all know better than that now.

Alison and Beth and Rand are all really good people, yet they say that's not good enough without believing in Jesus. Denice and Jones are two of the best people I know, but they don't really ever even think about God.

Maybe this is another area of my life where it's time that I quit just trusting what my father told me all my life and look for the truth myself. Really seek it out.

Regardless of what I find, it does seem to me that my Tennessee family has a certain peace that my "good" friends back home seem to be lacking. Peace is something I could use a little more of. Right now, sitting in a hotel room in Arkansas, it is so far removed from me that I'm not sure it even exists anymore.

I'm just sorry I won't be around Alison and Beth or Miss Birdyshaw anymore. They seemed to understand these answers. Perhaps in time, I would have, too.

On Saturday afternoon, Shane was wrapping up a day packed full of showings. His realty business was picking up, which was a good thing, because he needed to stay busy for the next month. Just one more month and then Kelli would be gone and maybe he could move on with his life as if she'd never been there.

In spite of the fact that he had been avoiding Dad's store like the plague for the past week or so, knowing she was still there left him restless. He couldn't get interested in any of the other girls in town, in spite of constant invitations from Amy and her friends. Once Kelli was gone, well, then he was sure he'd start to be interested in someone else.

He wanted to be mad at her, but even as he looked back on their time together, Kelli had really never done anything to lead him to believe she wanted to be anything more than his father's employee. He really couldn't blame her. In fact, maybe next week he would make a point of stopping by the store, just casually, to see if they couldn't get some sort of friendly rapport going again. He missed being around her.

He heard his father rumbling around in the kitchen as he made his way inside. "Hey, how's it going?" He rounded the corner and found his father at the kitchen table, wiping a tear from his cheek. "Pop, what's wrong?" He knew his father was upset about Beth's baby, but his father never cried. About anything.

Pop shook his head and looked away from him, toward the back window. "I'm fine. Just wallowing in a bit of regret, is all."

"Regret? For what?"

He continued to shake his head slowly. "So many things I don't know where to start." He turned toward Shane then and offered a strained smile. "Don't listen to me, I'm just an old man rambling on about nothing. What's on your agenda this evening?"

"Nothing that can't wait, if you're not feeling well."

"I'm fine. Like I said, just wallowing."

"How are Beth and Rand holding up? And Alison?" He knew that whatever it was that had his father so upset, it had something to do with the baby.

"They're making it through as best they can. They're heartbroken, of course, how could they not be?" He looked up toward the ceiling as if searching for something behind the antique white paint and plaster.

Shane needed to do something to cheer him up. There was only one thing he could think of, but it was something he really didn't want to do. Still, he'd never seen his father like this. "Why don't you invite Kelli over for dinner tonight? She always cheers you up."

"What?" That got his dad's attention in a big way. "Thought you two weren't speaking to each other."

Shane shrugged. "It's not that we weren't speaking—more like we were just avoiding each other. More like I was avoiding her, but you know what? It's time for me to get over it. Truth is, she wasn't as much to blame as I liked to think she was. If the two of you are going to be working together for the next month, then it's time for me to be a bigger person and move past my hurt pride."

Pop studied his face for several seconds and then said, "Unfortunately, you're just a little too late for that."

"What do you mean?"

"She's gone."

"Gone? Where?"

"Back to California, I reckon."

"You reckon? You mean she's left Shoal Creek and your store?"

"Yep."

"And she didn't tell you where she was going?"

"Nope."

"You've got to be kidding me. When's she coming back?"

"I expect she'll call me in the next day or two—whenever she's ready—and give me the details, but I already know the answer to the rest of it. She's not coming back. Ever."

It was Wednesday morning when Kelli finally pulled into the driveway of her apartment, exhausted but relieved to be home. Now she was thankful for the months of paying two rents—at least she had a place to come back to. She climbed the stairs to her little over-the-garage unit, somehow managing to drag her suitcase inside before she plopped across the sofa. The room felt empty without the six-foot bear looming above her. She both missed it and was glad for its absence, so bittersweet was what it represented. The man she'd loved but never really knew at all. The man who'd been so kind to her but had done something terrible to the rest of his family. She pulled out the remote and began to channel surf, not paying attention to anything she was seeing, just needing some mindless noise.

Mrs. Rohling came to the door. "I thought I saw your car in the driveway. Welcome back."

"Thank you."

"I've got a message for you. There was a woman who came by looking for you a week or so ago. She asked if I would give you this when you got home."

Kelli thanked Mrs. Rohling, who was already on her way out the door. She opened the envelope to find a handwritten note.

Dear Kelli,

You asked me to convey your message to my mother when she was ready to hear it. Now I have a message for you, from not only my mother but from the entire family. First of all, we would like to offer a heartfelt apology for betraying your trust and costing your job, when you were going out on a limb to help us. It didn't take long for Kevin to realize that his old high school buddy was indeed cheating our mother with abandon. If he were less of a coward he would have called you himself.

Long story short, Mom's house sold quickly, so while it's not possible for her to return home, she did find a cute little cottage in an adult living neighborhood fairly close to Kevin. She loves the place and the people, and still has her independence after all. She asked me to convey to you that she would love to see you if you are ever in the Bay area, so please stop by sometime. As for the rest of us, we again offer our sincere thanks and our profound apologies. I'm sorry that I did not find you at home so that I could tell you all this in person.

Best wishes,
Julie Layton

Kelli shook her head. Who would have thought? So many things had happened since that incident, she found it hard to believe it was part of the same lifetime.

After a while, she pushed herself upright and got into the shower. It was time to start facing the reality of her life, of what it was going to be and what it was not going to be.

It was going to be building up a fabulous new restaurant with her two dearest friends in a charming old Victorian in Santa Barbara. It was not going to be anything to do with country stores, or sweet next-door-neighbor ladies, or family members that she'd never even known existed.

She paced around the room for a while, then drove to Anna's Bakery for a cream cheese croissant and a large coffee. The bakery was busy as usual, but she found an empty table by the window. The sugar and caffeine flowed through her, and while it woke her up, it did nothing to give her any comfort. She watched families come in together, a mother holding a toddler, a teenaged boy with his father, a young couple holding hands. People who were committed to each other, living their lives together. Something she no longer had.

"Hey, Denice, it's me. I'm back in town. What's your schedule like today?"

Ten minutes later, Denice was sitting on Kelli's couch, a bag of potato chips in hand. "Okay, start from the beginning and tell me what's happened that caused you to stop taking my calls a few days ago, and now you've shown up here out of the blue."

So that's what Kelli did. She told her everything that had transpired, leaving out nothing. "That's why I'm back here. I couldn't stand to be there for even one more minute. You were so right when you said it was not the time for me to go back. Probably there never would have been a right time, I was just too blind to see it. I've not only messed my own self up, but I've hurt Beth—which is killing me. I know I hurt Kenmore, too, and Shane. I just made one big mess of it."

Denice hugged her tight. "I'm sorry you've had to go through all this. You deserve it less than anyone I know. You're back now, a bit older and a bit wiser, but things are going to work out, just you wait and see. Jones has been working hard on the menu and the arrangements. This is going to be a fresh start for you, and that's what you need right now." She looked at her watch. "Oh blast! I'm late. I'll see you tonight, okay?"

Denice hurried through the door, blowing a kiss as she went. She was such a good friend, had been for all of Kelli's life. Maybe Kelli didn't have any family left, but she had Denice.

The next day, Kelli decided to go for a drive by the ocean. She'd missed the ocean. As she merged onto the freeway, she thought through all her future possibilities. Denice was right—now was the time for a fresh start.

She slammed on the brakes so hard her car skidded to a stop. The driver behind her laid on his horn as he swerved around her. He made an obscene gesture as he passed by. Kelli's heart hammered against her ribs, and she hit the gas again, only then realizing what a stupid thing she'd just done. It could have killed her and several more people on the freeway. But in that moment she'd finally realized what she was trying to do. Leave all her problems behind and start fresh. She was no better than her father.

She was *not* going to be the coward her father had been.

After returning to her apartment, repacking, and making a few other quick stops, Kelli was on I-40 again. She knew she wouldn't pull off the road until she absolutely could not go any farther. The second day, she made it to Texas before exhaustion forced her to pull off the interstate. She found a rundown motel—it was clean enough, but it was old and had paper-thin walls, so she could hear every word of the conversation next door. It didn't matter. Within five minutes of entering the room, she was sound asleep.

It was still dark outside when she climbed out of bed the next morning, showered, and returned to the road. She had a sense of urgency, although she had no idea what she'd do after she got back to Shoal Creek. She had a very long drive during which to make a plan, so she started methodically thinking through her options.

She was still concerned that telling Alison and Beth would be more painful than helpful, but she thought about Beth and how devastating the loss of her baby had been. If she were to somehow miraculously find out that baby were still alive, even if it meant Rand had betrayed her, would she want to know? Kelli couldn't be certain, but she thought so. Since Alison was more even-keeled than Beth, she wondered if she should just go and tell her first, not telling Beth until after Alison agreed it was okay to do so.

Or should she tell them all together? Then they could kick her out of the house all at once, or they could rejoice, or they could ask all their questions, but whatever it was they were going to do, it would all happen at the same time.

At that moment, she knew where she would start. She would ask the one person she trusted the most to tell her the truth.

48

Kenmore was watching the Braves beat the Dodgers when the doorbell rang. "I got it," he called back to Shane, who was somewhere in the back of the house. At first, the glare from the setting sun outside left the visitor nothing more than a silhouette, but then he saw her. There were dark circles under her eyes, and her skin was pasty white, but she gave him a tentative smile.

He flung the door open wide. "Come inside and tell me what's happened."

She took a step in but went no farther. "I realized that I was trying to do the same thing my father did all those years ago. The truth was hard to face, so I was planning to go away and make a new life so I didn't have to be bothered with it all. But there is no way I'm going to make my father's mistakes. If there's nothing else good that comes out of this entire thing, it's going to be that I learned you can't change the truth to suit your desires. It's not fair to the people you leave behind to deal with carnage, and it's not the right thing to do as a human being."

He looked at the grim determination on her face. He nodded

once, then reached out his hand to clasp her shoulder. "I'm proud of you."

"Are you? Am I doing the right thing?"

"Kelli, I think—"

"The right thing about what?" Shane walked over to stand right beside them. He frowned at Kelli. "What are you doing here? Last I heard you were leaving town for good, going back to get married to some guy you never bothered to mention."

"Shane." Kenmore shook his head and took a step toward his son. "You don't have all the story. You need to back off."

"I don't have all the story because I've been purposely kept in the dark. That is not my fault."

"No, it isn't, and you're right." Kelli looked at him, then back at Kenmore. "Maybe I should start right here, right now, by telling Shane all of it. His reaction might give me a good idea about what I should and shouldn't do with the rest of them."

Kenmore nodded slowly. "There's probably some truth in that." He continued to nod. "Yeah, that's a good idea." He looked at the worn-down girl before him, her shoulders stooped as if the weight of a lifetime were upon them. Actually, Kenmore supposed the weight of a lifetime was on her shoulders—it was her father's lifetime that was crushing her beneath its weight.

Shane sat forward, elbows on knees, looking up at Kelli, who had paced through the entire explanation. "So, you're telling me that almost nothing I've known or believed about you was true?"

Ouch. It hurt. But it was the truth, so what had Kelli expected? "Yes, I guess that's what I'm saying."

"You guess?"

"No, I don't guess, okay? I know. I know that I didn't come in telling anyone the truth about who I was, for, well, for obvious reasons. But those decisions were made with good intentions."

"And this mystery guy you were going to marry, it was all just made up?"

"Yes. No. Sort of." Kelli dropped into a chair and doubled over, trying to somehow squelch the growing pain in her gut. "At the time, it seemed like the right thing to do. You were showing a fair amount of interest in me, and I was feeling more than a fair amount interested in you, but at the time, my plans were to leave here and never look back. It seemed like it would be the less painful thing, to just throw that out there, putting me in as the bad guy and letting you believe you'd gotten off the hook and were better off for it."

"That's what you thought, huh?" Shane shook his head. "If you ask me, I'd say you weren't thinking about much of anything. Otherwise, you wouldn't have made some of these bone-headed decisions you did."

"You're right, okay? I know you're right. But this isn't exactly a common situation. It's not like there are a bunch of self-help books about what to do after you've found out everything you ever believed was a lie—a lie told to you by the one person you trusted more than anyone else on earth." Kelli stood up and started pacing again. "Maybe I was right to go. Maybe I should leave forever before any more harm is done. It was crazy to come back again. I'm sorry. I'm sorry."

Kenmore, who had discreetly left the room while Kelli was telling the crux of it, now returned. "There is something you should know."

"What?"

"Alison suspects something. She hasn't quite figured out all the details. They are too farfetched for her to do that, but that horse figurine you gave to Beth? She recognized it as looking a lot like David's work. She asked me what I knew, and I played dumb. I don't think she quite believed me, but then again, what else is she supposed to believe? The truth is crazy."

"How did she seem, when she asked you all this? Was she upset? Angry?"

He shrugged. "She was a little worked up, but not hysterical or anything. Like I said, she asked the question, but she didn't really believe she could be right."

"If Shane is this upset, you know it's going to kill Alison and Beth."

"It will initially, you're right about that. When you first walked into my store three months ago, it stirred up some deeply buried feelings in me that were not pleasant and that I didn't want to face. But you know what? Since you came back, there's been something else, something else that surprised me."

"Like what?"

"Relief." He scrubbed his hands across his face. "All these years when I've had my suspicions about what happened—and then when you showed up and I knew for sure—well, it's been sort of like that feeling you get when a big flu epidemic is going around. You try to avoid it with all you've got, but when the symptoms finally start, it's almost a relief. You know the next little bit is going to be painful, but you also know that at least now you can quit dreading the 'what ifs' and just get on with what is. For me, it would be a relief to look at the people I love without secrets blocking my eyes, or theirs."

"He's right." Shane stood up and moved toward her. "He's absolutely right." He held out his hand. "You want to go walk for a bit?"

She looked at the extended hand, trying to think through everything. She couldn't make sense of it all, but there was one thing she did know. There were some risks that were worth taking.

"I'd love to." She took his hand, and the two of them walked out into the evening.

He kept shaking his head and muttering, "I can't believe it. I just can't believe it."

Kelli didn't reply. What could she say to that?

After they had walked for a while, and the muttering had tapered off, he turned to her with his most adorable boyish grin. "What was that part where you said that you were . . . what was it you said . . . feeling more than a fair amount of interest in me? I think that's something I'd like to hear more about. How'd it go again?"

She smiled up at him. "I can't quite remember."

"Let's see if I can come up with a little reminder." He drew her into his arms and kissed her deeply.

"I think it's starting to come back to me now."

"Maybe one more reminder."

"Sounds like a good idea."

Hi Alison, it's Kelli Huddleston. I'm back in town, and I was wondering if I could come over and talk to you for a few minutes."

"Kelli? Are you okay?"

"I'm . . . well, I'm fine. Would now be a good time?"

"Sure. I'm just washing dishes. Should I call Beth and tell her you're here? I know she'd want to see you."

"No. Please don't. I need to talk to you before I see Beth again."

"Okay. I'll be watching for you."

"Please take a seat." Alison gestured toward the sofa. "We've been worried about you."

Kelli nodded and stared at the coffee-table book about Ireland. The front image looked so fresh and inviting, just like the rest of Alison's house. Kelli was about to shatter that, but she didn't know what else to do. "I'm sorry I left like I did. Here's the thing." She shifted forward and leaned her elbows on her knees. "I grew up with a father and a stepmother. I think I might have told you that."

Kelli knew that Alison already was aware of this. She took a deep breath and made a concentrated effort to speak with intention.

"You know my father died a few months ago. What you don't know is what I found out after he died." She looked up and saw Alison watching her with a perfectly pleasant expression, yet there was a hint of fear in her eyes. "When I started going through my father's things, I found some newspaper clippings. They were pictures of a man and his young daughter who had apparently died in a boating accident near South Carolina."

Alison's hand went to her throat. "Was it David?"

Kelli nodded. "Yes. The clippings were about David and his young daughter named Darcy."

"Why would your father have those clippings?" Her voice trembled.

"I didn't know what it was about at the time. But I began to dig a little more, and I found other things, too." Kelli's throat began to close. "All my life, my father told me that my mother and sister and brother died in a house fire in Louisiana. He always refused to talk about it because he was so upset about it, but the more I sifted through his stuff, the more I realized he didn't want to talk about the fire because it didn't happen. My father, the man I knew, was Don Huddleston. But he had some old paperwork, and on it, his name was David Waters."

Alison's hand covered her mouth now. She nodded slowly, then shook her head, then nodded, as if she didn't know how to handle all this.

"When I came here earlier this summer, I just planned to stay for a week, hoping to get a chance to meet you all, to see you in person and know a little bit about what you're like. I planned to go back to my life and never say a word to anyone. Then Kenmore offered me a job, and I met you and Beth, and I couldn't make myself leave. And then I didn't want to leave, but I knew that it would be devastating to you if I told you the truth. And then when Beth was bedridden, and with Kenmore needing help at the store, I realized that in some small way I could make some amends for the wrongs my father did to all of you. Pay you back in some small measure. After Rose died, I knew I couldn't stay here and live a lie anymore, but after I left, I realized I was doing the same thing Daddy had done. I was running away from my problems. I didn't want to continue that legacy."

Tears were filling Kelli's eyes, so she wiped them away with the back of her hand. "I didn't want to think that my father could have done this. But I've had to accept it." Kelli reached into her bag and pulled out the manila envelope of clippings and notes. She handed them to Alison.

Alison said nothing, but she was shaking her head. "Where has he been all these years? Why did he never contact us and tell us he was all right?"

"From what I've been able to piece together, it appears that he faked our accident so that he could leave and start a new life. He went to California, under the name Don Huddleston. He married my stepmother not long after."

"You are telling me that my husband left me, took my daughter, and went to start another life with another woman?"

"I'm so sorry." Kelli stood, wondering if she should leave.

"If this is true, and it seems to be, it means that my daughter is still alive. It means that you, in fact, are Darcy. Is that what you're telling me?"

Kelli looked at the floor and nodded. "Yes, I believe that I am."

Alison burst into tears. "This is a little much for me to accept all at once."

"Believe me, I fully understand what you mean." Kelli paused. "I didn't want to tell Beth, at least not until I'd talked it over with you. She's so fragile now, I wasn't sure if she would be more happy to have a sister or devastated to learn about her father. That's why I came to you. And if you think it's best, I'll get in my car and leave right now and never come back."

"Oh, my darling girl. My darling, darling girl." Alison walked across the room and took Kelli by the hands while looking her over as if she'd never seen her before. "Welcome home, Darcy." She threw her arms around Kelli and squeezed her tight. "I can't believe it. You've been alive all these years. All this time that I've grieved your death."

"I know. I'm sorry." She held her mother tight. "There's something else we need to talk about."

"What's that?"

"Life insurance. Since Dad wasn't really dead when you got your payout, if we go public with who I am, I think there's a possibility they will ask for the money back. That's another thing that has kept me from saying anything. This could be financially devastating for you."

Alison shook her head. "Money is not something we're going to let ruin this for us. We will work this all out together." She pulled away and wiped her eyes. "Don't you worry about a thing. I do think we should tell Beth, and I think we should do it together. Tonight. She'd want to know, even though parts of this are going to be hard for her to accept. Then tomorrow we can meet with my lawyer and see what, if anything, needs to be done."

"Alison?"

"Yes?"

"I'm devastated about the way all this has happened, but I couldn't be happier to find out who my real mother is. If nothing else, I'm glad I got to know you."

Alison drew her into a hug again. "Welcome to the family, sweetheart."

"First of all, let me start by saying how sorry I am that I left you the way I did. So very sorry."

Beth reached over to take Rand's hand as they sat beside each other on their couch. "As much as I'd like to tell you to buzz off, for some reason I can't bring myself to do it." She paused for a minute. "What's this all about? And why is Mom with you?"

"It's a long and complicated story." Kelli took a sip from the glass of water Rand had brought her, drew in a deep breath, and said, "I grew up with a father and stepmother, as you know. . . ." The story spilled out from there. "After Rose died, when you sang the song about Scruffy, well . . . I dream that song sometimes. I never really knew the words, but it was a song about Scruffy—a stuffed dog I still have in my closet, by the way."

"That's why you fell apart when we sang it." Beth was on her feet now. "Mom, can this be true? Is there any way this story can be true?"

Kelli reached into her bag and pulled out the manila envelope. She handed it to Beth, who immediately dumped the contents on the coffee table. The three of them started picking up pictures and articles, gasping with each new piece.

"Unbelievable." It was the first thing Rand had said since the conversation started.

"Yes, it is. Unfortunately, though, it's the truth." Kelli looked up to find all three of them looking at her.

"How can it be?" Beth's voice was high-pitched as she looked to Rand. She stared at him as if she expected him to have the answers. When he offered none, she turned toward her mother. "I don't believe it. It's not true. My father would never have done that. He loved me. He loved us, and he would never have left us behind like that." She started crying. "Mama, why would he have done that?" Alison offered no answers, so Beth turned toward Kelli. "You're the one who got to live with him all these years, you tell me. Why? Why would Daddy do that? Why did he do it? He used to ride me piggyback all over the place. We built forts out of sticks and rocks, and we made s'mores over the grill in the backyard. Does that sound like the kind of man who would do something like this?"

"No. I don't know." Kelli scrubbed her hands across her eyes. "I didn't know anything until it was too late to ask him." She saw the raw grief on Beth's face and hated herself for having been the one to cause it. "I'm so sorry. This is a secret I thought I would take to my grave, and maybe I should have, but then again, I thought maybe it would be the right thing to tell. Maybe I was wrong. I would never want to hurt you any more than you've already been hurt. You've got to believe that. And if you think it's best, I'll get in my car and leave right now and never come back."

"So, you really are my sister? My true sister?" Beth moved a little closer.

Kelli nodded through tears. "Yes."

Beth threw her arms around Kelli and Alison. "I can't believe it." She was crying, and Kelli suspected the tears were both happy and devastated. Finally, she looked up at Kelli. "We've got lots of things to talk about and lots of things to do."

"Yes." Kelli added no more.

"First off, we have a call we need to make."

"To whom?"

"Max. We need to tell him his father was a lout." She started crying as she said the words but then took a deep breath and continued. "And that he needs to come home as soon as possible and spend some time with his sister, because he's going to love her. I know I sure do."

Alison looked across the big mahogany desk at Warner Brock, the man she'd known most of her life. He'd been her lawyer for all of her adult life—from helping David set up a new business to walking her through the mounds of paperwork following the "accident." Now, as she watched him stroking his gray beard and shaking his head, she realized that he, too, was at a loss.

"This is something else, I'm not going to lie to you. I've not come across anything like it in my practice." He looked over at Kelli, who was holding onto Alison with her left hand and Beth with her right. "Young lady, I will say that I am thrilled to see you alive and looking so well, in spite of the conundrum your presence brings along with you." He shook his head again. "We need to figure out Social Security numbers, death certificates, and any number of things, as well as the insurance issue you've mentioned. Most of this is out of my level of expertise, but let me make some calls, and then I'll get back with you as soon as possible."

"What do you think will happen, with the insurance money, I mean?" Kelli's voice was quiet.

He steepled his fingers together. "I can't say for sure just yet, but I have a strong hunch they're going to let this one go, and here's why. Have you heard about the Brinkman-Carrie scandal?"

Kelli shook her head. "No."

"Long story short, when Hurricane Carrie made landfall in Florida last year, it was going to cost insurance companies millions of dollars, right? Turns out a decision was made in the higher-ups at Brinkman Insurance several years ago to sell mostly bogus policies—with coverage so minimal that it was basically worthless—to the poorer areas of the state, to help bring in revenue to help pay off their more expensive claims after the next disaster. It worked great—their revenues were way up—but thankfully enough of the duped people came forward and got the attention of the media. Brinkman's got a massive PR nightmare on their hands right now. Bankrupting a woman like your mother due to circumstances completely beyond her control is not the kind of publicity they need at this point. My guess is that they will want to make this go away."

"I hope you're right."

"So do I. If I'm not, we'll start looking at alternatives we can explore. For now, just relax and let me see what I can find out."

"Thank you so much." Alison stood up and extended her hand. "You've always been such a help to our family."

He smiled toward Kelli. "And that's a tradition I plan to continue."

"Let's go get a bite of lunch, shall we?" Alison led the two girls—her *daughters*—outside to the sidewalk. "Shall we go to Country Kitchen? We've got to get Kelli eating like a southerner while we've got her here."

"Good idea, Mom." Beth smiled, but her eyes were sad. Between losing the baby and finding out about her father, the sadness and the happiness were warring inside her. Alison knew it was going to be a long healing process for Beth. The fact that she loved Kelli so much—and got to "keep her," as she'd put it—did help, though.

Two days later, Alison received a call from Warner Brock. The insurance company had agreed to forget any kind of claim they could make on this case, in exchange for a gag order on all the participants. While they didn't want to appear the bad guy, they also didn't want people getting ideas about setting up insurance policies and then disappearing as a great way to fix financial difficulties for their families.

"I think that's something we can live with." Alison smiled as she hung up the phone. They were going to make it through this one step at a time, and they were going to be just fine.

Kenmore arrived at the store early, wanting to get a head start on his day. When he pulled up, he was more than a little surprised by what he saw. Kelli stood in the parking lot, measuring tape in hand, drawing out a large rectangular area with chalk.

"And just what do you think you're doing?"

She grinned up at him. "Marking out where the gas pumps will go. You have room for two for sure. You could do three, but I think it would make it too tight of a squeeze."

"I told you, the store's closing in a couple months. I'm not adding gas pumps and deli counters, or anything else."

"Hear me out before you say no."

"I'm listening, but I'm not adding anything. Unless, of course, this means you're staying. If that's the case, we'll talk about it."

She shook her head and looked at the ground. "You have no idea how much I wish I could, but I can't."

"Why not? Everyone knows the secret now."

"Yes, but I've made promises back home, and unlike previous

members of my family, I intend to be known as someone who keeps her word, no matter what it costs."

"Good for you. You're making the Joseph kind of decision—it's always best to choose the way you know is right."

"Thanks, Kenmore. That means a lot to me. And now, I think I'd like to offer you the chance to make a Joseph decision of your own."

"This I gotta hear." He folded his arms across his chest. "But just so you know, I hate it when people throw my own words back at me."

Kelli laughed. "How can we help it? Your words are all just so brilliant."

"True enough." He looked at her and waited.

"You know how Beth had that project she was trying to get started before she got put on bed rest? The one that provided a place to live and job training to single mothers? Remember she had that one woman she knew from the thrift store that she liked so much, said was perfectly capable, but couldn't afford child care while she worked? It got me thinking. What if you hired her here?"

"You talking about the one who tried to steal her car?"

"No. The other one. The one she talked about being so good at displays."

"I like to do the right thing, but I'm not running a charity ward."

"And that's not what I'm suggesting. I'm saying why don't you hire her—I can stay for the next month and train her since I was supposed to be here until then anyway. She can bring her baby to work with her, just like you took this job so that you could bring Shane. Especially now with the little play area. It could be your way to pay it forward."

"Then what?"

"Well, you keep the store open, she gets a job, I teach her how to do what I've been doing, and you can cut your hours back or down to none at all. Maybe by then the store will be ready to hire another of Beth's projects."

"What about you?"

Kelli shrugged. "I go back to California and open the restaurant, just like I've always planned."

"What about your new family?"

"I'm sure there will be a lot of phone calls, and Skype chats, and visits back and forth. Maybe, just maybe, in a year or so, if the restaurant is up and running, maybe then I'll be able to leave it and come back here and work at the store again."

"You'd want to do that?"

She smiled. "I can't think of anything I'd rather do."

"But you're willing to give it up if things don't work out so well back home?"

"I promised Jones and Denice I would be there for them, and that's exactly what I'm going to do."

"I may be treading on a path that is none of my business, but what about Shane?"

"We talked about it last night. We're going to try the long-distance thing for a while, hoping I will eventually come back here. But if things work out to where I need to stay in California, he told me a real estate agent can find himself a job almost anywhere." She grinned and blushed a little.

Kenmore peered down at her chalk lines, feeling more hopeful about the future than he had in years. "Where did you say those gas pumps might go again?"

3 months later

Kelli, time to take this to the party in the back room." Denice breezed up to the hostess stand with the large birthday cake balanced on one hand. "Why don't you do the honors?"

"You got it." Kelli walked through the packed restaurant, taking care not to bump anyone. So far, Homestead had been a huge success. The critics had given it excellent reviews, the reservations were booked out weeks in advance, and it looked as though the dream of a successful restaurant was actually going to come true.

As soon as she entered the back room, a hush descended on the crowd assembled there, making Kelli very self-conscious as she set the cake on the table. Thankfully, Denice had followed close behind and announced to the room, "Jones has spent all day on this. You're going to love it. He was determined that this would be the finest cake he's ever made." Denice beamed with pride as she looked up at her husband, who had followed them in.

Jones grinned. "Any family of Kelli is a family of mine. I'm so happy to finally get to meet all of you."

For her birthday, Alison had requested a trip to California for the entire family. She wanted to come and see where Kelli had grown up and gain some understanding of where her husband had been all these years. They had spent the week visiting the places that had been important in Kelli's life. Max and Valerie and their kids had come, and Beth and Rand. Kelli had gotten to know all of them better. And then Kenmore and Shane had arrived at the end of the week to spend the last couple of days with them.

"You all have been just amazing and welcoming," Alison said. "I can't think of anywhere I'd rather be. What a fabulous restaurant you have here, too. We're going to miss the food when we go home tomorrow."

"I wish you didn't have to go home so soon." Denice frowned. "It's been nice getting to know you guys over the past week—even if it was under what can only be described as really weird circumstances."

"That's for sure," Alison replied. "I hope we'll see the two of you in Tennessee someday soon."

"I'd almost guarantee it." As Denice and Jones became able, they were planning to hire a floor manager, then gradually buy out Kelli's share in the restaurant. She would use that money to buy into Moore's More Store.

"As busy as this place is, I'm thinking we're going to need us a vacation. Tennessee is my number one destination from here on out." Denice couldn't seem to stop smiling. Neither could Jones.

"Okay, everybody gather round. Kelli is going to light the candles and then she has a surprise for Mom." Beth waved everyone over into a little huddle by the cake.

Kelli's hands were shaking as she attempted to light the candles.

Finally, Shane took the lighter out of her hand and said, "I'll handle this part."

"Thanks," Kelli whispered. She took a deep breath, looked at the assembled group, and began to sing "Happy Birthday" to her mother. When she finished, there wasn't a dry eye in the room.

"That was amazing." Beth jumped up and squealed. "Your very first solo, and you were amazing."

Alison hugged Kelli tight, tears gleaming in her eyes. She leaned forward and blew out the candles in a single breath.

Beth nodded her approval. "Good job, Mom. Did you make a wish?"

Alison glanced around the room, then looped her arm around Kelli's shoulders and held her close to her side. "Didn't need to. It already came true."

Your people will rebuild the ancient ruins and will raise up the age-old foundations; you will be called Repairer of Broken Walls, Restorer of Streets with Dwellings.

Isaiah 58:12

Acknowledgments

Heavenly Father—For your great love in all circumstances.

Lee Cushman—For being the amazing husband, father, and man of honor that you are. The whole family is blessed because of you.

Melanie and Caroline—For being the best kids in the entire world. You both inspire me to be a better person.

Ora Parrish—The embodiment of selfless love.

Kelli and Kyle—For answering my food/restaurant questions, naming Homestead and giving it direction, and being such fun members of the family (not to mention the yummy soups!).

Carl, Alisa, Katy, and Lisa—You are my rocks. I'd be lost without your love and support.

Kristyn, Judy, Brenna, Denice, Kathleen, Gary, Carolyn, and Lori—Great friends and supporters.

Dave Long—It is such an amazing privilege to work with you.

Charlene Patterson—For your willingness to take on this story and make everything better.

Carrie Padgett—Not only a writing friend, but a true friend.

Kelli Standish—For always cheering me on and for showing all of us it's possible to keep moving forward in spite of terrible pain.

For every single insurance agent/representative I have pestered with questions about how this story might play out, especially Nathan Thomas, Julia Tipolt, and Gayle Carroll.

Questions for Conversation

1. Has there ever been a person in your life whom you trusted with your entire being but then you later found out that your trust was not deserved? How has it affected your current relationships or your ability to trust?
2. In this story, Kelli's father began to search for "truth" that justified his choice, rather than making hard decisions because of what he knew to be true. Because of this, Kelli was raised with what might be called a "religion of convenience." In what ways do you see people doing that today? Have you ever tried to use the Bible to justify something you suspected might be wrong?
3. Denice comes from a very broken background. She has managed to cope for the most part through self-applied psychotherapy, yet Kelli notices that her real family in Tennessee has a different kind of peace. Do you think this is true to life? Have you ever met a person of faith who exhibited characteristics you envied?
4. Kelli's story is based on a hybrid of two true stories. Can you imagine a situation where "disappearing" is a better

choice than the alternative? Do you know of any real stories involving someone who completely changed their life situation?

5. Kelli left Beth in her time of greatest need because Kelli's own pain had become so great. Have you ever had to walk away from someone else because your own pain made it impossible for you to stay and help? Have you ever been the one left behind?
6. What kind of future do you envision for Kelli, Beth, and Alison? And for Kelli and Shane? Do you think Kelli will return to Shoal Creek? Do you think she'll remain close with her real family?

Kathryn Cushman is a graduate of Samford University with a degree in pharmacy. She is the author of seven previous novels, including *Leaving Yesterday* and *A Promise to Remember*, which were both finalists for the Carol Award in Women's Fiction. Katie and her family live in Santa Barbara, California. Learn more at www.kathryncushman.com.

More From Kathryn Cushman

To learn more about Kathryn and her books, visit kathryncushman.com.

After her Olympic dreams are shattered, can Sabrina Rice help a troubled teen runner find hope for the future in a life that's spiraling out of control?

Chasing Hope

With an entire nation watching, can two modern women survive the pressures of life, reality TV, and "going Amish" when nothing proves as simple as it looks?

Almost Amish

Grace Graham has been given one last chance to redeem herself. But when tragedy strikes her son, will she have the strength to resist running and stand strong?

Another Dawn

You May Also Like . . .

On the set of a docudrama in Wildwood, Texas, Allie Kirkland is unnerved to discover strange connections between herself and a teacher who disappeared over a century ago. Is history about to repeat itself?

Wildwood Creek by Lisa Wingate
lisawingate.com

Kate writes romance movie scripts for a living, but after her last failed relationship, she's stopped believing "true love" is real. Could a new friendship with former NFL player Colton Greene restore her faith?

From the Start by Melissa Tagg
melissatagg.com

When Eve discovers her uncle's bootlegging operation, she knows it's against Prohibition law. But can she risk exposing the man whose generosity is keeping her family from ruin?

Sweet Mercy by Ann Tatlock
anntatlock.com

BETHANYHOUSE

Stay up-to-date on your favorite books and authors with our free e-newsletters.
Sign up today at bethanyhouse.com.

Find us on Facebook. facebook.com/bethanyhousepublishers

Free exclusive resources for your book group! bethanyhouse.com/anopenbook